I0681493

WORTH MILLIONS

BOOKS IN THE ARGOSY LIBRARY:

UP JUMPED THE DEVIL

CLEVE F. ADAMS

THE BROTHERS OF THE SNAKE: THE
COMPLETE CHINATOWN CASES OF
JIMMY WENTWORTH, VOLUME 3

SIDNEY HERSCHEL SMALL

A CLUE TO THE COPPER: THE COMPLETE
CASES OF SILVER SKULL

RICHARD HOWELLS WATKINS

KINGDOM OF THE LOST: THE ADVENTURES
OF PETER THE BRAZEN, VOLUME 8

LORING BRENT

WORTH MILLIONS

RICHARD BARRY

TIGER DICK'S DOUBLOONS

DON MCGREW

PRESIDENTS: IMAGINARY MOMENTS IN
THE LIVES OF AMERICA'S GREAT

THEODORE ROSCOE

CROSS OVER NINE

MAX BRAND

ASOKA'S ALIBI: THE COMPLETE
ADVENTURES OF BEN QUORN, VOLUME 2

TALBOT MUNDY

THE LOST PUNCH: THE COMPLETE CASES
OF GILLIAN HAZELTINE, VOLUME 4

GEORGE F. WORTS

WORTH MILLIONS

RICHARD BARRY

ILLUSTRATED BY
ROGER B. MORRISON

COVER BY
PAUL STAHR

POPULAR PUBLICATIONS · 2025

© 2025 Popular Publications, an imprint of Steeger Properties, LLC

First Edition—2025

PUBLISHING HISTORY

"Worth Millions" originally appeared in the June 12–July 10, 1926 issue of *Argosy Allstory Weekly* magazine (Vol. 178, Nos. 2–6). Copyright © 1926 by The Frank A. Munsey Company. Copyright renewed © 1953 and assigned to Steeger Properties, LLC. All rights reserved.

ALL RIGHTS RESERVED

No part of this book may be reproduced or utilized in any form or by any means without permission in writing from the publisher.

Visit ARGOSYMAGAZINE.COM for more books like this.

WORTH MILLIONS

1

IN THE MAIL

OLD SCROGGINS WAS subbing for Mac, who was on his vacation. So when Victor drove up from the village in the station wagon, and handed out three thick bundles of mail, he remarked, apologetically:

"They must have made a mistake down town, super, and sent up business mail—and everything."

Scroggins glanced at the top letter on each bundle. The first was addressed to "The Hon. Peter Killigrew, Esq."; the second to "Mr. Peter Killigrew" and the third to "Mr. Peter Killigrew, V."

He bared the missives underneath, and convinced himself that the mail had been sorted, and that each top letter was an accurate sample of the pile it represented.

"These are all evidently personal letters for the master, Victor," he said, rather stiffly, but with a touch of that old-time elegance one sees nowadays only among servants of a former generation. It was beneath his dignity to address an inferior with any less respect than he would have accorded his superior.

Thereupon Scroggins, who was called "old" about the Killigrew estate to distinguish him from "young" Scroggins, brought down from Maine three years before to be head groom in the stables—the year Peter Killigrew IV died—proceeded leisurely to the library in the east wing where the June sun was struggling through the leaded glass.

A somber room, this library, about half an acre in extent, large enough for several modern apartments, and high enough for a handball court, but with narrow windows and tiny panes of glass; built a century before by the second Peter Killigrew, and with walls three feet thick.

There were books on three sides, pictures on the fourth— only four pictures, a Titian, a Rembrandt, a Romney, and the portrait of Washington by Stuart, said to be the third and best, which the librarian of Congress had repeatedly suggested ought to be purchased by the United States Government, but which no Killigrew would ever set a price upon.

The Ispahan palace carpet in the center of the room was forty-two and a half by seventy-three feet, eight and a half inches, but looked like a cocoa mat lost in a brown field of oiled oak boards. The field of the carpet was of umber-gine, with imperial yellow borders and jade green medal-lions—really a museum piece. Once the Metropolitan had borrowed it for an exhibition when showing authen-tic examples of fifteenth-century rug workmanship. The master of a Killigrew clipper in the '50s had traded it in for a cargo of shoes in Constantinople, the year after the Crimean War, when exchange was shot to pieces. It had been woven for a khan of the Turkoman empire—priceless.

But we cannot halt for a description of the Killigrew library. You will find a partial one in three octavo volumes, illustrated with colored plates, published in London by

Askew in 1897. The library hasn't changed much since then.

A family's social standing in Westchester County was measured by whether or not they had been received in the Killigrew library. A New Year's reception was always held there. Then, in June, the reigning Killigrew always sojourned there—for a week at least.

Inhabiting the Westchester estate, living in it, eating, sleeping, working there for a part of each June was a Killigrew tradition, an unwritten Killigrew law, even if the sunlight barely penetrated to the center of the library, even if the old pile of masonry was dull and youthless.

Scroggins was thinking of all this as he reached the long ebony table, bound with teakwood, in the far east embrasure, where the young master would presently arrive, following his horseback ride after breakfast.

He deposited the three bundles of letters and slipped off the cords which bound them, and reached for the letter opener of thin stag horn, prepared to do just what Mac had taught him to do.

Mac—Reginald McKenna, to give him his full name as he was known to his employer—was the high-powered, easy-running secretary who stood as a buffer between Peter Killigrew V and a designing world; a shrewd, soft-spoken, quick-thinking young man of irreproachable manners; college-bred, of course.

Old Scroggins, though, had never been to college. Hardly. He had been born on the estate in the dairy cottage farthest to the north, beyond the apple orchard, son of a farm hand and a kitchen maid. But he had risen far in the world, a self-made man entirely, for in little more than sixty years, he had become the superintendent of all the Killigrew properties in Westchester County—and lived in the Lodge, a very handsome stone structure at the entrance to the Towers.

Trustworthy, too, "honest as old Scroggins" had become a Westchester synonym. And smart, or else he would not have been considered competent to sub for the secretary while he was away; but perhaps a bit old-fashioned.

He was not exactly up to snuff, as one might say, not a 1926 model of a secretary. He belonged, rather, to one of those dependable brands that do not indulge in yearly models—in vogue any time, anywhere.

He opened the mail and proceeded to read it, and sort it into baskets labeled: "real estate," "bonds," "stocks," "new investments," "social," and "charity."

Not being inured to the confidential curiosities of a Killigrew correspondence, as was Mac, for instance, Scroggins could not help showing an occasional surprise.

When surprised in this way, he would click his teeth,

shake his head, and turn down the corner of the letter, for inquiry later on.

He was thumbing one of these missives when a quick step on the Ispahan carpet caused him to look up. An alert young man, well under thirty, in riding breeches, advanced to the ebony table, laid down a riding whip, and sat in the Byzantine chair said to have been used by Justinian in presiding over the institute of the codex.

" 'Morning, Scroggins," he asserted, briskly.

"Good morning, Master Peter," replied the sub-secretary. Only Scroggins of all the Killigrew employees, dared call him by his first name, even with the prefix "master," but Scroggins had dandled young Peter on his knee, and had spoken to him thus since he played ball with him on the lawn, down through his college days, and to the time when he came into his inheritance. Young Peter never asked him to change, though to all other servants he became, naturally, "Mr. Killigrew."

Killigrew picked up the contents of the baskets labeled bonds and stocks, slipped rubber bands about them, and laid them aside. He spent a few moments looking through the "real estate" and the new "investments," and then did the same with them, saying: "Let these rest until McKenna returns. There is nothing pressing."

When he came to the "social" letters, his face became more stern. A deep scowl appeared on his forehead. He labored through letter after letter. Finally, he tossed them across the table, exclaiming: "Have Miss Laffan answer those—the same to all—no."

"But, Master Peter, here is this invitation to the Hunts' ball. Surely—"

"No, Scroggins, I won't go, nor to the Brainerd's dinner, nor to the Artillery reception—not to any of them."

"But—" Old Scroggins relaxed with a helpless gesture; then nerved himself to voice his protest. "Won't you permit your father's loyal servant, sir, to urge upon you the necessity of a little harmless social diversion. Surely, it will do you good, sir, to mix with people of your own class, to pass a word or two with the ladies, sir—"

"You've hit it, Scroggins," young Peter replied. "If there was an invitation there to a stag party, I'd go. It's the ladies—ladies everywhere. And all angling for Peter Killigrew and the estate, but chiefly the estate, Scroggins, and you."

A smile came to him for the first time as he beamed on his old servitor. "I believe it's you they are after. They have heard what a jewel you are, Scroggins, and think that by getting me, they will annex you, with the Killigrew fortune!"

A wry smile came to Peter's face as he bent over the final pile of letters labeled "charity."

Scroggins, however, had another appeal. He put it softly: "I am sure, Master Peter, that Miss Hilary would want you to go out and meet the ladies, to have a good time, sir."

"Yes, I have no doubt." Peter gave no sign that he was affected.

Ann Hilary was to have been Mrs. Peter Killigrew V. Daughter of the next neighbor, a Westchester family as old as the Killigrews and only slightly less rich, and a childhood playmate of young Peter's, she had died six months before.

"Ann," Peter thought, "was not a gold digger. She is the

only girl I ever knew I felt was interested in me rather than my money." Aloud, he remarked: "You know that my father always said the only chance a Killigrew had in matrimony was to marry some one he had known all his life. That was Ann Hilary. There can never be another."

He dove into the "charity" letters again. Most of these he crumpled in a ball in his hand and consigned to the wastebasket. He came to one with the corner thumbed, and smiled across at the old man, chiding: "You wanted me to do something for this one, eh?"

"Yes, I thought, sir—" Scroggins hesitated. He had been cautioned before about this practice of turning down the corners, but he knew that young Peter's bark was worse than his bite.

"It's an application for a thousand dollars to save a young man from the penitentiary. I recognize the handwriting, and the letter, too, for I had one like it last month. I had it investigated. The man is a professional beggar; writes to every rich man in America every month of his life, and makes a good living at it, too."

The letter went into the wastebasket.

"Here's one," went on Peter, picking up another thumb-eared missive, "from an inventor, who wants a hundred thousand dollars to perfect his plan to make all streets in American cities curves instead of straight lines." Into the wastebasket.

"And this one wants anything to keep him from sending his son to work; wants him in college." Peter tossed this to Scroggins, saying: "Have Miss Laffan send him the list of self-help clubs. If he is on the level he will get by that way.

"Here is one with a tip on the stock market, will share

it with me; wants only half of the ten millions I am sure to make—by risking five millions." The wastebasket.

"This one needs coal for next winter. Forehanded, eh? In June!" The wastebasket!

"Here is one from an alleged World War cripple. Send it to the Legion; they will investigate—probably a fake; the real ones go there direct. And this is a trackwalker incapacitated with rheumatism—"

Peter was about to toss that in the wastebasket, too, but read on and added: "Why, he worked down in the village twenty years; says he has seen me every day. Look into that, Scroggins. If it is true, see that his wants are attended to."

The last one got a laugh from Peter. It was from a widow with four children who volunteered to come and live with him in the Towers, and be his housekeeper, on probation, and "not expect to marry you unless you fall in love with me." He tossed this in the wastebasket, remarking: "Sure of herself, eh?"

Then Scroggins handed him a letter which he had held back until the others were disposed of. "This," he said, "I did not know how to classify. It's registered, but Victor signed the receipt at the post office."

Young Peter read the letter. It was from the clerk of the probate court at White Plains, and notified Mr. Peter Killigrew that he was the sole heir of the estate of Patrick Henry Nelson, deceased.

Peter thought a moment, then shrugged his shoulders, threw the letter in the waste basket, and rose to go.

"But who," Scroggins asked, "is Patrick Henry Nelson?"

"How should I know?" young Peter lightly propounded.

"Not a relative?"

"Of course not."

"An old employee?"

"Never heard of him."

"Who is he, then?"

"Another crazy seeker of the Killigrew money. Scroggins, let me tell you. McKenna made a list last year of the amounts asked by beggars through the mail. If I had honored one-tenth of them it would have cleaned me out—taken every last cent of the Killigrew money, with nothing left for the other nine-tenths. And they think up a new dodge every day. This will is just another one."

"But an estate is left to you—presented—given!"

"Too good to be true," laughed young Peter, picking up his riding whip as he started across the Ispahan carpet.

But when he was gone old Scroggins dumped out the wastebasket and smoothed the crumpled letters until he found the one from the clerk of the probate court at White Plains. He folded that and put it in his pocket, along with the letter from the trackwalker.

2

LIKE A FLUTTERING LEAF

AFTER AN HOUR in the office, a new brick structure on
the edge of the farm, checking up reports from the dairy,
and the vegetable garden, Scroggins went to the Lodge for
dinner. Although he lived in as much comfort and luxury as
any millionaire—style, too—the Killigrew superintendent
dined at twelve o'clock noon, was up at five every morning,
to bed at nine every night.

The lodge had been Scroggins's residence for fifteen
years, ever since Peter Killigrew IV had made him superintendent. Of Vermont granite, slate roofed, it was set
three hundred feet back from the main road, just inside
the entrance on the road to the Towers. Fourteen rooms,
three masters' and two servants' baths, hot water heat, two
sun parlors, a lily pond in front, and a tennis court in rear,
half hidden in Japanese fan trees and rhododendrons trans-
planted from the Caucasus, it appeared to the casual pass-
er-by as the Killigrew mansion.

The usual rubberneck tourist always mistook it for the
chief Killigrew residence, for the Lodge looked the part,
flanked by four fat chimneys and bowered in English ivy.

Mrs. Scroggins, who presided, appreciated this. She
patterned the operation of the Lodge on the method

employed by the housekeeper at the Towers. The servants—
she had four: a cook, a handy man, and two maids—were
not allowed to speak to each other except after hours.

System and order were the rule of operation. Each room
must be cleaned every week and vacuum-cleaned at least
once a month, in studied rotation. Nothing was used on
the table until it was weighed on the kitchen scales and the
amount entered in a book.

The servants did not have the same food as was served
the superintendent and his wife. One got cream, the others
top milk. When one had the first cut of beef, the others
got the second. When one had ice cream, the others got
patent jelly—the same as at the Towers. And there was no
sneaking; Mrs. Scroggins saw to that.

On only one point had Mrs. Scroggins failed to score.
She had things her own way except as to the evening meal.
Scroggins would not copy the master and dine at eight
in the evening. He dined at noon, had supper at six, and
went to bed at nine—like the farm hand he had been. In
allegiance to that old custom, he stood out like a rock in
a weary desert.

Otherwise, Mrs. Scroggins maintained the social standing of their proud eminence. She never exchanged calls
with any of the employees, except an occasional surrep-
titious visit with the housekeeper at the Towers, for the
purpose, of course, of being kept up-to-date on how a great
establishment should be run; but these visits always were
restricted to the downstairs rear sitting room.

Scattered through Westchester by hundreds and thousands were well-to-do residents, the substantial professional and business men of the great city near by, but Mrs.

Scroggins would not have considered social relations with any of them. Which of them could live, as she did, in a Killigrew lodge, on a Killigrew scale, with a Killigrew background?

In fact, there were only two families in the world whom she considered fit to associate with on a plane of equality. These were the families of superintendents of estates as old and as large as the Killigrews'. Yet they lived at a distance and she saw them about once in six months.

But she was a worthy woman, was Maria Scroggins, scrupulously honest, as became the wife of the Killigrew superintendent. In fact, her whole life was devoted to the practice of thrift, to maintain the highest grade of living and service on the lowest minimum of money expenditure.

The ideal of Isaiah Scroggins—few knew his first name, but that was it, Isaiah—was the Biblical one reserved for the faithful steward, to expand one talent into ten, to make two blades of grass grow where one grew before. He looked upon himself as the vizier to the caliph, personally responsible for the estate.

His salary in cash was small. Not one of those near-by residents, whom Mrs. Scroggins looked down upon, would have thought his salary sufficient to more than pay their rent.

But Scroggins got his meager salary—got it twelve months of the year, and all the years of his life. And he got the Lodge, rent free, with all furnishings, fuel, repairs, insurance supplied. He also had his electricity, gas, and telephone paid out of the same meters as clocked the Towers. He had free all products from the dairy, and chickens, all kinds of vegetables and fruits, berries, honey, and cider, with home-made wine. He had unrestricted use of any of the eleven motor cars in the garage, and a chauffeur was his to command at any time, and he paid nothing for tires, gasoline, oil, or motor repairs.

He had to buy only the meat and the grocery staples such as flour and sugar for his table, and the clothes the two wore—and yet he was a poor man.

In all his life Isaiah Scroggins had never made one nickel outside his salary. Other superintendents did—"by investments" they said.

Once Peter Killigrew IV noticed in a monthly statement of income at the farm, an item, "graft—$225." He asked Scroggins to explain, and the superintendent said: "The salesman I bought the last six months' supplies for the farm from, sent me a check for that amount. I asked him what it was for, and he said 'graft.'"

To old Peter this was a very rich joke. He told it everywhere among his cronies as a proof of the stupid honesty of his superintendent. Scroggins had plowed his "graft" back into the land, just as he plowed back the manure.

But he talked things over with Maria—everything. And as he was the vizier of the Killigrew caliphate she reigned as the subtle power behind the throne.

So this day at the dinner table he showed her the letter from the clerk of the probate court at White Plains.

" 'To him who hath shall be given,'" said Mrs. Scroggins.

"But Master Peter threw it away. I fished it out of the waste basket." Scroggins pointed out the crumpled folds.

"Oh," gasped the frugal helpmate. "How could he be so careless? His father was never like that! I'm afraid, Isaiah, afraid—"

Whereupon Scroggins repeated what young Peter had said about beggars.

Mrs. Scroggins studied the letter, protesting, "But this is a gift."

"I told him so, but he knew better."

Scroggins had no idea of questioning the finality of the master's judgment, though he did look quietly over the top of his spectacles to see what his wife would say.

She reread the last paragraph of the letter: "A certified copy of the will, with sworn appraisal of the estate, will be furnished upon payment of one dollar and the notary's fee of twenty-five cents."

"Send for it, Isaiah," she admonished. "It would be wicked to ignore a valuable gift. Old Peter would turn in his grave if he knew this."

Out of his own pocket Scroggins paid the fee, and two days later received the copy of the will, with the appraisal.

As the letter was addressed to Peter he felt obliged to show it to the master, meanwhile avoiding his gaze, for he felt contrite, and dreaded a cross-examination, as he wished to shield Maria. He tried to forestall criticism by stating, "I paid the fee out of my own pocket, Master Peter."

A bit of a grin spread over the Killigrew countenance as young Peter read—on the outside:

LAST WILL AND TESTAMENT

of

Patrick Henry Nelson, Widower, of Dobbs's Corners, Town of Far View, Westchester County, State of New York.

And inside

> I, Patrick Henry Nelson, being in full possession of my
> faculties, of sound mind, and being moved to this act by
> no undue influence, do hereby express as my last will and
> testament that the entire estate, both real and personal, of
> which I die possessed, shall become immediately the sole
> and undivided property of the Hon. Peter Killigrew, of the
> Towers, Town of Far View, County of Westchester, State
> of New York.
>
> I am moved to this act by the benevolence and poetic
> insight of the Hon. Peter Killigrew, and by no other influ-
> ence whatsoever.
>> (Signed) PATRICK HENRY NELSON.
> Dated, January 4, 1920.
> Witnesses Ruth Goadby.
>> Joel Eckland

"How did he know about my 'benevolence and poetic
insight'?" asked young Peter.

"That's your father, sir," Scroggins corrected. "Notice the
date—1920. Your father was still alive."

" 'Poetic insight'!" Peter ruminated.

"He was very fond of dowers, sir," Scroggins suggested.

"I see!" Young Peter accepted this with literal exactness
and went on to read the second page of the submitted
document. There were three in all.

The second page was marked, "Codicil to the last will
and testament of Patrick Henry Nelson," and was dated
January 5, 1920.

The codicil read, following the introductory legal phraseology: "As a mark of my appreciation of his character and virtue I commend to the care and guidance of the Hon. Peter Killigrew of the Towers, Town of Far View, County of Westchester, State of New York, my beloved daughter, Imogen."

Young Peter did not smile. He regarded it, as he did all documents and their contents, with a cool impersonal judgment. "The codicil," he said, "is dated the day follow-ing the body of the will. It is—or was—apparently the main thought, not the afterthought, of Mr. Patrick Henry Nelson. Well, let's see. Of what does the estate consist?"

On the third sheet of the document submitted by the clerk of the probate court the fifth reigning Killigrew read:

APPRAISAL OF THE PERSONAL ESTATE OF
PATRICK HENRY NELSON, DECEASED.

One morris chair, leg broken, worn, value $1.00

One kitchen table, with two chairs, used, value. 2.50

Two beds, two chests of drawers, three chairs, much worn,
value 8.00

One rocker, painted, Windsor, antique, value. 12.00

One parlor table, oak, used, value. 5.00

One bookcase, stained pine, old, used, value 1.50

One hundred and seventeen volumes used books, no rarities,
value 20.00

Silver watch, Masonic emblem, very worn, value. . . . 3.00

Rugs, linen, kitchen utensils, all much used, value . . . 5.00

Total $58.00

Then came the notary's seal, with attestation and signa-ture.

"H-m-m!" Young Peter cogitated. "That's a new one all right." He looked up and out of the window silently.

"Yes, sir," Scroggins assented, and asked "a new what?"

"A new method of making an appeal for charity. An ingenious fellow, Patrick Henry Nelson, and daring. H-m-m! Out of the grave! Well! Well!"

After a few seconds more of consideration young Peter tossed the document across the table to Scroggins with the curt command; "File it, and have Miss Laffan communicate with the Westchester Division of the Association for the Improvement of Young Women. See that the case of Imogen Nelson is investigated. If need exists have her necessary wants supplied."

Scroggins placed the document to one side and waited until the morning's business had been completed. Then, as his employer was about to leave, he asked: "Did you notice that among the effects of Mr. Nelson was a masonic emblem?"

"I did."

"You remember, of course, that your father was a Mason?"

"Certainly, Scroggins, and also that I am one. That is why I wish everything to be done for Miss Nelson that seems necessary and proper."

"But, pardon me, sir," Scroggins insinuated, "would it not be a little more, shall I say, considerate, sir, to make a personal matter of the investigation?"

The thin lips of the young man pressed each other tightly. He appeared forbidding. "No," he replied, "and I wish you would not mention the matter to me again. I don't wish to have any personal approaches made in this fashion."

"Very well, sir." Scroggins appeared crestfallen.

Young Peter noted this as he passed the old fellow's chair, and placed a hand on his shoulder. "Your heart is in the right place, Scroggins, and if you saw a little more of this sort of thing, as I do in the New York office, you might feel differently."

"Yes, sir. Thank you, sir."

"And don't pay that fee yourself. Enter it in the expense account. See you tomorrow!"

"Good day, sir."

Scroggins lingered on to tidy up the desk. That passing reference to "the New York office," impersonally, as though both of them were members of some large firm, spread through his consciousness like a rare wine. It was the sort of thing Peter Killigrew IV might have said; like father like son.

It was through such subtleties as these that the Killigrews had always bound their trusted employees to them.

Scroggins felt emboldened to depart from the letter of his instruction in the matter of the will of Mr. Nelson, enough to slip it into his pocket and take it over to the lodge when he went to dinner.

There was time enough to file it and tell Miss Laffan what to do.

Thus the consort of the vizier to the caliph came to pass on the meaning of this fluttering leaf trembling in the June breeze—only one tiny leaf in the vast forests of the great Killigrew estate.

3

SOME RARE TREASURES

SCROGGINS WAITED UNTIL the serving maid withdrew after the midday meal. He knew better than to bring forth any secret he did not want peddled up to the Towers before he was alone with Maria.

Then he exhibited the will. Maria jumped immediately to the appraisal, scanned it eagerly and cautiously. "That 'Windsor chair, antique,'" she said, "cannot be worth just twelve dollars. If it's an old Windsor, a colonial, it's worth up in the hundreds. If it's merely worn, and painted, and a copy then it's not worth near twelve dollars. I wonder!" She speculated silently.

"Public appraisers are not specialists in anything," Scroggins offered. "They just make a stab and try to be conservative about it, but if it's anything special they're like as not wrong."

"And if the chair is a real Windsor the appraiser might have made a mistake on the other furniture. Old American pine looks very shabby when it's not been kept up. And it's peculiar, Isaiah, what the dealers find nowadays.

"Do you know that Aunt Mettie, over in Poughkeepsie, threw a bed on the woodpile and it was so worm-eaten Uncle Brent wouldn't bother to split it for kindling, when along come one of them dealers an' paid her five dollars for it; and what do you think? Up at the auction sale at the schoolhouse last April it sold for six hundred dollars."

"Master Peter got a letter yesterday," Scroggins contributed, "from the Metropolitan Museum asking if he would loan the bedroom furniture from the town house belonging to Peter Killigrew the First. Going to have a show of that stuff. Museum people can't get it any more. Real American."

Even Maria, who knew Scroggins better than any one else, failed to note the almost eager way in which her spouse waited her inevitable next suggestion.

"Isaiah," she asserted, the tone rendering certain the finality of the ukase from the consort of the vizier, "you must go at once to Dobbs's Corners and examine this Nelson furniture. You cannot permit the carelessness of Master Peter to cost the estate any possible income, either in money or credit, from this unforeseen source."

"Very well, Maria," assented Scroggins, as if the thought had never before occurred to his mind. "I will have Joyce drive us there this afternoon, in the old Mercury sedan."

He withdrew to the farm office for an hour with the foreman and the dairyman. The office was neutral ground. Here alone Scroggins ruled by direct action, and he could adopt a more commanding tone when the foreman asked his advice about the seven year pine grove which seemed not to respond sufficiently to the new patented humus, and when the dairyman confessed that the Holstein milk had fallen below the necessary centigrade test that morning.

Here one could see the real genius of Scroggins, the old Westchester farmhand juggling with scientific apparatus more deftly than a college professor. He always gave the new-fangled notions a chance, but when they failed he went back to the ways he had known from boyhood.

He told the foreman to scrape the patented humus from the soil of the pine grove, and to replace it with genuine pig manure mixed with old pine cones from the reservation. He told the dairyman to discard the electric milking machines on the Holsteins, and to milk by hand. Then he phoned Joyce, the second chauffeur, to bring around the Mercury.

He was ready to grapple with a more devious realm—the rule at the Towers, presided over by Master Peter, and the rule at the Lodge, presided over by Maria.

In neither the Towers nor the Lodge had Scroggins ever won except by indirection.

Long experience had taught him that there was one open sesame to the heart and mind of Master Peter. That was to show him the way his father or his grandfather had done, or would do. The Killigrew fortune was built upon reverence for the past; it was the fruit of the slow, cumulative power that came only from sticking to one conservative set of principles through generations.

Just as surely there was only one open sesame to the heart and mind of Maria. That was to show her some way of saving or making money for the Killigrews. If Scroggins was thrifty, she was penurious. If Scroggins was honest she was overconscientious—so conscientious that the only dishonesty she ever practiced was in saving pennies for the Killigrews.

Perhaps Scroggins was reflecting on all this as he left the

farm office shortly after four o'clock that afternoon in the Mercury and called at the lodge for Maria.

They drove into Dobbs's Corners half an hour later.

One of those hamlets suffering from arrested development, up to the very edge of it, and for miles in every direction, lay smart suburban estates—in brick, in stone, in stucco, in broad clapboards just from the mill but cut so as to look a century old. Everywhere was visible the effort to look old, to appear antique, to simulate age—in new paint, fresh varnish, expensive elaboration.

The one place in all the countryside where there was genuine age, real antiquity—the hamlet of Dobbs's Corners—these smart builders had abhorred as if it were the pestilence.

The newest building at the Corners housed Perkins's grocery store. It was of brick, put up in 1866, a parvenu. Then there was the "new block" of Gothic fronts, frames, with the boards showing the nicked saw lines of the early power mills. That went up in the 1840s.

Elsewhere in Dobbs's Corners practically every house dated back to the eighteenth century—at least in frame and sills. Nearly every house was separated from its neighbors by a board or picket fence, and, except in the block by the grocery store, there were sidewalks.

Over all lay the silt of neglect, the detritus of decay. No building in the community had had a coat of paint on it in over a generation. Less than half the houses were occupied, and those by slattern, slouchy people who looked out resentfully whenever the rare motor car plunged along the dusty main street.

The other houses were falling into ruin. Windows were

broken, doors hung in and out on rusty hinges. Fences were broken and trampled down.

By the side of the creek which ran through the edge of the hamlet was a two-story frame building, built originally as the warehouse for the grist mill during the Mexican War. A fading sign along its upper story read: "Mullins's Hairpin Factory."

Boards were nailed across the windows and the doors of the building. When bobbed hair came in the demand for hairpins had decreased to such an extent that the Mullins factory had been obliged to close.

Though some said it was because the railroad passed by Dobbs's Corners and ran seven miles to the east, despite the fact that the railroad had been laid down for fifty years, and the hairpin factory had been going nicely until very recently.

Perhaps it was because the new State cement highway had cut out Dobbs's Corners, choosing an easier rise from the valley, a mile to the west. Even the telephone line had not come that way.

Everything had passed by Dobbs's Corners. Railways, telephone, new roads, gas, building, electricity, women's barbers, prosperity—everything but the privilege of paying taxes to the sovereign State of New York, and the equally sovereign County of Westchester. More than half the property in town was offered for sale to pay taxes, with no takers.

The hamlet was the decrepit memory of an age so near that all the rest of the nation seemed over eager to forget it—except through painted lenses, framed in varnished veneer.

The Killigrew Mercury, with Joyce at the wheel, came to a precise and measured stop before the worn sign of the post office. Scroggins alighted and went in to the window.

"Could you direct me," he asked, "to the residence of Mr. Patrick Henry Nelson?"

A scrawny, bearded old fellow, in shirt sleeves and fireman's galluses, peered shrewdly over his spectacles, responded with a query; for no one at the Corners ever answered a query from a stranger except with another query.

"You mean old Pat Nelson?"

"Very likely. Were there two Nelsons in town?"

"Sure. Pat and Geeny. What y' want o' him?"

"I'd like to know where he lived."

"He ain't livin'. He's in th' cemetery."

"I understand. I refer to his late residence."

By this time the postmaster had descended from his high stool, had come out from his cage, and was circling his caller sideways, like a crab going around a strange fish. He got to the door, looked out and saw the motor car.

"Huh!" remarked the villager. "Yew fr'm Albany?"

"No," Scroggins replied, "but would you mind telling me where the late Mr. Nelson lived—when he was living?"

The postmaster scratched his head. After a close examination of Joyce and of Mrs. Scroggins, and then grudgingly, as if at a loss for legitimate excuse for further evasion, testily jerked his thumb over his shoulder, exclaiming: "Over there, crost th' street—cater-corner—whar th' firebush is."

"Thank you!" said Scroggins, going to the door of the

sedan and opening it for Maria, who promptly descended. Together they crossed the street in the direction indicated.

The postmaster watched them until they disappeared inside the broken picket fence, and then made a bee line in the opposite direction. Even while they were rapping at the door of Pat Nelson's late home he was breathlessly confiding, in a hoarse whisper, in the ear of a girl who was placing new colored paper on the tinned meat shelf in the brick grocery store at the far corner.

THERE WAS NO response to the knock, either front or back. Scroggins turned the knob on the front door. It opened readily. They went in, calling, but there was no response.

"Yes! This is it!" Maria cried, exultantly, pouncing upon a low rocking chair in the middle of the tiny room. Tied to its seat was a tiny cushion of cheap blue and white cretonne. It was painted a dull yellow, but the paint was very old, for in places it was cracked and chipped, though the chair, as did everything else, seemed well cared for, dusted and polished.

Maria reached into her reticule and brought forth a freshly sharpened paint knife, quickly tilted the chair and began scraping away the flaky yellow specks from the rear underpart of the seat. An almost feverish anxiety seemed to come into her eyes. In a few moments she was rewarded— after she had bared the old wood for a space of several inches.

"See! Isaiah!" she cried. "The initial—it's old Pegleg Williams's mark."

Scroggins took the chair to the window and there, under the light, was able to decipher a paint clogged crude monogram "AW."

"That was the mark of Arthur Williams of Stamford—the best chairmaker in Connecticut prior to the revolution," Maria asserted. "They called him 'Pegleg' to distinguish him from Henry Williams of Boston, though Henry made everything, including chairs, while Pegleg confined himself to chairs for forty years; but not more than seventeen of them have been found. The only one to reach public sale was auctioned last winter at the Audubon Galleries for eight hundred and seventy-five dollars. See! Didn't I tell you this would be a find for Master Peter?"

Scroggins placed the chair down gravely. "Yes," he admitted, "I guess you're right, though I'm not up on chairs."

"But I am. Haven't I been reading about them ever since Aunt Mettie lost that six hundred-dollar bed on the woodpile?"

Maria now darted from one piece of furniture to another with the speedy anxiety of a gold digger who has stumbled on a nugget of virgin metal and cannot wait to explore the pocket.

One glance at the morris chair and the oak table was enough. Cheap pieces of the last—the factory—generation. She came to the book shelves. Ignoring the books as of worthless content she scraped her paint knife along the joints of the simple shelves, until she had bared one. Again she cried out exultantly.

"Look! Isaiah! Not a nail in it—only dowel pins, and dove-tailed, and smooth as tallow. Real old pine. A hundred years, I'll bet. Worth a hundred dollars—a dollar a year.

"Come!" She led the way back to the kitchen, but passed up everything there with a quick glance, and mounted

narrow stairs, bending her head low to get under the upper
floor joists.

The house, a tiny one, had but two rooms upstairs, without a hall or entry way. Each contained the barest essentials, a bed, a chest of drawers and a chair. In the front room,
where the curtain was drawn, were two chairs.

Maria's first act was to raise the curtain and let in the
flood of late afternoon sun, for the room faced toward the
west. A dull, faded and much worn counterpane had been
pulled over the bed. Maria pulled this down and revealed
a straw matting. She rummaged under this, pulled it up
and revealed slats, without springs.

"The spitten image of Aunt Mettie's bed!" she cried exultantly. "Look! The slats are basswood. The base is cherry,
and the posts are straight comb-grained maple, with the
pineapple finials. It goes back over a hundred and sixty
years. There wasn't a bed like this made in the Colonies
after 1770. It may be two hundred years old! Oh, Isaiah!
What a find!"

She began coughing, and complained that the close
room was unbearable. She descended to the first floor for
a breath of air, Scroggins dutifully following her. When she
regained her breath she persisted: "And it is all the legal
property of Master Peter, isn't it?"

"I should think so," Scroggins assented.

They were so absorbed in their search that neither had
noticed that the outer door had been left open. Now a light
step sounded on the porch, and the entrance was darkened.
They turned.

Coming toward them was a girl in a printed cotton
frock that came just below her knees. Her hair hung down

her back in two braids. She stepped forward wistfully and shyly.

"I beg your pardon," she said with charming hesitation, "but I did not know you were coming—not quite so soon!"

4

THEY INVESTIGATE

THE GIRL'S LIP trembled, but she looked at them bravely out of wide-set eyes. The sun from behind flecked her reddish hair until it seemed she was crowned with an aureole. In that light the color of her eyes could not be noted. They seemed like lambent pools glowing from a far distance.

"The postmaster says you are not from Albany, and that therefore you must be from White Plains. I am sorry I did not answer your letter. I suppose I should have done so. You see, my father—" she faltered, gulped and struggled on—"well—I didn't write. I don't suppose there was any use. You see—"

While the girl spoke Maria seemed strangely affected. At first she started forward and was about to speak, but a slightly detaining gesture from her husband caused her to wait.

Scroggins also was silent.

This seemed to make it harder for the girl, though now she mustered a smile with great difficulty, and went on, as by a terrific effort:

"There was no use to write because I couldn't pay anyway, and I suppose you will have to take it, because—"

A great tear welled over her cheek and splashed to the floor, as she added: "My father is dead."

At this something happened inside Maria Scroggins. She seemed to forget instantly the avowed purpose of her visit. She went forward, opened her arms and clasped the girl to her breast without a word.

Scroggins managed to get the eye of his wife, and signed her severely to silence.

"There, my dear, don't cry. Everything will be all right, I am sure," Maria reassured. In a moment the girl hastily excused herself and scuttled upstairs, saying she would return immediately.

Scroggins got Maria outside, beside the firebush and under the butternut tree in the tiny front yard where, in a hoarse whisper, he said: 'She thinks we're from the county tax collector's office at White Plains. Probably they have notified her, as well as the State's office at Albany, she must pay her taxes or give up the property. She doesn't realize it is only a formal notice, and that probably every one else in town is in the same sort of pickle."

"I thought she was crying over the furniture. She made me feel like a thief."

"No. The postmaster tipped me off by asking if I was from Albany, the State capital, and then when I said no, concluding I was from White Plains, the county seat. The girl has been to him with her financial troubles—naturally."

"But she'll feel worse about the furniture—when she finds out."

"Don't tell her—not yet."

"But it belongs to Master Peter."

"I know, but he owes something for it." Maria Scroggins became stiff instantly. "Ah!" she opined. "It was a game then! This Patrick Henry Nelson was a shrewd one. I wonder if he is dead?"

Her lifelong training as the spouse of the guardian of the portal of the Killigrew estate came to the fore. Shrewd doubt mounted to her brain. "You had better leave it alone, Isaiah!" she warned. "Let the lawyers look after it. This is not your work."

She felt beyond her depth, and suddenly guilty of letting the master in for some strange graft through a laudable cupidity in his interest. She turned to go immediately back to the comfortable shelter of the Mercury and the amiable, secure Joyce across the dusty street.

"I must find out, and you must help me," Scroggins went on. "I want you to stay here with her. Find out all you can. Tell nothing. Meanwhile I am going around the village to investigate." He started across to the post office.

Maria reentered the small living room of the ancient house, and looked through the books on the shelves. There were a dozen or more school textbooks in standard subjects, and well worn. The others were poetry, essays and novels, mostly of the earlier nineteenth century American classics—Hawthorne, Longfellow, Whittier, Irving, Cooper. There was a large volume of Shakespeare, and an old commonplace edition of the Waverly novels of Scott.

While she was looking at the Shakespeare, which was well thumbed, the girl came down the stairs. Seeing that only a woman was present she seemed to gain confidence, exclaiming: "Do you know, it doesn't seem half so bad as I thought it would, now that you are really here."

"Tell me, my dear, all about yourself," said Maria, feeling again that her doubts were unworthy.

MEANWHILE SCROGGINS, AT the post office, was engaged in a duel of wits with the postmaster, striving to get information without giving any.

"Who was Patrick Henry Nelson?"

"An honest man, resident of this town all his life. What's your name?"

"Scroggins. What was his calling?"

"Bookkeeper. What's your'n?"

"Investigator. Where did Mr. Nelson keep books?"

The word "investigator" was rather a body blow for the postmaster. It smacked of authority. For the moment he did not counter so sharply with questions. "At Mullins's hairpin factory," he answered.

"When did he die?"

"Five weeks ago last Friday."

"But the factory has been closed for some time, hasn't it?"

"Three years last May. Women bobbin' their hair licked it. City women. No good to 'em."

"Then what did Mr. Nelson do after the closing of the factory?"

"Nothin'—only t' die!"

"But he lived over three years. How did he get on?"

"Didn't. If it hadn't 'a' been fer Geeny I don't know what he'd 'a' done."

"Ah! The daughter, Miss Imogen, I take it."

"That's the highfalutin' name Pat give her. Geeny we call her."

"How old is she?"

"Sixteen last September. Comin' on seventeen."

"A good girl, I presume?"

"Good as gold. None better. Kep' her paw alive three year an' more."

"How?"

"Workin' t' Perkins's store. That's the only thing 'at kep' th' souls an' bodies o' th' two o' them together after the hairpin factory closed down. Y' see, Mister 'Vestigator, this is how it was—"

Scroggins's rather benevolent, but firm and austere personality had made its impression by this time. Flanked by the imposing automobile with its chauffeur which the postmaster could—and did see with the tail of his eye—imagination easily went beyond to conjure visions of authority perhaps even as far as Washington itself. And perhaps it was better to curry favor. The postmaster grew loquacious.

"Ol' Pat Nelson," he waggled, "was born right over in that house 'cross th' street—'herited it from his paw. Kep' books all his life from the day he lef' school till the factory closed. Mr. Mullins once told me Pat was a born bookkeeper, never could be nothin' else, never wanted to be nothin' else.

"Married Betsy Rawlins—that's her folks' house 'round th' corner, on 'tother side, th' one closed up—been closed ten year now. Every one's dead of her'n, too; Betsy died when th' baby was born, and Pat looked after the kid hisself; never would have a nurse. My woman used to go in an' see him lookin' after her—to help if she could; nothin' doin'. Pat was nurse enough. My woman said that Mr. Mullins might think Pat was a born *bookkeeper*, but she 'lowed as how he was a born *mother*.

"You've no idea, mister, what Pat done for that girl. Everything, by gum, that a mother would do, and a father, too, and a school-teacher to boot. Yes, sir, a schoolteacher. Wouldn't let her go to public school. Learned her everything hisself outa books.

"They was a lota trouble about it one year, a time back. They come over fr'm the schoolhouse with a paper to serve him, an' make Geeny go to school. Pat jus' rared up an' told 'em to examine Geeny, an' find out if she wasn't eddicated. So the school board 'p'inted the teacher an' Horace Day— that was the year Horace was justice—t' give her th' once over. And do ye know she floored 'em—yes, sir, took 'em off their pins with what she knew. Everythin' they was in th' books, an' then some.

"Bright as a button, was little Geeny, but sly old Pat had pumped everythin' outa th' books into her nut, an' she jus' bowled over Horace Day an' th' teacher till they ups and says all right, she don't have to go to school none; they ain't nothin' they can teach her. That's what Horace Day hisself told me one day right into his office. So they gives her a paper pardoning her from school, an' she hain't never been—no more'n a rabbit.

"Only they's one thing queer about her. Bein' as how Pat learned her outa books she don't talk like you nor me, nor any regular human bein's. She talks jus' like a book, everything grammatical, as you might say.

"'Cept'n f'r that little queerness, which makes her a bit diff'runt, Geeny's all right."

"I see," Scroggins assented. "Then you say she went to work in Perkins's grocery store?"

"Sure. After the factory closed. Gets three dollars a week,

an' kin charge shelf vittels at Perkins's inside list price. That's wuth mor'n a dollar a week to her. Perkins says so. Least it wuz afore Pat died."

"Do you mean to say that father and daughter lived on three dollars a week?"

"Sure. Pat kep' a few chickens an' raised his own eggs, so to speak, an' he never did eat meat; didn' believe in it— nor Geeny, neither. That saved a lot. Only toward th' last Geeny would bring jellies an' stuff like that from th' store, Perkins tells me. An' she's got quite a bill to work out— thutty dollars, I believe. So she can't pay no taxes."

The postmaster chuckled, looked cautiously toward his mysterious caller and adding, as if to placate him: "Which is not much diff'runt from most o' th' rest of 'em in Dobbs's Corners."

"Evidently."

The monosyllables of Scroggins, his self-contained intentness, and a somewhat inscrutable calm which became more so as the story was unfolded, seemed to reassure the postmaster who felt he was succeeding in the presentment to authority of a very difficult case.

"Geeny," he further confided, "has been sore troubled over them tax notices that come to her now after Pat's gone. Pat never told her nothin' about them. So she never knew there was six years' taxes due. A course, she jus' reads writin' an' takes it fer what it says. No use tellin' her that fer th' State er th' county er th' town to take her property an' offer it fer sale don't mean nothin'.

"I tell her: 'Who's goin' t'buy?' That's all need worry her. A course, y' kin come down here fr'm Albany er White

Plains an' offer it fer sale, but long's there's no takers y' might save y'r breath. Ain't that so, mister?"

Scroggins nodded gravely, which seemed greatly to encourage the postmaster.

"I'd ask you t' tell her, only I know how it is. Y'll have t' leave that t' me. She's that worrit 'bout what she owes. Cried a heap 'cause she couldn't pay fer Pat's funeral. She wan't expected to. Masonic lodge over to the depot paid fer that."

"Did Nelson leave a will?"

The postmaster cackled loudly at the apparent silliness of this question. "Why should old Pat bother with a will? Hadn' no kith nor kin but Geeny."

"Who is Joel Eckland?"

"Why, he's th' attorney at law over by th' depot."

"At Havermill?"

"Sure."

Havermill was the new settlement seven miles away on the railroad. Quite a place now, three or four times larger than Dobbs's Corners ever was, but the Cornerites always spoke of it as "the depot," a contemptuous condescension toward its parvenu prosperity scarcely a generation old, as contrasted with the two centuries of the Corners.

Before going there Scroggins called on Mr. Perkins at the corner grocery. The calm of his personality with its background of expensive automobile, had an effect on the storekeeper similar to that achieved with the postmaster. Only that instead of thinking Scroggins a tax collector Mr. Perkins jumped to the conclusion that he was from the orphan asylum as soon as he asked questions about

Imogen; this without any statement from Scroggins to warrant the conclusion.

"Goin' t' take her away?" Perkins queried.

"That depends." Scroggins was noncommittal. "Will you tell me what kind of a girl she is?"

Perkins looked outside to make sure no one was near enough to overhear. Then he returned and whispered in Scroggins's ear: "A bit cracked."

Scroggins started. His glimpse of the girl had revealed one singularly intelligent and lovely. "Honest?" he demanded.

"As the day is long—but simple-minded—like her paw. Old Pat was that way, too."

"What way? Explain."

"Didn't like people. Lived in books. Read a million of 'em, I'll bet, fust an' last. Got Geeny that way. Why, do y' know, I'll bet Geeny ain't never had a boy or girl friend in her whole life—ain't been to school, ain't never went to no party nor dance, nor nothin'. It'd scare her to death if a fellow kissed her—don't know what it is—ain't went out, y' see. Jus' t' home, an' th' store here, and with Pat. Sort of a grown-up little old maid."

"But pretty—"

"As a picture, but don't seem to know it. Don't dress up none."

"Has she ever had a chance?"

"What difference does that make? Ain't there poor girls in this village 'sides Geeny? And is there 'nother one 'at don't ever even put on extra ribbons, er nothin'? No, I tell y', she's a bit queer."

"Reliable?"

"Y' c'n count on her, if that's what y' mean. Allus on hand; make change proper; wraps bundles good; speaks polite; an' all that; but she don't visit none with folks; an' that ain't good fer a store like this. Makes people think she's too good fer 'em."

"Stuck-up, eh?"

"N-no! Not stuck-up, 'xactly—jus' diff'runt. Day-dreamin', livin' in clouds, readin' poetry an' sich."

"I see! Literary!"

"Naw! She ain't lit'ry. They couldn' git her t' th' debatin' society that met wunst a month over th' post office. Asked her special, too, 'count o' Pat gettin' books all th' time from th' travelin' library. Jus' mopey."

"It all comes o' her not goin' to school I allus said. Horace Day's t' blame fer that—an' th' school-teacher. They let her off 'cause she passed examinations 'thout goin' t' school. 'Twan't right. Every boy an' girl is got to go t' school t' make 'em human—"

The storekeeper was willing to gossip on, but Scroggins felt he had learned all he could there, especially after finding that Perkins knew nothing of the will. He returned to the little weather-beaten house, Maria was seated in the painted Windsor chair, while the girl, beside her, in a glow of excitement was telling her the story of Leatherstocking, Uncas and Cora.

"Don't worry, my dear," he said to Imogen. "Everything will be all right." He led Maria out toward the car.

Imogen opened her mouth to speak, evidently to ask what they intended to do about the property, but subsided, lacking the initiative.

Maria waved a cheery good-by. The girl stood in the door and watched them drive away, plainly puzzled.

As soon as they were out of earshot Scroggins asked anxiously: "Did you let her know why we came?"

"Nothing."

"Good. I must first see Eckland, at Havermill, the lawyer who drew that will, There is a big mystery here."

"But she had a father and he certainly is dead."

"No doubt on that score. What did you think of *her?*"

Maria was silent for a moment, while her hand silently sought her husband's and rested there, as she looked out on the luscious summer landscape.

"She makes me think of Clara!"

Their daughter, their only child, dead in her eleventh year, and gone from them now for a dozen years.

After a long silence Scroggins asked: "Why, Maria?"

"Because she's what I wished Clara might be."

"An orphan—destitute—with no background—and no prospect!"

"Oh! Isaiah!"

His wife looked at Scroggins with deep reproach, while he concealed his satisfaction with the progress of the situation.

"Don't you see," Maria pleaded, "but, of course, you wouldn't!"

"Wouldn't see what?"

"That Imogen makes you feel how utterly useless money is, and everything connected with it."

"Imogen!" Maria was already calling the child by her given name. Scroggins said nothing.

The wife continued: "It wasn't what she said, or did.

Perhaps it was all she didn't say, and didn't do. But some-how I felt the freshness, the purity of her—and her strange beauty, different from anything I ever saw before in all my life—something apart, divine."

"Ah!" said Scroggins.

He thought, "Imogen!" Maria had leaped instantly, to calling her by her first name!

5

AN OLD COLLECTOR'S GEM

AS THEY DROVE to Havermill Maria related what she had seen and heard while Scroggins was at the post office and the grocery. The girl had taken her out the back door to the garden. And such a garden! It seemed to extend far beyond, though in reality the space was small, yet inclosed in high privet hedges. The village could hardly know what was there—such wonders.

Even to Maria, accustomed to the Killigrew greenhouses, they were wonders, triple petaled and ruffled hollyhocks all along the borders, enclosed in multi-pasteled phlox. Then in one corner a riot of nicotiana, something quite new. And opposite a strange artichoke, with lavender flowers three feet in diameter. And near by tight, little, yellow buttons with scarlet centers. And giant sweet peas, big as tea roses. And much, much else.

The culture of the late Patrick Henry Nelson, the girl had said, a bit proudly and yet wistfully. She had spoken of each flower as if it had a personality, as if it lived, separate and distinct from its kind and from humans—something above an animal; perhaps even above humans, but different, quite different.

"And how she loves her flowers!" exclaimed Maria. "It would be a crime to separate her from them!"

"Unless she could have something much better," Scroggins corrected.

"What do you mean, Isaiah, better?"

"Wait till I see this man Eckland."

They halted across from the "depot" beside the chief business block of the prosperous little suburban town which the railroad had built up to ruin Dobbs's Corners. Over the stationery store a sign painted on the window announced:

JOEL ECKLAND, ATTORNEY AT LAW

Real Estate Insurance Notary

Scroggins climbed the stairs, knocked at the door, and was bidden to enter. He went into a small office, severely plain and scrupulously neat. A map of Westchester County hung on one wall, an engineer's plot of a subdivision in South Havermill on another, a calendar on a third, and a framed campaign lithograph of President Coolidge on the fourth. A lone man at a desk said, with measured courtesy:

"What may I do for you, sir?"

"Am I addressing Mr. Joel Eckland?"

"You are."

"Do you draw wills?"

"Why—on occasion—yes. Do you want a will drawn?"

"No. I came to consult you about one already drawn."

"Sit down, Mr.— Did I get your name?"

"Scroggins." The caller took from an inner pocket a legal

document in an envelope and laid it before the attorney. "I am the acting secretary for Mr. Peter Killigrew."

"Mr. Killigrew, of the Towers?" Eckland's little eyes went wide open, and he rubbed his hands nervously.

"Yes, sir," said Scroggins. "I have served the Killigrews, father and son, all my life, and I have come to you confidentially for an explanation of the meaning of this will of Patrick Henry Nelson."

Eckland opened the document, glanced hurriedly at it, and placed it back near the hand of his caller.

"Surely," he said expansively, "I will tell all I know. It was drawn on the dates there noted, in 1920, the will proper on one day, and the codicil on the following day. A little peculiar, I thought at the time, as it involved a walk of fourteen miles each day, on two successive days, on the part of Mr. Nelson. He was obliged to walk from the Corners over here and back."

"You knew Mr. Nelson well?"

"No. My acquaintance was almost casual. It began when I was the attorney for the Mullins Hairpin Factory, and he was the bookkeeper. Mullins was in legal difficulty the latter years of the factory's existence, and would frequently call me in to stave off judgment from various creditors. Then I usually had to refer to the books, and in that way came to know Nelson.

"Several times Mullins had trouble with him. If it had not been for me, I think he would have fired Nelson, but I pointed out to him that there was no one else available at the Corners to take his place. Besides, he had inherited Nelson with the business from his father, and really did not want to let him go—though he was exasperating."

"Troubles! Exasperating! Please explain, Mr. Eckland."

The attorney hesitated, looked out the window, and rubbed his head. Then with a chuckle as though he had overcome an unspoken objection, he continued. "As they have both passed on, and as the factory is out of existence, I suppose I may speak frankly—though, of course, it is confidential, Mr. Scroggins."

"Quite."

"Well, Mullins—to speak plainly—felt it was necessary on occasion to conceal certain items of income which appeared on the books, when the creditors came in, to spare him from bankruptcy; and to do that, he asked Nelson to make—ahem—alterations. This Nelson refused to do. Mullins told him he must make the alterations or get out of the factory.

"So Nelson did get out of the factory; but Mullins had to go and beg him to come back, for he was helpless himself in keeping the books. Then Mullins tried to make his own alterations, and when Nelson found it out he told Mullins that if the items were not kept exactly as he entered them, and thus in strict accord with the facts, he would quit of his own accord. A bit of a bully, in his way; but it worked. Mullins was obliged to obey."

"Mr. Nelson was an honest man," said Scroggins.

"Yes—and old-fashioned about it. Of course, it was best for Mullins in the long run; for through strict adherence to Nelson's system, which was quite correct, I managed to save Mullins's personal property for him when the final crash did come. I thought he would do something for Nelson on account of this, but he didn't; just turned his back on the old fellow and left him flat, and moved over by the river into the Yonkers district. He has since passed away.

"I rather liked Nelson, though he was a taciturn and silent individual, and when he turned up here one day and asked me to draw his will, I obliged him, of course. He said he had only five dollars—which I could well believe—and hoped that would be enough for my fee; but I charged him nothing, except a quarter for the notarial seal. Then the next day he came in with that codicil—and another quarter."

"Do you think he was in his right mind?"

"Legally? Yes—beyond the shadow of a doubt; and it was a powerful mind, too, in its way, a very powerful mind. Don't know that I ever came in contact with a more determined individual, though he was most reserved and almost completely self-effacing. Although the time he defied the school board about his daughter and the time he defied Mullins showed the spunk that was in him. A village Hampden, I'd call him, 'born to die unknown.'"

"A Hampden?" asked Scroggins. "I thought you said he didn't talk. Wasn't Hampden an orator?"

The attorney laughed. "Pardon the simile. I should have said 'a violet born to blush unseen,' only old Pat was hardly pretty enough for a violet. Now, if it had been the daughter—"

"What do you think of this will?" Scroggins brought the argument back.

"I think it is one of the great curiosities of jurisprudence. Eventually I expect to write an article about it for the Law Journal. But I have been waiting for the denouement—for something to happen—and this call to-day, sir, may be the beginning of that denouement!"

"Ah!" Scroggins hitched his chair closer. "Now, Mr. Eckland, you begin to interest me. Just what do you mean by that?"

"I mean nothing at all, and I mean everything. Somehow I have had a feeling all along that that will, innocent on its face, apparently the strange vagary of an obscure man, might eventually lead to something beyond—well, beyond the ordinary imagination."

"Please be definite, Mr. Eckland. You believe you see in this a deliberate plan on the part of the late Mr. Nelson to ingratiate his daughter into the good graces of Mr. Killigrew?"

"Well, that is in the face of it," responded the attorney, "and looking at it from the viewpoint of an outsider, yourself for instance, or any one who never knew Pat Nelson, it might seem merely the presumptuous effort of a destitute old codger to fasten his orphan onto the estate of the richest man in the neighborhood. But, knowing Pat, I feel it was a brave, a pathetic, and—a psychic thing to do."

"What do you mean by 'psychic'?" Scroggins demanded.

"Something beyond the legal or the moral code—though not inimical to either—something cosmic, elemental, something that only a self-contained, deep-thinking, wide-reading, upright old philosopher like Patrick Henry Nelson would understand fully."

"I thought 'psychic' meant something to do with the soul."

"So it does. That's what I mean. Nelson's body is gone, and of worldly possessions, as we know them, he left practically nothing at all; but he put his soul in that will. He has rendered it alive, potent. Why, sir, he has begun to achieve his ends right now while you and I sit talking about him!"

Scroggins smiled, not without amiability, saying:

"For a man who received no fee you seem to be arguing his case rather well."

"I have neither the ingenuity nor the directness to state his case as well as he states it himself in that document"— tapping the envelope—"but I know that a man in his will is likely to reveal certain characteristics, certain hidden strengths, unprobed virtues which those who knew him a full lifetime did not know he possessed."

A frown appeared on Scroggins's practical forehead. He felt almost as if Mr. Eckland was becoming too bold an advocate.

"Did Nelson ever come in contact with Mr. Peter Killi-grew—I mean the father of the present Mr. Killigrew, for it is plainly to him that he refers as of the date in 1920?" he asked.

"That is an important question. Even if my fee was nil in drawing that will, still I did try to conscientiously perform my service as an attorney."

"I don't quite follow that remark, but please answer my former question."

"I mean," said Eckland, "that if Nelson never did come in contact with the late Mr. Killigrew, his obvious purpose in calling the attention of your employer to his daughter might be easily dismissed. Otherwise— But that is just why I asked him myself."

"What did he say—what did he say?" Scroggins was getting impatient with the lawyer.

For just a moment the attorney thought the caller was as eager as he was himself to establish a just claim.

"He said that one day he had met Mr. Killigrew, the elder, while the old gentleman was riding along the road near the Corners, that he had secured some flowers from him—Nelson—and had parted with the remark that if Nelson found any more rarities to send them to him, and he would be glad to see that they were properly appreciated."

"Rarities? Did he explain what was meant by that?"

"Not exactly; but Nelson was a lover of flowers. He grew them in his garden, was an amateur of some importance, developed hybrids in a small way, and always in the spring hunted the fields for wild flowers, especially rare varieties. Did the senior Mr. Killigrew pay much attention to flowers?"

"He was regarded as one of the chief patrons of horticulture in the country. He never failed to exhibit at the annual shows in New York, Boston, and Greenwich. He took many prizes. You must have heard of his head gardener, the Dutchman, Herr Verhens."

"Ah! You see! Flowers level rank. Nelson and Killigrew, horticulturists, met on an equality. What more natural than that one should leave his estate to the other?"

Scroggins suddenly remembered Maria's report of the garden behind the Nelson home. Mentally he upbraided himself for not having examined it. Perhaps it contained exotic rarities even more valuable than the Pegleg Williams rocker and the pineapple bed.

But there was the codicil—and its barbed shrewdness!

"Why have you not notified Miss Nelson of the will and its contents?" Scroggins suddenly asked.

"I thought it better to let Mr. Killigrew first make what decision he desired."

Mr. Eckland surveyed his caller calmly.

"I see," said Scroggins, giving no hint of what that decision might be. "Then I would advise you to notify her, and suggest that she personally go to the Towers and present herself to Mr. Killigrew as soon as possible."

An inscrutable man—Scroggins—not to consult Maria about a matter so delicate as this. Evidently he realized the liberty he had taken, for he leaned over and said softly:

"And be sure you do this on your own, Mr. Eckland—not as coming from me."

"Quite right, Mr. Scroggins—quite right."

The "acting secretary" rose. As he stood at the door he remarked, almost casually:

"Has it occurred to you that when Nelson walked over here that day—fourteen miles, you said—"

"That is, both ways."

"Seven miles each way. Well, when he walked that first fourteen miles he thought he had said all he had to say in his will, that he had left his entire estate to Mr. Killigrew. What was not expressed, but what he meant, and what he expected Mr. Killigrew to understand, was that he was leaving his rare flowers, the cultivation of a lifetime, to another connoisseur, a horticulturist of rare insight who had promised to 'appreciate' them. And that that was really all he had to say. Do you follow me?"

"Quite. My mind has traveled even ahead of yours, I believe."

"Merely because you have had a previous possession of the facts. Has it also occurred to you that Nelson's second trip of fourteen miles—quite a hike for an old man, especially the second day running, when he was not used to it—was brought about only through his fear that perhaps Mr. Killigrew might not be quite so 'appreciative' as he had promised to be; and to insure the inclusion of the masterpiece of all his flowers, the gem of his collection, his daughter Imogen, he felt it necessary to specify her in the codicil?"

"Ah!" sighed Mr. Eckland with satisfaction. "Then you have seen Imogen?"

"Exactly. Good day, Mr. Eckland."

6

HOW IT ALL HAPPENED

AS THEY DROVE home in the early June twilight, Scroggins related to his wife the attorney's version of the will, adding: "When he told me of the meeting with Master Peter's father I remembered it myself."

"You remembered it!" exclaimed Maria.

"Yes. I was driving. We had the bays and the Brewster victoria. Carl was sick that day and could not go: so I was alone on the coachman's box."

"Really! Tell me!"

Scroggins recreated the scene:

FIFTEEN YEARS BACK; before the Great War. Westchester. June. Daisies dripping over the meadows like a fog. Violets lush in the woodlands. Wild roses climbing over the fence rails. Trees in full leaf. Skies clear. A gentle breeze.

Peter Killigrew IV, in the full flower of his robust old age, at the accustomed four in the afternoon, started on his daily ride in the carriage he had used for twenty years, the well made and once fashionable victoria.

Most of his friends and neighbors had long since given up the horse-drawn vehicle in favor of the motor car; but not Peter Killigrew. He was not one lightly to accept every passing fad and fancy. Mechanical toys he left to children;

he was a full-grown man, loyal to horses, as was his grand-father, just as he was sure his children would be loyal to horses.

Loyal, too, to old servitors; for there was Scroggins on the box, driving—Scroggins, the new superintendent of the estate, a competent executive, a highly intelligent fellow, worth and getting much better than a coachman's wages. Yet each afternoon, just the same, it was Scroggins and none other who personally drove the master along the countryside.

This day the customary footman was absent, ill. No matter. Scroggins was equal to a regiment.

The bays pranced with the tang of June freedom, Toby Belch and Semmy, winners of the blue ribbon for pairs in gentlemen's sulky, the fall before at the Dutchess County Fair. Twelve to fourteen miles an hour was easy for them—much better on a track.

An hour or so after leaving the Towers the victoria sped along the creek bottom a mile beyond Dobbs's Corners. It was Saturday afternoon. The hairpin factory, which they had just passed, had closed down for the week earlier in the day.

As they were about to enter a wood, Master Peter—the elder, of course, for young Peter was there, too, about eleven years old, sitting primly beside his father on the rear seat—called to Scroggins to stop.

In a near-by field, close to the edge of a creek, and almost buried in daisies and queen's lace handkerchiefs, was an old man delving among the grasses and flowers.

"Call to him, Scroggins. Tell him to bring his flowers."

Scroggins called, the victoria being dutifully stopped

in the dusty highway. The old man looked up, then calmly turned his back and resumed his occupation.

"Go get him, Scroggins. Tell him to come here," testily from the master of the Towers.

Scroggins was obliged to descend from his box and wade across the springy loam. The land became marshy as he advanced, and he feared he would get his feet wet, but he escaped dry shod and delivered his message from the vantage of an oasis of high ground a few yards from the flower picker.

Thus he could see the man was occupied with a trowel and pieces of gunny sacking. Some of these had been placed aside, forming a smooth dry spot, and on them sprawled a baby—a curly-golden-haired baby, laughing, and twining through her fingers a chain of violets and stars of Bethlehem.

The man reluctantly laid aside his trowel to obey the summons, picking up the baby in his arms.

"The flowers! Tell him to bring the flowers—the long-stemmed ones!" yelled Mr. Killigrew from the victoria.

Scroggins communicated his message, and was a bit annoyed to see that the itinerant stranger seemed little impressed by the importance of the summons or the eminence of its source.

The old man carried the baby's flower chain and a handful of huge blossoms on extremely long stems, picking his way stolidly over the meadow to the side of the road, where he stood by the wheel of the victoria and peered up into the wrinkled countenance of its owner.

As they confronted each other they seemed to be of about the same age, perhaps seventy, although the face of the flower hunter was unwrinkled as that of the baby in his arms, and his complexion as fair, while Killigrew's seamed brow and sunken cheeks testified fully to his years.

"What are those flowers?" demanded the multimillionaire rather gruffly. "Mallow?"

"Yes, sir." The other handed over the long-stemmed posies, the huge petals already drooping. "They don't last when you pick them, sir, not at first, though if you take them home, cut off the lower stems, sear the ends in hot water, and imbed them in wet mud, they will revive by morning."

Killigrew reached in his pocket and drew forth a silver dollar. With his right hand he extended this to the flower hunter, while he took the flowers in his left.

The smooth-faced old man refused the dollar.

"Thank you, sir," he said. "The flowers belong to anybody. They are wild. This is railroad land—only the railroad never came through."

"Take it anyway. For your trouble."

"No, thank you. I am only an amateur."

He persisted in refusing the money, and no persuasion could induce him to take it. Eventually Killigrew was obliged to pocket the silver piece, while the other went on to explain that mallow was a hard thing to transplant; that he had tried it in his own garden for several years, and at last had discovered the secret. It lay in digging up roots fully as long as the stem of the flower, and then in transplanting them in soil always wet.

"Of course," he concluded, "it is not the best time of year for transplanting, but if the conditions are observed carefully the mallow will thrive another spring. Would you like a few roots?"

"Perhaps, but—"

"Then I will get you some. I have a trowel with me. Wait a moment."

The old man turned back toward the field with his child still in his arms.

At that there was an outcry—from both youngsters, from the baby, and from Master Peter, lusty with the full vigor of his eleven years. While the elders had been talking flowers over the wheel, they had been getting acquainted across the open space of the victoria.

For the first time the seams came from Killigrew's brow. It was seldom that Master Peter wanted anything, but now he wanted the baby, and said so with that petulant childish authority which was a futile replica of his father's.

"Let the baby stay here," said Killigrew.

The old man regarded him severely, but without relaxing his hold. He seemed held between an innate sense of courtesy and an intense concern for the child.

"I'll look out for him, never fear," assured Killigrew.

"She is a girl," corrected the man.

"Ah! A girl, eh? And her name?"

"Imogen."

"Imogen? A pretty name. Imogen what?"

"Imogen Nelson, sir."

"And you are the father?"

"Yes, sir."

"Well, Mr. Nelson, trust me. My name is Killigrew. Peter Killigrew. I live over there a ways." He gestured indistinctly across the hills toward the far distant Towers, a dozen miles or so beyond.

If Nelson recognized the name, and realized the significance of the casual meeting, he showed no sign of it, either with word or look, beyond accepting the assurance that his daughter would be carefully guarded while he went back to the marsh to dig up some roots of the elusive mallow.

While he was gone she sat on the rear seat of the victoria, between Peter Killigrew IV and Peter Killigrew V, and showed them how to untwine violets from stars of Bethlehem without breaking the stems, rather an appalling feat in a child not able to talk distinctly.

Young Peter marveled at this. "It's a girl, my boy," his father explained, "with the feminine instinct with flowers. Now, with you, you young rascal, even at your age, you would tear those to pieces in unraveling that chain."

Imogen smiled at Peter, and Peter smiled back at Imogen, and it wound up by the boy and girl climbing off into the grass, where they proceeded to pick fresh flowers from the field, while old Peter watched them indulgently.

Evidently this was the very recreation he had sought in driving away from the musty, stuffy atmosphere of the old stones, of the Towers that lush day of early summer.

Nelson returned presently with a gunny sack filled with well-mossed roots, which he deposited by the feet of Scroggins in the coachman's seat. Again he refused money, firmly, decisively.

"Well, then," said old Peter at length, in one of his best moods, his face almost unwrinkled at last, "perhaps you will exchange with me. Come over to the Towers some day and let me present you some roots from my garden."

"Thank you, sir."

Loud protestations from the children in the field attracted the attention of the old men. They turned to see the baby apparently remonstrating with the half-grown boy. In placing the flower chain impatiently around her neck, he had broken it, and then had crushed several of the violets in his hand, perhaps inadvertently, perhaps in boyish sport.

"Come, Peter!" his father sternly commanded. The youngster advanced ruefully to the carriage.

The reigning Killigrew reached down and took from his son's hand the bruised blossoms. "That is wrong, Peter," he said, taking the petals from him gently. "You should never crush a flower."

Nelson, holding his little girl by the hand, looked on, mouth half open, as though with a stunned respect. It was the first time that Scroggins, from his coachman's seat, felt satisfied that this wayside wanderer had shown the deference due from every one to the chief of the great house of Killigrew.

The flower hunter gravely nodded in silent approval.

Killigrew told Scroggins to drive on. Nelson picked up Imogen and held her in his arms, while she waved to young Peter, and young Peter blew her a kiss.

Old Peter saw the kiss, smiled indulgently, and added, as Scroggins flicked the end of the long whip over the backs of the bays, "If you have any more rarities in the floral line send them to me. I will appreciate them."

The victoria drove away, with young Peter leaning over the lowered top of it, waving his hand as long as the flower hunter and his baby girl were in sight.

As Scroggins finished his reminiscence, Maria sighed, "Just like old Peter! What a dear he was!"

"I'm thinking of Nelson," said Scroggins. "He never came to the Towers. At least I never heard of it if he did, and I would have heard of it. I was superintendent, and no one ever entered the outer gate without my knowing it."

"But he did not forget."

"Forget! I guess not! It was evidently the great incident of his life. He built on it, and banked the future of his girl on it. I wonder if Eckland is right?"

"How?"

"In thinking Patrick Henry Nelson a great man. We'll see."

They made the trip to Dobbs's Corners on Friday afternoon, late. When they got back to the Towers it was to find that Master Peter had gone away for the weekend. He did not return until the following Tuesday.

On Monday Mac came back to the secretary's desk, with news that he was to pick up the loose ends and prepare to take all business back to town. Master Peter had done his required "bit" at the Towers for the year, would return for only a day or two, when he would be off to New York, preparatory to sailing for Europe the latter part of the month.

Scroggins waited rather anxiously in the superintendent's office for a summons. Instead, Master Peter walked in on him about noon of Tuesday, saying briefly, "Did McKenna tell you my plans?"

"Yes, sir."

"Good. Then you will get on all right until I come back in the fall. You can always reach me through McKenna."

"I have a report to make, Master Peter; something a little—well, unusual, sir."

"What is it?"

"It's about that will of Patrick Henry Nelson."

"What will? I don't remember any will."

"The man in Dobbs's Corners who left you his estate."

"Yes—and the daughter. I remember. I thought I put it in the wastebasket, and told you to turn her over to one of the charitable societies?"

"You did, sir; but I ventured to investigate myself."

"Ah!" The look was not encouraging.

Scroggins hastened on. "Mr. Nelson knew your father, Master Peter. I remember him."

"Knew him? What was his occupation?"

"A bookkeeper."

"How did he know him? Work for him?"

"No. He met him by the roadside."

"That couldn't have amounted to very much. Come!" Young Peter glanced at his watch. "I can't wait. What is it all about?"

"This young lady, sir; Imogen Nelson."

"Young lady!" Peter's face became very set. One could see the same lines that deepened and hardened with age in his father; lines formed through resistance to efforts to dissipate the Killigrew fortune. "Turn her over to the Westchester branch of the Society for the Improvement of Young Women."

Scroggins felt baffled in something that seemed very simple until he confronted what he so well knew to be the glacial side of Master Peter. "But this is different," he insisted. "She does not even know about the will, and yet her father has left you some valuable old furniture. Mrs. Scroggins says it is worth thousands, maybe, and some flower roots, rarities, something Verhens ought to report on."

"What has that to do with the young lady?"

"They are all she has, sir, and yet they are left to you. She is destitute, and she was commended to your care by her father. Besides, her home is about to be sold for taxes, and she is in debt."

"Just what I thought when I first looked at the will, a new species of foxy trick. The man knew father; it is immaterial to what extent. He knew him. You have investigated. You say the case is deserving. Very well. Attend to it."

"But it requires your consideration, sir?"

"Why? What do you recommend?"

"That you do not claim the furniture nor the flowers unless the girl wants to give them up."

"For a price, I suppose. No. Don't bother. Let her keep them. If they require special supervision, you attend to it. What else?"

"Her taxes, her debts. They are really trifling, but—to her—appalling."

"How much?"

"A few hundred, I should say."

"Will five hundred dollars cover it?"

"Undoubtedly."

"Then attend to it. Is that all, Scroggins?"

"But Master Peter, I want you to hear about it—to consider—to understand this case—to—"

"About the young lady? No, Scroggins, you take care of it. And let me out."

Which ended that.

Wednesday morning, about ten o'clock, between the tall granite pillars at the entrance to the Towers, walked a girl wearing an old cotton printed slip, brown cotton stockings, worn black shoes, and an old woolen tam-o'-shanter.

She was laboring under a rather large bundle of dull brown coarse cloth—gunny sacking, from which protruded the ends of earthy roots.

She surveyed the lodge in its setting of rhododendrons and ivy, evidently under the same misapprehension that took most passing tourists, that this was the main residence of the Killigrews. She rested her bundle on the slate flags before the door, and rang the little bell.

A maid in trim cap and apron answered.

"I want to see Mr. Peter Killigrew," said the girl.

The maid looked at the bundle. "Service entrance is up there." She pointed to a long winding drive, lost in the trees.

"But I want to see him personally."

" 'Personally'? What for?"

"It's a private matter. Just tell him Miss Imogen Nelson is calling, please." She looked aside demurely.

Rather a scornful smile came to the face of the maid. "If it's personal I'll call Mrs. Scroggins," she said, and quickly disappeared.

In a moment Maria came, greeted Imogen warmly, and took her into the reception room of the lodge.

"Mr. Eckland told me to come," Imogen explained, "and bring father's prize dahlia roots. It's not too late to put them in. He always said the latter part of June was the best time of all; then they flower right up to frost. Where is Mr. Killigrew?"

"Just a moment, my dear," Maria dissembled, excused herself, and phoned Scroggins at the farm office. In a few minutes the superintendent appeared.

He found Imogen in the living room with his wife.

"Why didn't you tell me about father's will the other day?" the girl expostulated.

"I thought it better to let the attorney notify you. Did he?"

"The next morning. I don't understand it at all. I am so excited, so mystified. What did father mean? Mr. Eckland thought it might be the dahlia roots. He inbred them for a good many years. They bore well last year. I have them outside.

"And does it mean that Mr. Killigrew will want the house? And what will he do with it? And where will I live? And what will I do?"

Her blue eyes snapped. The red curls escaped rakishly from below the rim of the tam-o'-shanter. She appeared unconcerned, free-hearted, almost gay.

"How did you get here?" asked Maria.

"Walked, of course. How else?"

"It's over twelve miles!"

"Nothing at all. I started right after breakfast."

SCROGGINS SEEMED QUITE satisfied with the situation, as if he had planned it. He excused himself and went to the estate phone, calling the Towers, and learning that Master Peter was there, at work with McKenna in the library.

The superintendent went to Imogen at once. "Come," he said, "I will take you to Mr. Killigrew."

They started up the drive. Imogen wanted to get her roots. Scroggins told her to leave them.

The thing had come to pass as he—and her father—had planned it. The girl was to confront the man! And what young man could fail to note the beauty, the youth, the sparkling light in this girl's eyes?

Master Peter had avoided her on general principles, as he avoided where he could, all young women, but this was different. This was unique.

Scroggins thought of the painting of "Cleopatra Before Cæsar," with the dutiful but intriguing merchant discreetly in the background as he removed the carpet from his precious bale of goods, revealing the superb loveliness of the young queen to the austere melancholy of the conqueror.

Only in this present case the queen was fully clothed, and the conqueror was not bald.

They reached a little anteroom adjoining the library. Scroggins told Imogen to wait until he called her. He went on into the library. She could hear distinctly.

"Well, Scroggins?" The voice was level, hard.

"That young lady is here, Master Peter. I want you to see her."

"What young lady?"

"Imogen Nelson from Dobbs's Corners."

"I told you to attend to that matter. I have no desire to see her."

"But she has walked all the way—"

"Send her back, then—in a car—and quickly—"

"I am oure your father—"

"My father often warned me against affairs of this kind.

He said every woman in Westchester County in the last hundred years had been breaking her heart with schemes to get hold of the Killigrew money. I don't want to see her. Give her five hundred dollars. And let that be the last of it."

Scroggins bowed before the blast. As he turned to go, Master Peter thundered after him, "And get a signed quit claim. No come backs."

In the anteroom the superintendent faced a seething tempest. He saw the flare of anger mount Imogene's cheeks, and rushed her outside. Once in the grounds she faced the superintendent.

"What a conceited little beast!" she cried. "Why, Mr. Scroggins, I wouldn't touch one penny of his money if I were starving—and tell him so!"

She started off rapidly, but halted long enough to call over her shoulder, "And *you* can keep the dahlia roots. *You're* a dear!"

He was unable to overtake her, and she paid no heed to his voice. The last he saw of her she was racing between the granite pillars into the freedom of the public road.

7

THE ATMOSPHERE OF ANTIQUITY

MARIA WAS THROUGH, so she said. When Scroggins related to her the result of the interview with Master Peter she saw no further hope for Imogen Nelson. The spirited *volte face* of that young person made no impression on her beyond rendering the solution of the situation easy.

"The spiteful little urchin!" she commented, when Isaiah repeated what she had said about the reigning Killigrew. "Master Peter has the long head. He sees farther than you or me. After all, I suppose it is only a bold attempt by a nobody to make Master Peter feel he owes something when he has no obligation at all. I think he is the prince of generosity to give her five hundred dollars."

Maria was nothing if not servile. Scroggins's life long habit of mind and action was to accept any and every Killigrew dictum as final, but in this case the female of the species was more deadly than the male.

"I am afraid she won't accept the money," Scroggins offered tamely.

"Never fear! Just watch her grab it!"

"I am at a loss how to get it to her."

"The mails are still operating, and Dobbs's Corners has a

post office." Maria was quite scornful. She made a motion as if to wash her hands of the matter.

"I'll bet she sends the money back."

"Not much—she won't. Five hundred dollars in real money—out of the sky, and in debt and about to lose her home, the penniless orphan. If she were not a bold little minx she would not have had the nerve to walk over here in person and try to horn in to the Towers."

Scroggins discreetly said nothing about his share in that episode. Evidently it was not desirable that Maria should know that he was still planning for Imogen. He was careful to let his wife read the quite formal letter in which he sent to Miss Nelson a check for five hundred dollars.

By return mail it came back with this letter:

> DEAR MR. SCROGGINS:
>
> Please do not think me unappreciative, but I cannot think of accepting this money from Mr. Killigrew. I know you will understand how I feel, and thank him just the same.
>
> Yours ever respectfully,
>
> IMOGEN NELSON.

Maria was not impressed, apparently. "Like her father," she said. "Bigger game on foot."

By this time Scroggins believed Young Peter was on the Atlantic, bound for a summer in the North Sea on his yacht. He could not be told of the failure of his casual charity, and Scroggins held the five hundred under compulsion to deliver it where it was intended.

A few days later he suggested to Maria that he might manage to deliver the money tactfully, through the guise of

buying the ancient bed they had seen in the upper room of the Nelson house, the one of the maple finials with pineapple tops.

"Splendid!" endorsed Maria. "Offer her five hundred dollars for it!" She held the mental reservation that Aunt Mettie had been paid six hundred for hers, and that there might be a little chance for trading here, killing two birds with one stone—or three; delivering the Killigrew charity in the form of paying the stipulated five hundred, selling the bed for a profit and crediting the difference to the Killigrew account, to say nothing of retaining the principal intact. A neat piece of business worthy of a Killigrew' stewardess.

The success of this enterprise, however, was thwarted, through the fact that Scroggins himself undertook to put it through. He rode over to Dobbs's Corners a day or two later, having transformed the check into cash—five one hundred dollars bills.

When he rapped at the door of the Nelson home there was no response. He walked around the side, and there, in the garden, he saw an earthy young person in khaki knickers spading and weeding.

It was Imogen busy about a bed of mammoth drooping scarlet tassels that matched her radiant hair. Chenille-like, they had only begun to come into bloom.

"Oh, Mr. Scroggins!" she greeted him, "I can't shake hands. I'm helping along my new *amaranthus abyssinicus.* They need lots of sun and free earth. Last year I didn't get them to bloom until August, but this year I've been babying them under glass since February, and—look! It's only the end of June!"

The brilliant tassels flopped about lustrously, two or three feet long, as though responding to the caress of her fingers.

"They look like Hawaiian leis," said Scroggins. "Verhens has shown me pictures of them. He says they can be grown only in tropical climates."

A silvery laugh leaped in his face. He felt strangely elated.

"I grew these in Westchester." Her voice fell; her face straightened. "Or rather father did. He worked four years to learn how. He always said he could grow anything in Westchester that was grown anywhere, only he did need more room and better heat in winter. Here!"

She plucked a stem of the furry amaranthus and bestowed it on her caller, while the momentary cloud passed from her face. "And let me pick something for Mrs. Scroggins. I'll send her a *cactus pitajaya.* That's tropical; but see the flower, six inches across. Father bred that to stand ten degrees below zero. It took him ten years, though. A long time, isn't it? And a lot of patience. My! I often wonder if I will ever have the necessary patience to keep on as he did!"

She sighed. Now Scroggins saw the wistful child look in her merry eyes. He had been fascinated by the oddity of the long botanical names falling from her lips and remembering the postmaster's remark that she did not talk "like you and me," but only "grammatical." And he was more and more piqued by the sense of the mature mind hiding behind that girlish brow.

He came to his business. "My wife," he said, "saw what she thought was an old bed upstairs in your house the other day. She thought it might be a Colonial—something quite valuable.

"In the front room?"

"I think so."

"Father's bed. It has been in the family for about six generations, I believe."

"Then it is valuable. I wonder—now please do not misunderstand me, Miss Nelson—"

"Imogen, Mr. Scroggins."

This emboldened him, for he was strangely bashful. He even blushed to think that Maria was not present. "Would you sell it?" he plumped out.

"Why—"

He could see plainly that she was at first pleased. Then her pale skin mantled a rose pink. Finally she burst out into the gentle little silvery laugh which was so disconcerting.

"For five hundred dollars, I suppose."

"Yes, that would be fair." He reached in his pocket for the money, the five crisp hundred dollar bills just from the bank.

"Oh, Mr. Scroggins, you are not at all clever!" She ran her hand through his arm. "Come into the house. I must get you some tea."

He was warmed and thrilled by her touch. Could Maria have been right? Could their Clara, if she had lived, ever have been so eerie, so nimble witted, so elfin? "What a daughter!" he thought. He experienced a strange spasm of ghostly jealousy of the departed Patrick Henry Nelson. He dwelt on the happy years of the old bookkeeper in this decayed cottage with this leal spirit and the responsive flowers.

Inside he produced the money. She gave him one reproachful look, and thrust the bills back into his coat pocket.

"Of course I'm not going to let you give me Mr. Killigrew's money *that* way. I tried to let you see I couldn't take charity."

She busied herself with the tea.

Scroggins stoutly protested his purpose was not ulterior. His wife was an expert on old bedsteads. She had seen the one upstairs. It was valuable. In fact, her aunt had one not so good that had sold for more than five hundred dollars. He really felt, so he said, ashamed of himself for trying to take advantage of an orphan and buying something from her worth more than he had offered.

"In that event," she laughed, "I'll take advantage of you, Mr. Scroggins. I'll sell you the bed, on consignment. You take it, sell it for what you can, subtract your commission, and send me the balance. How's that? Fair?"

"Done! And I think you are a wonderful business woman. Where did you learn it?"

"Have I not been working for Mr. Perkins for three years? And do I not buy all the merchandise he sells in his store?"

"But you deal in new goods—not antiques, where the values are so difficult to estimate."

"I know what consignment is. *You* can do the worrying about the value."

"You authorize me to sell at any price?"

"Except five hundred dollars—and—" She seemed greatly embarrassed, but looked at him rather roguishly, "will you let me see the bill of sale, please?"

He was taken aback by this and must have shown it clearly. The girl was revealing shrewdnesses of which he would not have suspected her. He made no immediate reply.

She divined his feelings, ran, and placed an arm through his. "Oh, please, Mr. Scroggins," she pleaded, "I want the bill of sale to be sure you really do sell it. You see, if I hadn't overheard Mr. Killigrew that day, it might be different. I do need a friend like you, but I am sure father would not want me to take money from Mr. Killigrew."

"Did you read the will?"

"Yes. But I can't—I can't—oh!"

She stood piteously before him, looking pleadingly into his face. All his paternal instinct welled up and overwhelmed him. Nature had made him to be a father, and he had been denied expression. He seemed to feel and to justify every contrariety of her longings.

He reached forth both his hands, and she placed hers in them.

"It's a bargain then," he said.

"Good!" said she.

Neither of them defined the bargain.

He added impulsively: "I'll get you the best price I can, and it will be more than five hundred dollars, with a clean bill of sale, Miss Nelson."

"Imogen, Mr. Scroggins."

"Imogen, then—only I wish you would do something for me."

"Of course—anything!"

"Call me 'uncle'!"

She passed an arm playfully about his broad waist and walked with him toward the gate. "Uncle Scroggins?" she tried.

"No. Uncle Isaiah!"

"I like that. It's Biblical. Uncle Isaiah!"

THE NEXT DAY he sent Victor with the one-ton truck for the bed. He had it taken to the carpenter shop, washed and cleaned, but gave careful instructions not to have it touched with tool or sandpaper. The basswood of the slats and the cherry of the frame seemed equally hard, though one was known as a "soft" wood, as hard as the maple of the posts.

The carpenter explained the action of time on soft woods, vitrifying them. The carpenter thought it was probably very old, though he wouldn't give it "house room." "Those old timers had no idea of comfort. Look at those slats. Man might as well sleep on the railroad ties."

A corn husk mattress, however, completed the bed; not the original mattress, of course, but one going back a good piece.

Then Scroggins told Maria and rode over with her to Aunt Mettle's at Poughkeepsie, and got the address of the man in New York who paid six hundred dollars for her bed. He wrote a letter saying there was one he might look over at the Towers.

The dealer came up the following Monday. Scroggins and Maria went with him to the carpenter shop while he made his inspection. He was a wary man, quite non-committal. He examined the marks of the conical chisel on the finials with a microscope, and finally said he would give two hundred dollars for the bed.

This made Maria furious. She revealed that she knew the dealer had paid six hundred for a similar bed in Poughkeepsie. He smiled sheepishly when thus faced down, but began to depreciate the Nelson bed. He said one side sagged below the other. Scroggins countered that this improved its antiquity. The dealer took out the slats and examined each in the daylight. He protested because they were basswood; should have been pine.

The carpenter broke in: "Basswood was from Connecticut, pine from Maine, but the cherry came from a Boston house, and the pineapple tops were done at home, right on the farm."

Scroggins got the glint from the dealer's eye, and when he suddenly jumped to four hundred dollars in his offer, the superintendent walked away, apparently too busy to listen longer. The dealer came to six hundred, to six fifty, and, before he left, to seven hundred and fifty dollars. He almost wept, and when Scroggins refused it, he pretended to be grateful, as he declared that the price would ruin him.

After the dealer was gone, Maria took her spouse to task. "You'll never get another offer like that, Isaiah. It's a crime to let the man go away!"

"Wait! I'll get twice that! Did you see how he winced when the carpenter pointed out the assembly of the frame in different colonies. I don't know a thing about it, but I'll bet there's a catch in that worth double the value."

THE FOLLOWING MONDAY at ten in the morning, a motley crew drove through the granite columns at the entrance to the Towers—in all manner of vehicles, from tin lizzie to straight eight brougham. From outside the gate protruded a red flag, with the insignia: "Henry Matthews, Port Chester, Auctioneer."

To the horror of Maria, watching from inside the secure shelter of the Lodge, these traders, this *hoi polloi*, drove straight on up the circular road to the front entrance of the legendary Towers, where stood Victor and Carl to conduct them inside the sacred precincts.

Straight on went the horde of money changers and antique hunters across the entresol, through the hall, into the library itself—the Killigrew library; into the presence of the Rembrandt and the Romney and the Stuart Washington.

There, in the very center of the Ispahan carpet, had been erected a small auctioneer's pulpit: before it about forty canvas camp chairs, and, by the side, on a beautifully polished handwrought dais of newly quartered oak, stood, under an electric spot light, the ancient bed, with its fluted finials and its sagging basswood slats.

Twenty minutes past the appointed hour a glabrous-faced little Yankee from Port Chester, the eminent and highly respected Mr. Matthews, in person, mounted the pulpit.

Behind, and peering out cautiously from moment to

moment, wondering how his stage management would work, stood Scroggins, his rubicund countenance the picture of bland benevolence. No one looking on him could, for an instant, suspect him of a devious or of an untoward act, "Gentlemen," shrilled the thin little Mr. Matthews, "I thank you for coming, this morning, to this sale. Before proceeding with the business of the day, I wish to make a few remarks. This sale is held under rather peculiar circumstances.

"I have accepted its conduct with the proviso that I am not to mention in either written or spoken advertisement the exact spot on which I have pitched my pulpit. Nor am I to certify that the article of furniture which I am presently to be privileged to offer for your pleasure comes from any member of the family of the estate whose guests we are to-day. At the same time—"

Mr. Matthews smiled broadly, adding, with an unctuous inference, as though all could well appreciate his sly joke, "We are here, and we all know where we are!"

Isadore Gitstein from Ossining, of the People's Furniture Emporium, glanced out in sheer awe at the Rembrandt and dug his broad felt toes well into the silky Ispahan. Even his polished neighbor, Mr. Flers, of the Flers Antiques, Inc., Fifth Avenue, New York City, felt oppressed both by the actual splendor of his surroundings and by their historic meaning.

Mr. Matthews proceeded in his precise style: "I am offering for sale this morning, gentlemen, this early American bedstead and slats. The mattress of cotton ticking, stuffed with cornstalks, goes with it, but the mattress is no older than perhaps fifty or sixty years."

He took a drink of water, rather pretentiously; and continued: "I am not permitted to specify the exact origin of this bedstead, beyond assuring the purchaser that it has been in the same room, within a few miles of this residence, for more than one hundred and fifty-five years.

"No warranty goes with this bed. Here it is. Examine it. The purchaser accepts all risk, and I will thank him if he will see that it is removed from this residence before four o'clock this afternoon. Packing and moving at his own risk and expense.

"Now, one word as to warranty. While no positive guarantee is made, I am willing to state, as an expert frequently employed by the inheritance tax appraisers of the State of Connecticut and of the State of New York, that, in my opinion, it is a perfect sample of the pure Colonial, while it differs from any other known bed of the period, in the fact that its slats came from one colony, namely Connecticut; the base from another, Massachusetts; and the tops from still a third, New York. This renders it, you will agree, unique.

"Now, gentlemen, your pleasure. What am I bid? Do I hear two thousand dollars to start it?"

Mr. Matthews appeared almost shocked that he did not immediately receive a bid of two thousand dollars. After dwelling for several minutes on this figure he dropped, gracefully, to fifteen hundred.

Then, swiftly a finger was lifted, and the cabalistic sign quickly flashed to the pulpit was instantly translated into a sonorous announcement.

"One thousand dollars! I am bid one thousand dollars for this early American colonial bedstead, with slats—and mattress. The mattress, gentlemen, you must understand, is probably not more than sixty years old.

"One thousand dollars! One thousand dollars! A fraction of the worth of the bed, of course, but it will do for a start—merely for a start."

Some one called: "Twelve hundred and fifty."

Mr. Matthews gravely shook his head and assumed a more conversational tone. "Gentlemen," he said, "merely because, for the sake of getting some action, of expediting matters, I accepted the absurdly low starting point of one thousand dollars, please do not misunderstand me. I will not accept raises of less than five hundred dollars!"

He was promptly rewarded. Another finger bid fifteen hundred. Then another two thousand—and a quivering eyelid somewhere satisfied the sign reading Mr. Matthews that one of the assembled hard heads was willing to fork over twenty-five hundred dollars for the bed of Imogen's father.

At three thousand the figure stuck. Once! Twice! The auctioneer's mallet fell. Poised for the third time a squeaky nasal voice—perhaps Isadore Gitstein's from Ossining—tolled out, petulantly: "T'ree t'ousand, vun hundred!"

Quick as scat, Mr. Matthews said: "Three thousand, two hundred and fifty!" And in a jiffy the bed was up to thirty-five hundred.

There it seemed to stick. It quivered and hung in the balance, and eventually Mr. Matthews capitulated. It was five minutes of eleven, and he had carried on his climacteric for nearly forty minutes. He compromised, and took a raise of fifty dollars.

Three minutes later the bed was being scrambled for at

the rate of ten dollars a raise, and there were half a dozen
bidders. At the stroke of eleven the price was at three thousand eight hundred and seventy. Then a deep bass voice,
hitherto unheard, said:

"Four thousand dollars!"

Every one looked to an elegant figure draped below the
Romney. It was Mr. Flers himself—Mr. Antoine Flers, of
Flers, Antiques, Inc., Fifth Avenue.

The country fry dropped out. The ex-junkmen from
the river and Sound towns quit instanter. The "gallery"
was gaping. Mr. Matthews prepared to knock it down. By
infallible auction signs he felt he had plumbed nearly to
the bottom.

But he was wrong. As his gavel hung in mid-air, a pleasant voice spoke from the arched doorway, saying, "Forty-
five hundred!"

It was from a figure in knickers and plaid waistcoat,
carrying a cigarette in a long holder.

"Forty-six hundred!" said Mr. Flers. "Five thousand!"
from the knickers.

"Fifty-one hundred!" Flers.

"Six thousand!" Knickers.

Flers threw up his hands in disgust, plumped himself
into a wide divan, and savagely bit on a pencil.

In a trice Mr. Matthews, who knew when enough was
enough, knocked down the bed for six thousand dollars.

"Name, please?" he inquired blandly.

The young man in knickers came forward languidly,
whispered in the ear of the auctioneer, secured the loan of a
fountain pen, drew forth a check book, and began to write.
The excessive deference in the attitude of Mr. Matthews

fired the curiosity of all, but none dared advance to ask the name of the unknown bidder. Slowly and reluctantly they left the library, glancing surreptitiously toward the paintings and the bric-a-bracs as if wishing they might too go under the hammer.

As Scroggins came forward Mr. Matthews greeted him with a facile grin.

"Satisfied?" asked the superintendent, when the buyer was gone.

"Quite."

"How much was the bed worth? Come, now—the low down?"

"In an open dealers' market?"

"On the level—without boosting."

"Twelve hundred dollars, I appraised it before the sale; but you never can tell at an auction."

"Thank you," said Scroggins. "I appreciate your efforts—and the price you got."

The auctioneer winked, made sure they were quite alone, and whispered:

"It was the atmosphere, Mr. Scroggins, the atmosphere of many millions in Mr. Killigrew's library. I'll name you a pretty penny if you'll hire me this hall for my regular auctions."

8

PLANS FOR A VACATION

THUS SCROGGINS SECURED six thousand dollars, minus the auctioneer's fee, and—a complete conquest over Maria. She forgot instantly that she had ever referred to Imogen as "a bold little minx," or "a penniless orphan."

And she tried to induce Scroggins to credit a part of that money to the Killigrew account. Neither for her own pocket nor for her husband's would Maria have been guilty of graft or diversion. She was too much a product of the Scroggins training for that. But for the Killigrew exchequer, already fabulously bloated, she would skin pennies.

Scroggins showed her the auctioneer's bill, duly discounted and receipted, which he proposed to carry to Imogen, with the full amount of the balance, fifty-four hundred dollars. Maria insisted that he keep out the "commission" promised. He refused.

"But Master Peter is entitled to it for the use of the library as an auction room," Maria protested. "The bed is no better than Aunt Mettie's that went for only six hundred, and the child would be well satisfied with that, which is a heap more than she expects."

"What would Master Peter say," Scroggins asked, "if I itemize 'Rent of library to auctioneer, $4800'?"

"He would be furious, but avoid that by itemizing it some other way."

"There is only one way to be honest."

Defeated, Maria countered: "What fool paid all that money for those old sticks?"

Scroggins lowered his voice: "Dean Hilary!"

Maria gaped. Ann Hilary's brother, next to Master Peter, the wealthiest man in the neighborhood. "But he will tell Master Peter about the auction. How will you explain?"

"With the facts. Truth is always best."

"Facts! Truth!" Maria snorted. "You are a great stickler for facts and the truth, and then led all those poor dealers to believe that bed was a Killigrew piece!"

"Don't waste any pity on a secondhand furniture dealer. Anyway, this was a means of beating them out of their profits, not of fooling them into parting with any."

"What do you mean?"

"I mean that Dean Hilary bought that bed because he believed it came from one of your relatives, and to mate with the one from Aunt Mettie's."

"Mr. Hilary has Aunt Mettie's bed!" Maria was dumfounded.

"Paid fifteen hundred for it to the dealer who bought it for six. And this is a rarer piece—wood from three colonies."

"Well, drat my stars!" Maria was startled into profanity.

The two faithful old servitors surveyed one another in mutual amazement, contemplating the same thought—the vagary that had taken possession of the inheritors of many millions. After squandering fortunes to bring from the Old World rugs and tapestries and paintings and potteries, they were elevating to the pedestal from which these works of art were temporarily displaced the worn-out and discarded furniture of their servants.

Accustomed to the whimsies of the overrich, it never occurred to them to question this latest peculiarity. Their chief object now must be to minister to it.

"The will!" Maria exclaimed. "That bed belonged to Master Peter under the terms of the will of Mr. Nelson. So the money all belongs to him."

"Only he told me not to claim the estate, and to let Miss Imogen keep it."

"I see!" Maria was crestfallen. "Then you must take all that money to her!"

"Naturally—and this afternoon. Do you want to go along?"

AS THEY DROVE again toward Dobbs's Corners, Scroggins tactfully recalled Maria's first impression of the girl— of the memory of the departed Clara. And now that she was in her way an "heiress," Maria appeared to forget all she had said or thought against her.

Ever since the day Master Peter had turned his back on her she had been to Maria "that girl," but now, after contemplation of that clinching check for fifty-four hundred dollars, she was again "Imogen."

On arrival at the Nelson home there remained one more reversal of form to completely cement the regard of Maria for "that girl."

It was mid-afternoon, and Scroggins had to send the chauffeur over to Perkins's store to get her. She came in breathless, a little abashed to find Maria, for she seemed more herself in the presence of Scroggins alone. She felt his complete sympathy, and perhaps easily sensed the volatile weathercock in the veins of the ductile Maria.

She revealed this feeling by greeting him as "Mr. Scroggins," when he had been hoping to hear "Uncle Isaiah." Perhaps it was just as well, however, for Maria to get that later.

Scroggins told her of her good fortune. She was incredulous at first. Then Scroggins produced the check and laid it before her.

"There it is, my dear!"

She looked at it, made out to Miss Imogen Nelson, signed by Henry Matthews, public auctioneer. She looked up shyly, carefully refraining from touching the marvelous piece of paper.

"An auction," she commented. "Oh, my! They had one here of Josh Trimble's things, but nobody paid anything more than a few dollars for them."

Despite the vigorous frowns of her husband, Maria spilled the beans. She told what an auction it had been—and where; the Ispahan carpet, the Killigrew library, the old bed enshrined in the midst of priceless objects of art like a rare gem, the subtle effect of vast wealth.

Imogen turned impulsively, embraced Scroggins until he blushed red to the roots of his hair, and exclaimed:

"Uncle Isaiah! What an old dear you are!"

This revelation of an intimacy in which she had not as yet shared caused Maria to freeze up.

Perhaps it was this, or perhaps it was "that girl's" intention all along. In any event, Imogen then did the wholly unexpected—again

She waved toward the check airily, laughing: "Then, of

course, that isn't for father's bed. It's for Mr. Killigrew's library!"

"It's yours, Imogen—all yours!" Scroggins protested.

"Josh Trimble didn't get more than two dollars fifty for his bed; that is probably all father's was worth. Come!"

She led them to the garden.

"But it is hers, isn't it, Maria?" Scroggins appealed.

The thrifty Maria assented rather halfheartedly.

Neither, however, could persuade Imogen again even to look at the check. Whenever they mentioned the subject she diverted the conversation. She showed them her evening primrose, just beginning to unfold in the late afternoon. She led them to her calacanthus, plucked a stem for each, and made them whiff its pungent scent.

As they departed she slipped the check into Scroggins's pocket. After Maria was inside the car she bade them wait a moment and darted back into the house. She reappeared bearing the Windsor chair.

"There, Mrs. Scroggins," she said, depositing it by the step of the Mercury. "You said you liked my chair. Take it—please."

"Why—why—" Maria sputtered, looking at her husband in the vague hope he might approve. She had wanted that chair from the moment she first saw it, with its eleven back spokes, and its cracked yellow paint, and the faint mono-gram—AW—on its seat.

Before either could say more, Imogen had thrust the chair through the door of the Mercury, where it rested lightly on Maria's feet, and whirled back through the gate, waving merrily to them.

"What shall I do, Isaiah?" Maria asked.

"Get out and thank her," said Scroggins.

Mrs. Scroggins did not alight, but she opened the door on her side, called Imogen to her, and embraced her.

"You adorable child!" she exclaimed. "And why have you not been calling me 'Aunt Maria'?"

Scroggins later declared Imogen winked over his wife's shoulder at him as she replied in Mrs. Scroggins's ear:

"I am so glad you want me to, Aunt Maria!"

They drove off in a glow of—something, they hardly knew what.

"The weather is very fine!" said Maria.

"Best day of the year!" Scroggins assented.

They were halfway home before Scroggins remembered that the check was in his pocket, made out to Imogen Nelson. He made a rapid calculation. All right. Matthews could give him another—made out as he directed.

"Master Peter told me to attend to everything in connection with Imogen," he ruminated, "and I must obey instructions."

"The latitude was wide," Maria assented.

"Turned the estate back to her, with five hundred to boot."

"And told you to look after it, didn't he?"

"Yes, personally."

"You will have to do just as he said, Isaiah!"

"Of course, Maria."

Both seemed quite satisfied.

But after they had dined, in semistate as usual, and alone, in the Lodge, and the long June twilight was at an end, and it was about time to retire, Scroggins said:

"Seems as if the Lodge's terrible lonely, Maria."

Mrs. Scroggins sighed. "It is lonely, Isaiah!" she admitted. "Strange you never noticed it before."

"I notice it now."

Again, as they turned out the lights and withdrew to the upper floor, Maria remarked:

"It's not hardly right for a young girl to live alone."

"Very unsafe."

"Dangerous!"

"Especially in a half deserted village."

"Like Dobbs's Corners."

They looked at each other grimly. They were thinking the same thought.

Maria voiced it first. "But she's awfully sot in her ways. And very independent!"

"Independent as a wood sawyer!" Isaiah responded.

"I wonder if you couldn't persuade her, for her own safety, to come over here—"

"I can try," Scroggins assented rather half-heartedly.

"Just on a visit—to me—to us—to Uncle Isaiah and Aunt Maria. She hasn't anything against us. It's only Master Peter. And she wouldn't see him."

Maria was pleading with her spouse, though neither realized the intentness of her manner, the anxiety with which she was estimating her chances with "the penniless orphan."

"I'll go back to-morrow and invite her," Scroggins suggested.

"The very thing, Isaiah—and she can have the southwest room, over the porte-cochère. The sun doesn't get there until one o'clock, and those new awnings protect it fully anyway. But we'll have to buy her some clothes. I wonder if she will let us!"

"We'll try to manage."

"It will have to be done very carefully—not to let her know we're giving her things."

"Not to let her know Master Peter's giving them."

"He won't be. She has money of her own."

"If I can get her to admit it."

SO THEY WENT on, long after the lights were out, discussing ways of adapting themselves to the vivid, definite, and poignant personality of the "bold little minx."

Imogen had captured them both—completely.

The next day Scroggins decided he would have to act boldly. He drove to Dobbs's Corners, and, instead of stopping before the Nelson home, as he had been doing, went directly to Perkins's store.

Inside, Imogen, her long legs incased in white cotton stockings, her hair braided down her back, was wrapping an order of tinned milk and bag sugar for a customer. Perkins was perched behind his high desk in the rear, reading the weekly *Argosy-Allstory.*

Imogen saw him enter, but went on with her duties. Scroggins passed to the rear and engaged Perkins in an animated conversation. When it was over the customer had gone. He called to her. She came to where he was standing with the grocer.

"Imogen," he said, "I have been talking with Mr. Perkins, and he agrees with me that you need a vacation."

"What for?" she demanded.

"For a vacation—to rest—to get away from routine."

"I'm not tired. I sit down more than half the time in the store. Don't I, Mr. Perkins?"

The grocer assented glumly, regarding the caller, whose limousine he was watching with one eye, with pent-up interest.

"That's not the point. It will do you good to get away for a bit—to have a change of scene."

"Oh, I don't know!"

Imogen was puzzled. She cocked her head to one side like a bird regarding a change in the weather.

"And Mr. Perkins has agreed to let you go—for a few weeks."

"But—" Imogen flushed and looked down, embarrassed. "I—I can't afford it."

"It won't cost anything."

"But—oh, Mr. Perkins—" She regarded her employer in embarrassed dumbness.

"If it's yer bill, Geeny, 't needn't bother y' none." Scroggins punched the grocer with his elbow, reminding him of his promise that nothing was to be said of the money that had just passed between them. "An' I'd advise y't' go. 'T'll do y' good. Y' needn't worry. C'm'n back when y' feel like it."

"Let's go over to the house and talk about it," Scroggins interposed.

Imogen went with him, wonderingly and protesting.

When they reached the garden she turned on him, exclaiming:

"I know why you did that. So I could have more time for my garden. But the garden doesn't need so much attention now. It's summer. If I only had more time in the spring I could have separated the iris and the peonies as father told me I should."

"Good!" said Scroggins. "Then the garden won't miss you so much while you are visiting your Aunt Maria."

She appeared suddenly to shrivel up.

"No! No!" she protested.

"Why not?" he added softly, as if answering her unspoken objection. "Mr. Killigrew is in Europe, and you will be a guest of the Lodge, and that is Maria's home, you know—Maria's and mine."

Tears came to her eyes. She hid her head in his coat front.

"Uncle Isaiah," she sobbed, "I feel almost as if you were another father to me. You seem to know how a girl feels—just as my own father did."

He kissed the stray reddish hairs on the top of her head.

"You make me very happy, my dear," he said. "Come!"

She was suddenly distraught again. "But the garden! How can I leave it to the weeds—and without water."

"You can drive over every day or two and look after it, if you like."

"How wonderful! What a dream! And does Aunt Maria want me, too?"

Once determined, she became a fever of preparation. She had no receptacle for her things, but she packed them into a bundle, tied in an old piece of cretonne left over from the year before in making a bed cover.

An hour later the Mercury, Carl at the wheel, drove between the granite columns of the Towers, and stopped before the Lodge. Maria, evidently on the watch, came through the front door, embraced the cotton-legged girl, and led her inside with her cretonne bundle. Up the wide stairs, along a spacious corridor, and to a huge room with wide windows on three sides, the whole top of the porte-cochère.

From it one could survey the valley below for miles in all directions. From a comparatively small window in the rear Imogen could look into the dour magnificence of the stately Towers, set back spaciously in its ten acres of lawn.

"Will this do, my dear?" asked the scrupulous Maria, fearful lest she make some slip to offend her eerie visitor.

"Is this your room?" Imogen asked, abashed, as she surveyed the burnished silk set in the walls in place of paper, and noted the tasseled silk coverings on the low hung lamps.

"No. It's yours!"

"Mine!"

Imogen looked at the bed, a three-quarter mound of snowy sheets, surmounted with a pure linen covering of pale lemon color worked in medallions of silhouetted lavender. She saw the landscape on the rear wall, a rather pretentious thing by William Keith, discarded from the Towers several years before. She saw the chaise longue, with its sateeny tongue of overstuffed downiness; the nice table of old walnut inlaid with stripes of cherry, surmounted with a gold-topped vacuum bottle—and beyond—a little bookcase with its tantalizing array of morocco-bound classic titles.

"Well!" she murmured. "Ivanhoe never did as well for Rebecca!"

Maria left her and went below to Scroggins, who was waiting to learn if all was well.

He was not easily reassured.

"We will have to be very careful not to offend her," he said. "She's as flittery as a wild bird."

"And as adorable!" added Maria.

9

A GREAT NAME COUNTS

WHEN PETER KILLIGREW reached his town house that June he found it not so easy to command the skilled workmen he required to complete the equipment on his yacht, the Tumbleweed. That was rather a gypsy name for a vessel that cost more than the usual ocean liner, that carried every modern equipment, and some things known on no other vessel.

What other ship, for instance, could boast possession of a set of microscopes capable of measuring any known minutiae of sea life, or a chemical laboratory competent to carry on over a course of months any species of experiments? To say nothing of a heterodyne radio, a movie theater, and all the casual luxuries, such as a swimming pool, and a flower garden with tropical humus and sixty varieties of growing plants.

Peter had crossed the Atlantic once on a regular liner, in the presidential suite, of course, but never again! Too much curiosity on the part of fellow travelers. No privacy! Too many ingenious schemes to induce him to meet marriageable daughters. The world seemed filled with determined, ambitious, and extremely resourceful mammas!

However, the securing of privacy in crossing the ocean

was the least of reasons for equipping the Tumbleweed as it was equipped. The chief reason was Peter's hobby of oceanography. Except for the Prince of Monaco and Billy Van Pelt, his chief crony, there was no other amateur in the world who knew as much about deep-sea life as did Peter Killigrew—nor cared as much.

Of this absorbing love—or passion—Scroggins knew only vaguely, for Peter had never brought evidence of it to Westchester. The Towers was only a formal residence, the ancestral seat. It bored Peter. He only kept it up through fidelity to the family traditions.

His heart was in his aquariums and the Tumbleweed. He never even spoke of it to Scroggins, but it was the underlying reason for his scant courtesy in considering problems connected with the Towers. When he told Scroggins he was going to Europe that summer he did not consider it necessary to specify how or where. Scroggins's only touch was through McKenna and the town office.

So the letter Scroggins wrote about the auction was forwarded to him at his Long Island estate, on the south shore, near Montauk, where he had his aquariums, beyond which, in the drydock, the Tumbleweed was being fitted with a larger coffer dam, capable of trawling in very rough seas. The letter said:

> DEAR MASTER PETER:
>
>   In regard to your instructions concerning Miss Nelson I wish to report that the official appraisal of the estate was most inadequate. The bed, alone, proved to be an antique of considerable value. As it was left to you I caused it to be auctioned, and have realized from the sale the net sum of five thou-

sand four hundred dollars. Pursuant to your instructions, I tendered this to Miss Nelson, together with the five hundred dollars you instructed me to give her. She has refused to accept both, and, therefore, I am holding to your order the sum of five thousand nine hundred dollars. What shall I do with it?

Yours very truly,

Isaiah Scroggins.

As it happened, the day that Peter got this letter Billy Van Pelt motored over from Southampton to look at the new tanks, and the cartouches painted over them by Twilling, the great marine artist—wonderful studies of marine life, held sacred by Peter to a few intimates.

Billy had with him in his Scrappy roadster a guest, Dean Hilary, Peter's neighbor in Westchester.

At dinner that night Hilary asked, "Why did you let that old American bedstead get away from you, Peter?"

"What American bedstead?"

The fat was in the fire. Hilary, after a bit of questioning, told the story of the auction in the Killigrew library, the bedstead enthroned on the Ispahan carpet, the ex-junk-men vying with the Fifth Avenue dealers, with the prize eventually carried off by a neighbor.

"Hm!" said Peter. "First I heard of it."

"Your superintendent had his nerve then. That's all I can say!" Hilary remarked.

"Scroggins has always been dependable," Peter lamely defended his father's servitor.

But the next morning, over the long distance, to McKenna, in New York, he was not so sweet. "Take a letter to Scroggins," he said. "Tell him to give that money to the girl in Dobbs's Corner. I don't want it. Get it to her somehow. That's up to him. But no more auctions. Make this very plain. I am astonished that the Towers should be used in that way. If there are any more auctions let him hold them in the cattle shed."

McKenna toned this down for the letter, but he got Scroggins on the long distance, for he liked the old superintendent, and admonished him in friendly fashion. "Mr. Killigrew," he phoned, "seems much put out about some auction you held—didn't tell me much about it—but thought I'd pass on the tip; lay off auctions in the Towers."

"Yes, Mac. I understand."

"What have you been doing, you old rascal?"

"Living up to instructions. I guess Master Peter forgot."

"I know nothing about it. I am merely telling you."

"Thought he was in Europe."

"He is—publicly. Privately he's on Long Island. Sails from Montauk, though, in a couple of days, on the Tumbleweed. So long."

Scroggins did not tell Maria about this, but he said to himself, "The cattle shed—huh!" Fortunately, there was no need for more auctions.

There was need, however, for some way in which to get rid of that six thousand dollars. He had slipped a little of it, a trifle of thirty or more, to Perkins the grocer. Then he paid the overdue taxes on the Nelson home—a few hundred more.

Now Imogen was free from debt and had a balance in the bank of more than five thousand dollars, and didn't know it—and he was afraid to tell her.

Master Peter did not know she was a guest at the Lodge. She did not know that Master Peter had wished on her a sum that her father would have regarded a comfortable fortune.

Scroggins felt like a conspirator in a drama whose denouement he could not possibly foresee.

July sped away on wings of light. The Oriental poppies grew lush on their mammoth stalks. The rainbow corn quivered in the brilliant heat. Westchester mellowed in the supremacy of its luxurious beauty.

Imogen was in fairyland. Verhens, the Dutch gardener at the Towers, initiated her into the mysteries of the Killigrew flower acres. There were four of them back of the greenhouses, but in all those acres were no *cactus pitajayo,* no *amaranthus dbyssinicus.*

When Verhens discovered that he was dealing with a flower expert he gave particular attention. He respected only a knowledge of floriculture. Any one of several millionaires would have welcomed him and given him employment on a day's notice. So he cared little for millionaires, but to Imogen's knowledge of root growth he "took off his hat," as he said himself.

Perhaps it wasn't jealousy that gave Scroggins the great idea. Perhaps it was just his mounting paternal love for Imogen, though his idea did furnish a good excuse to get Imogen away from Verhens, with whom she was spending most of her time.

He confided it to Maria one day toward the end of July, when Imogen had said finally—for the steenth time—that she must go back to Dobbs's Corners and Perkins's store.

"We'll have to put her in school in the fall!"

"She's exempted from public school."

"A private school, Maria, of course. You can't pay a public school; and there's that five thousand I got to spend on her."

"A private school!"

Maria had served enough in the house of the great to know that there was only one private school a girl of a really exclusive family should be permitted to enter.

"Then it must be Mrs. Morton's!" Maria asserted with a finality which became her.

Mrs. Morton's—on the Sound, at Pumice Bay, twenty miles away. Ann Hilary had gone there; the sort of school that new money could not get into, and that no old family could enter without money. It took old money to get a girl into Mrs. Morton's; money at least three generations old, and plenty of it.

The more Maria thought of it the better she liked the idea. If Imogen could be entered at Mrs. Morton's—at present, she admitted to herself, a desire seemingly impossible of realization—she would secure an enormous advantage. As guardian, or next of kin, she would be privileged on visitor's days and at the end of the school year to appear at Mrs. Morton's, where she could associate on terms of equality with the mothers or the guardians of the other girls.

That would be a society which her severe restrictions would approve. To be a frequenter of Mrs. Morton's! What a coup! No other superintendent's wife in all Westchester could boast *entree* like that! She urged Scroggins to get busy.

He did, and the letter he wrote, signed Isaiah Scroggins, came back, in due time, with a polite but firm finality.

Sorry, but the rolls at the Morton School in Pumice Bay were filled.

Maria was not to be so easily put aside. She ordered the Mercury out, and drove to Pumice Bay the following day. A precise young woman received her. Mrs. Morton, she said, was engaged. What could she do? An entry? Sorry. The rolls were all filled.

Maria, dressed for the occasion in summery flounce, and with a manner even more haughty than that of the young secretary, remarked, rather languidly: "Too bad! Mr. Killigrew will be disappointed!" and turned toward the Mercury.

The young woman gasped, and hastened after her. "Mr. Killigrew!" she exclaimed. "Mr. Peter Killigrew?"

"The Fifth," amended Maria, seating herself in the Mercury's rear seat, and opening her mouth as if to instruct Carl to drive on, though noting with scientific accuracy the fluttered manner of the young woman, who was devouring the unmistakable Killigrew crest and the entwined monogram of "PG" on the door of the limousine.

"But," stammered the young woman, plainly beaten, "you said the young lady's name was Nelson."

"I did," frigidly admitted Maria. "That is her name— Imogen Nelson."

"But how will Mr. Killigrew—where does he come in?" floundered the young woman.

Up to this moment, Maria had not known how she would get around the situation—to capitalize the name of Master Peter and yet remain within the strict bounds of truth. But an inspiration came to her. She knew it would.

"Miss Nelson is the ward of Mr. Peter Killigrew," she said.

And she thanked her stars that she was certain, *via* Mac in town, that Master Peter was near Archangel in the North Sea on the "Tumbleweed," Still, it was the literal truth, she solaced herself.

"Well—" gasped the young woman, "you must please pardon—pardon me a moment. I am sure Mrs. Morton would want to know about this. Please wait." And she darted back into the office of the school.

A moment later Mrs. Morton received Maria, and began explaining that the young woman had been only recently employed and did not know the exact condition of the school. Yes. There might be a vacancy for the coming term, very fortunately. The ward of Mr. Peter Killigrew could be accommodated. Of course, and with great pleasure.

WHEN HE HEARD that night how it had been accomplished, Scroggins said, ruefully: "When Master Peter hears of it, I hope he won't discharge me—after sixty years of faithful service."

"That's not worrying me," Maria objected, "but I am puzzled to know how to get Imogen to agree to it—and to pay the tuition!"

"How much?"

"Five thousand—for the first year!"

"If necessary," said Scroggins, after careful consideration, "we can sell the chair."

10

QUALITY AND QUANTITY

MRS. MORTON—ANGELA MORTON, head of the Morton School—was driving slowly along the shore road to Pumice Bay, having been down to Beechmere for a hand at bridge in the Agawam Club, when she saw a car on Lynhurst Drive that caused her to step on the gas and spurt along in her coupé.

Angela knew cars-the outside of them—from their bifocal tail lights to their reversible cowls. That is, eights. She passed up fours and sixes as of no importance. Fours and sixes carried persons of the lower nine-tenths, though it was becoming harder each year to discriminate, now that eights were becoming so plentiful.

She could not be mistaken about this car, a foreign trap, surely, with its torpedo hood, and its silvered mounts, bronze-tipped, and its plate glass jointed so neatly there appeared to be no supporting posts. It had an air—an air of angled precision quite different from that smooth rondure of American smartness.

Close enough to note the occupants, she saw the liveried chauffeur in the outside drive—in dull black whipcord with no visible monogram on his clothes, a long melancholy, intellectual countenance. Might be a grand duke in moderate distress.

Then the detail quite convincing, if the car itself and its obvious destination were not enough—the upright, prim little girl alone in the low-hooded tonneau.

An entrant for the school beyond a doubt; for it was Monday of the second week in September, and the assembly was scheduled for Tuesday.

Angela slipped in the rear way, behind the vegetable gardens, parked the coupé behind the "temple"—for so she had renamed the offices this year—and managed to get through to the high-ceilinged room in front before the strange car rolled majestically along the curve and came to a halt before the entresol to the temple.

Then she deciphered the brass wheel caps, with their insignia of hare and arrow—a Deisel-Mascisti. Angela sighed with relief. Her curiosity was appeased. There were only three of these Austro-Italian double eights in the United States. Girls from the families owning two of them were on the waiting list of the Morton school.

The third was owned by Mr. Peter Killigrew.

Thus, by a process of elimination, infallible as a model detective, Mrs. Morton knew who her caller would be, even before the melancholy grand duke descended with exact leisure, and assisted to alight a reddish-haired girl in rather long skirts which accented her scant seventeen years.

This palpable grand duke was only Carl, wearing the black house livery of the Killigrews, its only distinguishing mark being a tan seam along the trouser leg, but above the tunic line—a mark of identification, as it were. Impeccable taste, approved Angela.

The Deisel-Mascisti had been a two week toy of Master Peter the summer before, and discarded for being too fragile with its inclined stabilator—and it took six months to get parts. It would have rusted into an idle grave at the Towers if the chauffeurs had followed their inclination. No one wanted to bother with it.

But there was a proper time to use it. Trust Scroggins for that. Despite Carl's mumbled protestations, the old superintendent had ordered him to take it out that morning for the trip with Imogen over to Pumice Bay.

Scroggins was right—as usual. If anything more was needed to complete the conquest of Mrs. Angela Morton, the Deisel-Mascisti was it. Mentally and spiritually she salaamed.

How could she know that this clear-eyed young feminine person who presently entered to her was neither kith nor kin of any Killigrew and that her whole fortune, though without her knowledge, was represented in the check received from the Towers a few days before?

And that her whole fortune paid for only thirty-eight weeks of registration and tuition in the regular curriculum including dormitory rent, and board, with the exception of week-ends and of the Thanksgiving, Christmas and Easter holidays?

But not for extras, not for dancing instruction, not for athletic outfits, which included complete equipment for tennis, riding, golf, motor and ice boating, ice hockey, and basketball. Nor pocket money—the chief of all items with most of the Morton girls.

Imogen knew nothing of this, of course, and cared as little, though "Aunt Maria" was doing, and had been doing a great lot of very tall thinking. Indeed, Aunt Maria sorely wanted to accompany her on her first trip to the school, but had been dissuaded by the mortz discreet word of her spouse.

"Don't take any chance," Scroggins had urged. "They have accepted the check, but there is a reservation in the contract—I read it—the girl must pass the entrance examinations. And"—he halted significantly, surveying sensibly the broad-hipped, lantern-jawed, plebeian Maria—"you had better not be one of them."

Maria bowed to superior wisdom. Despite the acuteness of her feminine intuitions, she realized that her spouse had long had a more intimate touch with the great world. Chiefly, it was to remedy this defect in her experience that she had connived at getting Imogen into the Morton school.

"But don't kill the goose that you want to lay the golden eggs," Scroggins had urged, "not before she lays one, anyway."

If either of them could have known the real predicament in which Mrs. Morton was struggling they would not have felt any apprehension. For the apparition of the Killigrew machine had been a godsend to her. During the past several years, she had been doing constantly what in a short time would prove to be a fatal error for the Morton School; she had been letting down the bars of eligibility.

Angela Morton, in her day, had been the ideal governess for aristocracy, had been, in fact, the chief governess to the children of the second Mrs. Anstruther, leader of the Four Hundred when there was a Four Hundred.

When she founded the Morton School, naturally, all the

women of the Four Hundred, to say nothing of the myri-
ads who longed to be of that sacred circle, overwhelmed
her with applicants. The secret of her success, naturally, had
been discrimination, to stick to the Four Hundred and to
avoid the climbers.

All would have been well—and perhaps in due time she
would have quickly seen through Imogen—but for her
great weakness. One season she called it bridge; another
the stock market; again she put off the tradespeople with
constant references to her real estate investments. The plain
name for it was gambling.

Angela Morton was an inveterate gambler, and when
she lost, her only sure method of prompt recovery was to
take in a few more pupils—at five thousand a year. These
were not always forthcoming, without question and without delay, from the Four Hundred.

So far they had always been forthcoming from parvenus,
from mammas who read the smart chatter in the flashy
society pages, from wives of war millionaires, from wives
of bootleggers. Yes, Angela had fallen to that, or almost
there, she feared, the day the Killigrew Mercury rolled
along the curvex.

Now she longed for all who had turned her the cold
shoulder for her perilous promiscuity to see that Killigrew
Deisel-Mascisti, and Carl's manner a la grand duke—and
this wisp of a young lady.

"Surely," thought Mrs. Morton, as she surveyed Imogen,
"the girl is every inch an aristocrat. So simple! So *svelte!*
Such an *air distingue!* Aloof! Cold! Yet piquant! Ah!
This will put Mrs. Throckmorton in her place! And Mrs.
Limberling!"

Already there was printed in the fall announcement, among the list of "Freshwomen, class of 1929"—"Miss Imogen Nelson, ward of Mr. Peter Killigrew of the Towers, Fairview, Westchester."

And let her fail to pass the "examinations!" Not much!

CARL ENTERED THE office, following Imogen at five paces, bearing a black portmanteau, the rather huge affair Scroggins himself used to carry accounts to the town house.

He touched his cap respectfully. "Is that all, Miss Imogen?" he asked, but with a manner worthy of the soliloquy in Hamlet; and stood aside at attention, with no touch of the military, but with vast deference. Carl had the faculty merely in the way he bent from his waist of indicating that stretch of ten-acre lawn that rolled in front of the Towers, the seepage of a lifetime of association!

Without looking at him, but very simply, she said: "Thank you, Carl. You may return!" Casually, gently, as one might speak, when preoccupied, to a pet housedog. In reality, her heart was knocking wildly away.

"Thank you, miss!" He withdrew. Outside, he became again the grand duke, condescending to pilot a Deisel-Mascisti.

Mrs. Morton was enchanted. Here was something to work on—something to start with—instinctive breeding. The worst thing she had to combat was the tendency of her girls to be familiar with their chauffeurs. Either they chatted with them, or abused them, or flirted with them.

Not the ward of the Killigrews, it was evident! Not one associating for generations with the selective blood of America! Not a member of one of the first ten families of the western hemisphere.

"Come to me, my dear," she said, with purring affection, indicating a seat by her side, and patting Imogen's hand as she sat down.

Imogen looked at her levelly and clearly, studying her as she might a new plant, remembering her father's dictum: "Human beings are no different from flowers. Don't spoil them, and don't neglect them. Study each one to know its peculiarity, and treat it accordingly."

"I want you to feel at home and I want to spare you the preliminary examination that is usually required at the school," Mrs. Morton glibly asserted, "so if you will merely answer a few questions all will be well, and I can show you to your room. As you know, perhaps, we take girls here only who have what would be the equivalent of a high school education."

Imogen instantly shriveled inside, though she tried not to show it. Without "education" what could she do?

Mrs. Morton rattled on: "You, I understand, have not been to a formal school."

Imogen managed to murmur: "No."

"Very well, my dear. Don't be alarmed. Some of my very best pupils never went to school before they came to me. Your education has been confined to tutors, of course."

Imogen pursed her lips and looked away shyly. "I had only one tutor," she corrected, wistfully, her heart fluttering at the memory of the long days and nights at the knee of Patrick Henry Nelson, while he struggled with her and the school books.

"Good! Good!" purred Mrs. Morton, determined not to be outdone. "One good tutor is often better than a faculty of superficial instructors."

"He worked hard with me," Imogen assented. The perspiration came to her brow. It was a very warm September day.

"Then, of course, you have all the elementary studies. I need ask you no more about them," Mrs. Morton sighed with relief, in which Imogen joined. "And French? How about French?"

"I read it—rather badly."

"Ah, well, we will remedy that. We will converse. Mlle. Renoir will attend to that. And what is your favorite study?"

"Flowers."

"Ah! Botany!"

"No. Roots. The perennials take longer, but you get more from them."

"I see! Floriculture!" Mrs. Morton made a note. "And what is your favorite exercise?"

"Walking."

"Indeed! You play tennis, of course?"

"No."

"You ride?"

"No."

"Surely, with all of Mr. Killigrew's riding horses—he has taken so many ribbons at horse shows—you will have found mounts to please you?"

"No. I never ride. I prefer to walk."

"Indeed? Basketball?"

Imogen sadly shook her head. Then she laughed gayly.

"I am afraid, Mrs. Morton, you will find me out of place in your school, because I don't know any games at all. I have spent my whole life alone—with my tutor—and flowers. That's all! Except for a few books! Nothing else."

"How charming!" Mrs. Morton patted her hand.

There remained to secure the more important information which she sought. She felt she had better get it now under the guise of the "examination." "You are the ward of Mr. Killigrew," she asserted.

This being a statement of fact, Imogen made no effort to dispute it, nor did she affirm.

Mrs. Morton felt a bit put out, just a trifle distraught in the presence of this self-possessed girl, but she felt she must know a little more than she did. Every one would demand information about the "ward of Peter Killigrew."

"Mr. Killigrew is a very charming man," she ventured.

"I am told so," Imogen admitted, half shrugging one shoulder, remembering her, only direct knowledge of him, barring the baby experience which she could not recall, but of which she had heard Uncle Isaiah tell.

"You see him, I suppose, frequently," Mrs. Morton encouraged.

"No. I have never seen him." Imogen said this more casually than she had dismissed Carl, lifting her eyebrows and looking out. She would not lie, and she figured now the cause was lost.

Mrs. Morton felt really abashed in the presence of this superiority, but she struggled on for the essential facts—if she could get them. "Ah, I see!" she ventured, "Then your relationship is formal, in a way, is it not?"

"Very."

"Mr. Killigrew is a formal man, I hear."

"So do I."

"Your families have been acquainted for a long time, I imagine!"

"For about fifteen years, I believe."

"Ah! Indeed! Well, that may be a long or a short time—according to how you look at it. Then you are not a blood relative?"

"No." The blue eyes of the girl looked out toward the lush trees as if to say this was a most unnecessary catechism.

But Mrs. Morton was relentless, for while the other phase of the "examination" might be glossed over this was imperative, "Pardon me, my dear," she insinuated, laying her hand over Imogen's sinewy palm, "but I am so interested. Please tell me how you became the ward of Mr. Killigrew, for he is such a very great man?"

"Through my father, I believe!" Imogen was almost ready to burst into tears.

"Your father! Then he was a friend of Mr. Killigrew's?"

"No. Of Mr. Killigrew's father!"

"I see! I see! Then how—"

With this the storm descended. Imogen turned on her tormentor with icy fury. "I believe you suspect me of some untruth, Mrs. Morton," she cried. "No one in my whole life has ever talked to me like this! Will you please call up Mr. Scroggins and ask him to send the car for me at once?"

"Oh! My dear! My dear!" Angela Morton now promptly revealed how "motherly" she might become under necessity. She seized both hands of the girl. Soothed her with a volume of endearing assurances, carefully avoided any further reference to Peter Killigrew apologizing humbly, and would only be content when Imogen recalled her plea for Scroggins and the Deisel-Mascisti.

"Now! Come!" she concluded. "You have passed your

examinations brilliantly. I predict a wonderful future for you in the Morton School. And let me have you shown to your room."

She pressed a button. A porter appeared. He took the huge portmanteau and led the way across the lawn to the freshman dormitory which Imogen was to share with thirty other entering girls.

There in her room, half an hour later, while she lay sobbing her heart out on her bed, giving way to the second great grief of her life—an unnamable nostalgia—a gentle knock came.

Mrs. Morton entered and tried to calm the quivering girl, from whom she could pry no further word. Her eyes meanwhile restlessly took in Imogen's belongings—the real purpose of her visit.

She saw a pitiful array; one little dimity frock, a change of under things and of ordinary quality, only one extra pair of stockings and a worn set of toilet articles in somewhat battered silver. Of the latter she managed to satisfy herself that they bore the Killigrew crest—Aunt Maria had salvaged this from the Towers's cast-off—which seemed to fill her with an immense satisfaction.

Thereupon the head of the school withdrew to let Imogen cry in peace and settled herself in her office with her assistant.

Angela rubbed her hands. "Not since Emmeline Anstruther have I known such a girl!" she exclaimed. "Only once before in my twenty-seven years of striving to keep the daughters of the rich in bounds have I seen anything in her class.

"Emmeline Anstruther was the granddaughter of Old

Commodore Anstruther, the builder of the Great Western! And made of the same stern stuff! Blue blood was written all over her. Delicate! Reserved! Æsthetic! Living in the clouds! And as parsimonious as a church warden. But with perfect taste! The most exquisite!"

"How is this girl like that?"

"Imogen Nelson?" exclaimed Mrs. Morton. "Why, if one doubted that she came from the richest family in the world, almost, one need only see her wardrobe. Only one extra frock! And lisle stockings! No one else could *afford* to dress like that!"

If Scroggins could have overheard. He would have been fully repaid.

11

IMOGEN'S FRIENDS

SCROGGINS DID NOT overhear, but as the weeks went on he was satisfied his calculation had not been amiss; for it was chiefly due to his guidance that Maria had refrained from outfitting the girl with her idea of elegance, which Scroggins had very greatly feared.

The five thousand and a little more left from the bed and Master Peter's beneficence was largely gobbled up by that atrocious "tuition" fee at Mrs. Morton's. What was left Maria wanted to spend on dresses and silk stockings, and a well fitted traveling bag. Scroggins was tempted, loving the girl, but he stood firm. He felt sure Maria's taste would give the snap away.

"Safer to let her have only lisle stockings and one change of clothes, and my old bag," he asserted. "Believe me—I know. This Mrs. Morton is a cagey old dame, and she will be much quicker to believe Imogen is a ward of Master Peter if she goes in niggardly things than if she parades in the sort of department store stuff Maria Scroggins thinks is swell."

Maria protested vigorously, but in her heart she knew Isaiah was right. Yet she wanted Imogen to have everything any other girl would have, and before the term was over she enjoyed all the torments suffered by any mother with a girl in boarding school if her bank account is limited.

Only she had to enjoy them in imagination. Imogene would give her no inkling of hardship.

Indeed, Imogen was quite ignorant of the curious sensation she caused; for Mrs. Morton proceeded to point her out as a model to the aping flock of young femininity. Whether newly rich or more securely set in the ways of the world the pupils at the school were urged to copy both her behavior and her wardrobe. One they were unable to achieve. The other, however much they may have honored it under compulsion, they were unable to copy.

What girl at Mrs. Morton's, for instance, would willingly have limited herself to a single party frock?

Imogen appeared to be sadly lacking in the modern spirit. This was thoroughly established at the first hop. It was the second Friday night of the school year. Each girl was permitted to invite one boy, and all adjourned to the country club near by.

Before they started two of her classmates invaded Imogen's room.

"Perhaps I don't care to dance!" Imogen suggested rather tentatively, not informing them that she never had danced.

"Oh!" cried Clare Holliday, daughter of the newest sensation on the Stock Exchange. "There is no surer way to be poodly."

"Poodly?" asked Imogen. "What's that?"

"Lonesome."

The girls chattered, and proceeded to puff at cigarettes, which they offered Imogen and which she refused. There was a rule against smoking at Mrs. Morton's, but no one tried to enforce it inside the rooms in the dormitories, or on the grounds if concealed behind hedges. Tobacco had become too much a staple of feminine necessity to be longer listed as a vice. It was regulated, not prohibited. In spite of this there were quite a number of girls at the school who did not smoke, and thus Imogen did not arouse special comment for her abstinence.

Even Gwen and Clare, who belonged to the wilder set of girls—the "gold plate gang," they were called, derisively, to distinguish them from the few remaining relics of the Anstruther period, "the solid gold crowd"—made no comments on Imogen's abstinence from tobacco.

A girl could smoke or leave it alone—to suit her own taste—at Mrs. Morton's, and not get into Coventry thereby. Final proof of the very subtle empery of Angela Morton, a tight rein was for girls of an earlier generation, not for those beginning the second quarter of the twentieth century.

At the same time, Angela contended, there must be no snobbery about vice. That was not social. A girl must not be ostracized because she was not vicious. Irrespective of her vices she must be accepted solely for what she was—or is. Even without vices she might thus become, all other things being equal, a pattern, a model.

This was lucky for Imogen. It made her feel less "out of it" for not smoking, and for persisting in her plebeian and antediluvian ways. The Morton girls were too well bred to persecute her for peculiarities like that.

And in the "solid gold crowd"—Angela's private classification to her intimates—not a few began looking up to Imogen for her dignity and her self-restraint. Natural, of course; for, after all, she was a Killigrew, however distantly connected.

The leader of the solid gold crowd—before the advent of Imogen—was Selene Henton, now a senior. Selene had no use at all for any girl who smoked.

Selene, in her twentieth year, and shortly to graduate, was fully aware of her purpose in the Morton School. It was to be properly "finished" that she might enter upon the fulfillment of her destiny, marriage with a man of social eminence and high fortune. No other purpose in life seemed to her worth consideration, and, indeed, none other in her case would be considered.

Selene was entirely at one with her mother in this dominant ambition. If anything she was shrewder and more hardheaded than her mother. Every one in the family, including her father, declared her to be the elder of the two. For it was Selene who had confided to her mother, only the semester previously, that in her opinion the character of the girls in the school was falling off, that Mrs. Morton was becoming too lax, and that she seriously doubted if it was advantageous to continue there.

This was rather a serious dilemma in the Henton family, having invested an important three or four years of Selene's life in acquiring the prestige that ought to inhere with attendance at the Morton School. So when, at the beginning of the fourth year, Mrs. Henton heard that "a ward of the Killigrews" was matriculated she hastened to Selene with the glad news.

Selene listened gravely. "I wonder!" she offered.

"What do you mean?" her mother demanded. "Mrs. Morton has printed it in her fall announcements."

"Even so," Selene persisted, "I wonder who this ward may be. Peter Killigrew has only male relatives living."

"This is not a relative—a ward."

"Strange nothing is known of her."

"Are you sure?"

"She is not in the Social Register—or Dau's."

"That makes no difference. She is going to Mrs. Morton's this year," Mrs. Henton stoutly asserted, "and it's a great chance for you, Selene!"

The calm eyes of the twenty-year-old tuft hunter gleamed dully. She had announced to her mother two years previously that there were only two men in the world she would marry—the Prince of Wales or Peter Killigrew. She had met the prince on his visit to America, and had danced with him at a Long Island country house, but as yet there was no further prospect of her marrying him. She had not even met Peter Killigrew.

"I'll find out," Selene asserted calmly, and went to the phone, where she hunted in the book for the number of the Killigrew estate. Presently she had the housekeeper on the wire.

"May I speak to Miss Nelson?" she asked.

"Who?"

"Miss Imogen Nelson."

There was some delay, and a bit of whispering on the other end. Then the prim voice responded: "She does not live here; you may find her at the lodge," and gave another number.

Selene did not call again. Instead she remarked to her mother: "Something queer about it. Why should a 'ward of Mr. Killigrew' live in his lodge, with his superintendent? Peculiar, to say the least."

"How do you know who lives at the lodge?" Mrs. Henton demanded.

"Oh, mother! Foolish question number ten thousand."

Indeed it was a foolish question to want to know why or how Selene had information about Mr. Killigrew. She had made it her business to know all about him. She knew more about him than Scroggins did—knew about the new outfitting of the Tumbleweed, for instance, and his friendship with Billy Van Pelt. She had her wires out in that direction. She knew a friend of Billy Van Pelt's who thought she could arrange it through Billy next winter.

Meanwhile, of course, Selene would pursue any advantage that offered. She made herself very agreeable to Imogen, and on the night of the first dance, when Clare and Gwen dropped her "like a hot cake," as she seemed not readily to enter the spirit of their festivities, Selene, from her secure senior heights, saw her chance to make the ground solid for the advance she planned.

She sought out the lonely girl in the brown thread stockings and the rather shapeless long frock, whom as yet no boy had desired to meet, and proceeded to make her feel happy and important.

Selene did it well, too—trust her for that—tactfully, without a single reference to Mr. Killigrew, and as sweetly and as democratically as if they had been friends all their lives, and bosom confidantes.

It did not lessen Imogen's warmth of response to discover that Selene was far more rigid than any dowager in her attitude toward tobacco, and—boys! But she did not talk about it. She had a way of letting every one know how she felt, without saying so. She saw that Imogen had partners, saw that she met any of the girls she desired to meet, and hovered over her like a hen over a lone chick. And before the evening was over she had achieved the satisfaction of a promise from Imogen to visit her in her room on the morrow.

This visit naturally produced an invitation from Imogen—rather shy and reluctant, but nevertheless an invitation—to Selene to visit her room.

When she reported this visit to her mother, Selene exclaimed: "The poor little thing! I really felt sorry for her. Why, mother, she has almost no clothes!"

For a moment Selene was speechless.

Mrs. Henton laughed. "Proof of your suspicion that she is an impostor, I suppose!"

"On the contrary," Selene came up proud of her insight, "proof of her consanguinity. The Killigrews are the stingiest people in the world, I've been told."

"Why not invite her home with you for the next week-end?"

"I will," Selene assured her mother; for she expected to lay a substantial basis for a genuine campaign which might take years to be successful.

The girls at Mrs. Morton's who lived within motoring distance usually went home for week-ends. The Deisel-Mascisti called every Friday afternoon at four for Imogen, and its swank had its effect even on the crowd of swagger eights and double sixes which cluttered the drives of the school at that time.

The third week-end—arrangement having been made

with "Aunt Maria" over the telephone—the Deisel-Mascisti was about to turn back, when Imogen suggested that perhaps Selene would like her car to take them home.

The ensuing hour was the proudest of Selene's life—when the foreign car with the Killigrew crest and monogram on the door drove up to the Henton estate in Connecticut, just over the border—and deposited her on her own doorstep.

A premonition of the future, her palpitating heart said to her.

Mrs. Henton was peeking from an upper window. It was a great moment for her, too. But she met a severe frown from Selene when she informed her later that she had invited a number of guests in for the evening.

"I wanted to be alone with Imogen," Selene pouted.

"My dear, but think—" Mrs. Henton would not put in words what she meant, but she could not forego the chance to have it known, among certain persons, that "the ward of the Killigrews" was their house guest for the week-end.

So quite a crowd came.

And thus, to the quivering alarm of the intuitive Selene, Imogen met Darcy Jennifer.

12

DANGER

MRS. HENTON HAD not invited him, she protested to Selene, but that was no alibi, not in Harbor View, where everybody went anywhere if there was a party on—a good reason for Selene's detesting the place.

It was enough to pass the word that a few were expected in during the evening. Cards, dancing, anything might happen. With the Hentons there was a little movie theater on the top floor, which boosted the stock. But not like having a "ward of the Killigrews." When that word spread through Harbor View, every one under thirty for ten miles swarmed to the attack.

Selene said she didn't know half of them; nor did she; nor Mrs. Henton, either. They just oozed out of the drives and roadways like shore fog on a moist day.

Dozens, scores, the Henton butler declared he prepared sandwiches and punch for forty, and then had to double— twice. Mr. Henton said he'd be dashed if they could have his Bourbon.

In the mob was Darcy Jennifer and his sister, Lenly. They had dropped in for a call on a neighbor, and had been urged to "come along." The Hentons had never seen either of them before. No matter; the house looked like the scene of a public auction or a charitable bazaar.

Selene was furious—and icy proud. She wandered among them like a sheik in a harem, and condescended to occasional utterance, and kept watch over Imogen as if she were the favorite sultana.

Before the evening was half over the whole thing degenerated into a sort of public reception, with Selene and Imogen at the peak, and the grist of curiosity seekers being fed along with more or less snappy introductions. How Selene hated it! The reverse of what it should have been! And due to the stupidity of her mother!

When Darcy and Lenly Jennifer first hove in sight, she paid no more attention to them than to any of the Harbor View residents. They were strangers, but so were nearly half the others. She asked their names, like the aide to the President at the White House during a reception, and then turned and introduced them to Imogen, inwardly protesting, though she felt obliged to pretend to know them.

Imogen had been acting the part of "the ward of the Killigrews" just as easily as it had fallen to her from the first. Which is to say that her natural shyness and inherent timidity made her seem, as the actors say: "upstage." She accepted the enthusiasm of her new acquaintances with embarrassment, responded in monosyllables to all they said, which was nothing at all but the merest homily, and looked as if she would give a great deal to be far away from the maddening scene.

Which was the necessary touch to render her eminence real—even to Selene.

And Darcy Jennifer was the first to see through it, or to

appraise it at its true worth; for he managed to stick along by her side as the line swirled past him, and to remark, during a lull in the storm: "I'll bet you'd rather be somewhere else, Miss Nelson."

She glanced at him quickly, and said: "Oh, no! I like it here!"

"It's more of a crowd than you are accustomed to."

"Yes," hesitantly.

"I knew at once. Harbor View is rather a lively place."

"It seems so."

"A bit too lively for you, I take it."

"No. I—"

"Come. Miss Nelson, you can be frank with me. I am almost as new to Harbor View as you are. We have lived here only a few weeks."

"But I like it. Really, I do." Imogen felt she must be loyal to Selene.

"A change, I suppose, from the wonderful quiet of the Towers! Ah! That is a place for you! I rode by there yesterday!"

Imogen began to feel a terrible longing for the Lodge, and for Uncle Isaiah and for Aunt Maria. Darcy had touched just the right spot. She did not tell him that it was the Lodge she was thinking of, rather than the Towers.

He rattled on, while Selene tried to hover near enough to overhear. "The Towers is quite the finest place in all Westchester—or in New England, either, for that matter. They say Harbor View is the gateway to New England— but the Towers is New England, though strictly not in New England at all. I suppose it would be nearer truth to say the Towers is old England. Of course, you have been there, Miss Nelson."

Imogen shook her head.

"You are not like the rest of the Killigrews, then," Darcy ventured.

Selene near by wanted to break in and stop this conversation. The stranger was proceeding aggressively, more so than she had dared yet to proceed. Curiosity stopped her.

"By the way," Darcy went on, "to which branch of the family do you belong?"

There it was direct—the question Selene had not dared yet to ask. She wanted to hear the answer, but she felt something sinister in Jennifer's quick probing of the essential point. He was a fast worker, and she dared not be.

Imogen was well aware of the underlying motive in all this hubbub about her—its centrifugal hum about the spokes of the Killigrew wheel, and her vicarious relation to it.

More than once she was tempted as she had been on several occasions at the school to break out and face every one with the facts, and inform them frankly that she was the orphan of the late Patrick Henry Nelson of Dobbs's Corners, and had never seen Peter Killigrew, and never expected to, and was no more related to him than they were.

But a sense of self preservation—and the imp of mischief, for she was developing a latent sense of humor—kept her silent.

So now she replied cryptically to Darcy Jennifer, while Selene Henton listened, eagerly: "I am from what would be called the distaff side."

"Ah! Then your mother."

"No. My father!"

"But that would not be the distaff side!" Darcy paused, pondering, then a light broke as he added hastily: "I see! On Mr. Killigrew's mother's side. Well! Well! Interesting, is it not? I rather believe in genealogy and all it stands for, don't you, Miss Nelson?"

"Geology? The science of rocks?"

"What?" Darcy was about to explain the meaning of "genealogy," but hesitated. Was she really dense, or stupid, or unread? Most likely so—a part of many millions. He decided to say nothing in elucidation. The plan for the thing already spinning in his head would be so much easier to effect. So he replied hastily and a bit irrelevantly: "Just so!"

Imogen was keeping a straight face with difficulty.

Selene was listening avidly.

"I want you to meet my sister," Darcy said, and Lenly came up.

Then he had the supreme audacity—so Selene thought—to link one arm through his sister's and the other through Imogen's and to say boldly: "You two must be pals, and Miss Nelson must come and visit you at the Larches. Now go ahead and book Miss Nelson. The quicker the better. Next week if you can!"

This was the thing that positively convinced Selene that Darcy Jennifer would bear much watching, and that filled her with foreboding. Imogen was hers. Why had that stupid mother rendered her seizable by the whole community?

She could hardly wait for the company to disperse. Some

of them hung on and hung—as people will when there is plenty of refreshment, and a free movie show, and the nearness of an alleged inmate of the Four Hundred—until after midnight.

It was only when she was at last alone with Imogen that Selene ventured to ask in the most casual way she could summon: "Tell me, Imogen, what was your mother's name?"

"Betty," said Imogen.

"I mean her last name."

"Rawlins."

"Oh, yes. A distinguished name."

"I don't know."

Selene could not get away quick enough to her own boudoir, and her collection of registers and "Who's Who," and to glance down the indexes under "Killigrew." For an hour she hunted and hunted. It was well on toward morning as she exclaimed to herself: "Not a Rawlins in all the Killigrew line. Something queer about this."

Next morning, her mother pointed out to her that to be "a ward" did not imply, necessarily, that one must be of blood kin.

"I know," Selene sniffed, "but if she amounts to anything as a ward there is some blood relationship—somewhere—at least with the Killigrews."

"What do you know about the Killigrews?"

Selene tried to kill her mother with a glance. Failing, she sought her father to learn about, some one less elusive. "What do you know about the Jennifers?" she asked.

"Just moved up to the Larches?"

"I suppose so, blew in here last night—bounders!"

"That's the Jennifers."

"Who are they?"

"Jennifer is a western Pennsylvania man, solid enough, I take it; but the boy, Darcy, is a whiz-banger—stock market rocket. Would be in very bad if his father had not helped him out on several occasions. He just tried to rig a corner in Billing Tire stock, I hear. Missed it by a good margin, and was trimmed for all he had and a good slice of his father's; and has been cautioned not to run loose again or he will be refused his place on the Exchange."

"In other words—as I said—a bounder!"

"Financially, yes."

Selene added significantly: "I mean socially."

She went back to her room to send an order to a family-finding expert to trace the Rawlins family in Westchester.

Imogen, apparently innocent of its meaning, though shrewdly seeing into it, often too late to prevent its devotees from overreaching themselves, was the center of much intrigue, both at Mrs. Morton's school and outside.

Visitors were permitted on Wednesday afternoon. The first Wednesday after the Henton party, Lenly Jennifer called at Pumice Bay, bringing to Imogen as presents a bottle of perfume and a huge box of candy, and would not leave until she had been promised that Imogen would visit her at the Larches the second week-end.

Imogen felt it necessary to get the consent of Mrs. Scroggins, and when this was not forthcoming, she phoned to Lenly saying she must postpone the trip. There ensued pleadings and cross-phonings to the Lodge, with the result that it was arranged Imogen should go for Friday dinner and to spend the evening, and would afterward go home.

Lenly called for her at the school at four. An hour later they rolled into the grounds of the Larches at Harbor View. Darcy permitted his sister no such folly as inviting the neighborhood in, as had been the case in the visit to Selene Henton's.

This was an *intime.* Mr. and Mrs. Jennifer, Lenly and Darcy, Imogen and a boy Lenly liked, young Percy Grilling. They dined and played billiards, listened to the radio, and passed the time pleasantly until nearly ten.

Then Darcy thought a bit of air might do them good. It was November, but not yet very cold. The young people went onto the veranda, in wraps, of course.

The Sound lay off, hazy under a new moon. They could hear the New London steamers laboring down the channel, and see Long Island, very dim, much to be taken on faith, on the horizon.

Darcy, standing beside Imogen, very close to her, pointed out the bits of distinction on the landscape—Indian Head over there, Inchcape Light beyond, Huntington Harbor five miles off, and in the foreground, Pelican Island, half a mile away.

"How about a spin in my motor boat," he suggested.

"No," Imogen asserted. "I must leave in half an hour. My car will be here."

"I'll bet," Darcy softly intoned, "I can take you around Pelican and get you back here in half an hour."

"Really!" Imogen was tempted. The night was soft with a languorous tang of late Indian summer. The Sound seemed a sheet of silver. And she had never been in a motor boat.

"Bet you a box of candy against a kiss!"

"Wouldn't bet something I couldn't pay."

"Oh! A slap on the wrist, then."

"That's easy enough."

"Then it's a go!"

Imogen hastily told Lenly they would be back in half an hour. Then, her arm through Darcy's, she slipped with him toward the boat landing.

AN HOUR BEFORE, in the Lodge, Scroggins was called to the phone. A girl's voice, so he believed, on the other end, when she became satisfied it was the superintendent talking, said: "I wish to warn you about Miss Imogen Nelson."

"Who are you?" demanded Scroggins.

"A good friend of her—and of yours. I want to warn you that she may be in danger to-night. That is all." She hung up, Selene Henton.

Scroggins ordered Carl to bring out the new roadster. It was surer than the Deisel-Mascisti, and fast enough, seventy miles, if necessary.

He reached the Larches, in Harbor View, in less than half an hour. When he rang the bell, the butler answered and asked him to wait. The word came: "Miss Nelson stepped out for a few minutes. She will return immediately."

Ten minutes later Scroggins demanded to see Mr. Jennifer, told who he was, and said he had called for Miss Nelson.

Then Lenly and Percy Grilling came in, and said that Darcy and Imogen had gone off in the motor boat, just for a spin around Pelican Island; ought to be back any minute.

Scroggins asked young Grilling to show him the lay of the land—and water. Grilling pointed out Pelican Island from the rear terrace. Nothing was visible on the water near by.

"Maybe they got off on the island. It's surely a pretty moonlight night," Percy suggested.

At eleven o'clock Scroggins was more nervous, more fearful than he ever had been in his life. He asked the Jennifer butler to direct him to some public boat house where he could hire a vessel. The nearest place was the landing of the yacht club, three miles away.

Carl got him there in the roadster in defiance of all speed laws. Scroggins found the club launch the only thing available. A bill of good size induced the skipper, against the rules, to take it out for a nonmember passenger.

As they started off, the skipper said he knew Pelican Island. Yes. It had a cabin, with one room, accommodations, he believed, for picnickers.

The night, the hour, the circumstances filled Scroggins with strange fears. He would hold Maria for this! She had let Imogen accept these invitations from strangers. Desperate! People living in hovels like that had no honor. "Hovels!"—the Larches, with its three and a half acres. Of course, three Larches could have been planted on the lawn of the Towers.

A jumble of such stuff, irrelevant, foolish, diverted Scroggins until he reached Pelican Island. He leaped ashore, and pushed a stolid way to the dim cabin. The whole island was not a hundred yards across. He saw at a glance no one was on it—unless in the cabin.

He almost feared to enter, for there was no light.

Had a catastrophe occurred to his adored Imogen?

He knocked at the door. No answer. He shoved on it, for he could see it was not latched. It gave before him. He turned his electric flash inside and swept its dusty corners, its two bare cots, its rustic furniture.

The cabin was empty.

He explored every inch of the island, its least lichens, its barren tangled shrubbery. It was deserted.

13

A SURPRISE

WHEN DARCY JENNIFER said it would take him half an hour to make the round trip to Pelican Island from the boat landing at the foot of the Larches Terrace, he was mentally counting on a stay at the island, a romantic spot in the moonlight.

He reached the island with Imogen in the motor boat in less than five minutes. It lay offshore only a few hundred yards. He beached the boat and stepped out, giving her a hand.

She avoided his hand and leaped lightly to the beach, ran lightly to the top of the nearest rock, and poised herself there, breathing deeply of the mystic night air.

He followed her, but found no place convenient, where he could stand beside her without crowding.

"Lovely, isn't it?" he commented.

"Like moonflowers and poppies," she said. "Shirley poppies, and Iceland poppies, and a field of shasta daisies!"

Her eyes dilated with the mellow shine of the moon on the inland sea. Her hair fluffed with the breeze. Her whole personality seemed distended with the night, and with the exhilaration of the remoteness of the tiny isle, weirdly alone and yet so near the high-built homes twinkling among lights just beyond.

As a rule, Darcy cared nothing for flappers, but Imogen was different.

"Come!" he urged. "Let's see what is in the cabin!"

He took a step toward the dark outline of the log structure a few paces away, along a winding path.

With a light, silvery laugh she darted ahead of him, reached the building, looked in its nearest window, which was quite dark, passed beyond to the door, shoved it partly open, glanced quickly inside, and was back meeting him as he came along, just outside the shadow, and in the moonlight.

Darcy liked to think himself quite an athlete. He was a runner up at metropolitan tennis, and on the sunny side of thirty. He had gone up the path as rapidly as possible.

Yet this girl had beaten him, and apparently without effort. It was disconcerting to say the least. She seemed self-sufficient. He had anticipated timidity, little squeals of fright which he could quell in an approved masculine manner.

Almost before he realized it, Imogen was back in the boat, seated by the gunwale, and without so much as laying a finger on his arm, or rendering it necessary or possible for him to so much as touch her.

And yet she had entered heartily into the spirit of adventure, and had added a poetic appreciation which was a little beyond him.

As he pushed off he suggested a ride across the harbor, but Imogen vetoed that. It was time for her to go home, she said. So reluctantly he put back for the landing. When

they rearched it he looked at his watch. They had been gone just twelve minutes.

"Well!" he exclaimed, in an attempt to conceal his disappointment. "I will have to pay you that box of candy."

"But you won, Mr. Jennifer. It's not half an hour."

"Then have your slap."

She clapped her hands in front of his face, and ran up the terrace. This time he caught her before she could reach the house, and ran his arm through hers.

"I'll produce the candy!" he announced.

"But you won. You don't owe me any candy."

"I want you to have some."

He diverted their path along the terrace toward the brick garage at the far end. In a moment she sensed he was not headed for the house. She loosed her arm from his, saying, "I must go in. The car will be here for me any minute."

"Oh! Come along! I'll get that candy for you."

"It's too late!"

"Shank of the evening. And I want you to see my sport phaeton."

He opened the garage and led the way to his low-slung, cream-colored eight, not a month out of the factory. The collapsible top was down.

"It's a perfect night for a spin," said he. "Jump in. I'll get that box of candy for you in Greenwich."

Still she hung back.

"We've been only fifteen minutes so far. I'll make it to Greenwich and back in another fifteen. I made good on the island. Trust me this time."

She assented. "Not for the candy, though, but for the phaeton. I like an open car. Wait till I get my hat and coat."

Thus it was that Scroggins missed her. He passed them on the Shore Drive, but it was under the linden arch where the darkness was intense.

At Greenwich, Darcy declared he could not find a shop open with the candy he considered fit. After ten o'clock at night one cannot buy good candy in a small town. It was now eleven, nearly.

"We'll hop over to Port Chester—only a few miles. There'll be places open there." Darcy silenced her protests, and presently they crossed the Byram River and slid along Main Street in Port Chester.

There were some drug stores open, but Darcy declared drug-store candy was not fit to eat. He wanted a special box—Templeton's Honey Spice—the best candy in the world, he said. Nothing else quite the thing for a girl. They kept it, he believed, in the stationery store on the square in Mamaroneck.

Imogen seriously objected, now, to going farther. She knew Aunt Maria would be expecting her, and that Carl would probably be at the Jennifer home with the car, waiting for her. They must have been gone the fifteen minutes. Darcy was obliged to admit they had been gone more than that.

"Never mind," he said, "when we get to Mamaroneck we can strike the cement road over to White Plains, and from there I can get you to the Towers in no time. I'll take you home, and about as soon as you could ride back now to the Larches."

"Well, I wonder—"

Imogen hesitated—and the penalty of hesitation is proverbial.

The phaeton went through Rye at sixty-odd miles an hour. At Rye Beach Avenue a "crossroads cat" hopped their trail. This motor-cycle cop overtook them as they passed the Jay mansion, halting them, and handed Darcy a ticket.

"Thanks!" said Darcy, gayly. "Meet you in court in the morning."

They loafed into Mamaroneck, but the stationery store at the square was closed.

"What a shame!" Darcy exclaimed. "Well, no matter!" He climbed into his seat, and again they were off.

They passed through Larchmont, and when they reached the Main Street of the next town, with its well-lighted vistas, Imogen asked, "Is this White Plains?"

"No. It's New Rochelle!"

"But you promised to go to White Plains. Isn't this the opposite direction?"

Without lessening his pace, for the street was clear of traffic, Darcy replied, "We'll go back that way. Must get that candy for you."

Imogen became alarmed. As they passed under a dark

culvert and into Pelham, she protested. "I feel you are taking me a long way around. Please go right to the Towers, Mr. Jennifer."

"We'll be there soon enough."

A few minutes later they were sliding down the long crest of the Pelham-Hutchinson hill. A myriad of lights filled the foreground.

"My!" exclaimed Imogen. "What town is that?"

"New York!" said Darcy, as they slipped over the city line.

Imogen opened her mouth to protest, but it stayed open. Then slowly it closed, and she said nothing. It was her first sight of New York. Born less than forty miles from the city limits, she had never before seen the city. She had never been fifty miles away from it, and she had never before been in it.

Darcy accepted her silence as acquiescence in the lark.

Imogen had never let her father know she wanted to see New York; she had never mentioned her desire to Scroggins or to Maria; she had never mentioned it to any one. She certainly was not going to let Darcy Jennifer know now how much she had always longed for a sight of the city.

Her protests at his detour ceased. She slouched a little lower in the front seat of the phaeton, and let the street cañons, both dull and lighted as they came, ripple over her.

They crossed the Harlem River, and after ten minutes or so of a long, wide avenue, passed among trees, and beyond the sight of buildings.

"Ah!" Imogen sighed. "We are back in Westchester. How did you do it so quickly?"

"No. This is Central Park."

"But how far from the Towers are we?" There was a wee note of fear in Imogen's voice.

"About thirty-six miles. I could make it in half an hour if it weren't for the traffic cops. We'll go back by the Drive and the Albany Road."

"Well, please start right away. Please turn here."

"In just a moment, I must get the candy first."

"Don't wait for the candy."

"It'll not take a minute."

They passed through the midnight splendor of Columbus Circle at that moment. Imogen gaped like any country girl at the river of molten incandescents burning down the Great White Way. They were not an old story to her, but a Gargantuan fairyland, leaping up like the instantaneous illumination of illimitable Christmas trees.

"This is Broadway!" Darcy explained, as they slid along.

"This little narrow street. Why, we came through bigger ones!"

"I know, but this was broad a hundred years ago. Those streets were made yesterday."

"It's as old as Dobbs's Corners," she said.

"Dobbs's Corners! I know that village—a quaint place!"

"Oh! Mr. Jennifer! You know Dobbs's Corners!"

"Of course. How did you know it?"

"I was born there. It's my home!"

Instantly she regretted she had said it, for it was her policy not to speak of herself or her origin. The next moment she felt repaid, however, for her apparent indiscretion.

"It's just the sort of a place to come from," Darcy laughed.

She liked this when he said it, but later she thought it over and wondered how he meant it.

The car turned into a side street in the upper Forties, crossed under the L, and came to a halt before a canopied door. A very tall man, in the uniform of a Russian Cossack, with a bandolier of cartridges slung across his shoulder and chest, stepped to the door and opened it, reaching forth his hand for Imogen to alight.

"But we are not getting out!" She looked toward Darcy.

"Yes, just for a minute."

"But why?"

"For the candy."

Imogen laughed. "I don't want any candy. Let's go home."

"We came this far to get the candy. Now we simply can't go back without it."

Darcy stepped out, and stood opposite the Cossack waiting for her to alight. Imogen stepped to the walk, feeling very much like a princess in a fairy tale, and quite unconscious of the disapproval in the appraising glance of the Cossack as he surveyed her modest frock and her old straw hat from his seven-foot eminence.

Just inside the doorway they were halted, while Darcy signed something in a book which was passed inside. They were obliged to wait.

"This is a funny shop," said Imogen.

"Particular," said Darcy. "They sell their goods to only a limited clientele."

In a moment they were admitted past the outer door, only to find themselves before a velvet rope, behind which stood two boys in buttoned light blue uniforms.

"Name, please?" asked one.

"Jennifer—Darcy Jennifer."

The name was repeated. Imogen could hear it passed, three or four times along like an echo. Then, after another wait, one of the boys slipped the velvet rope over its detaining hook, and beckoned. Darcy stepped aside so Imogen could precede him.

They passed into a little hall. At one side stood a narrow table about a foot wide and perhaps three feet long. It was piled high with boxes of candy. Near by stood a girl in the costume of a French peasant, with very low-cut bodice, tightly laced, and wearing wooden shoes, without stockings.

"Ah! Meestair Jenniver!" she called. "I know vat you like. A t'ree-poun' box of Honey Spice—*n'est-ce pas?*"

She produced a gaudily ornamented metal box, curtsied, and presented it to Imogen, as if by prearrangement.

Darcy passed over some bills.

Imogen, fascinated, exclaimed: "How did you know we were coming?"

"Ha! Ha!" laughed the French peasant, winking broadly at Darcy. "A leetle bird she wheestle—lak dat!"

She pursed her lips and shrilled. At the sound a man in faultless evening clothes came through some curtains.

"Good evening, Mr. Jennifer," he bowed low.

"Good evening, Tony. How about a table?"

"Certainly. This way. We are filled, but there is always room for you."

Darcy started forward. Imogen, clutching the box, now clung closely to his arm with a sudden revulsion of feeling.

"Where are we?" she exclaimed. "What is this?"

"Just a little private night club—something exclusive—

the Old Toasted Cheese." The man in evening clothes parted the curtains. Beyond was a room filled with men and women in evening clothes, eating, drinking, dancing. A saxophone orchestra was thrumming a sobbing moan.

"Please, let's go home?" protested Imogen.

"Come along. It won't bite you!" Darcy laughed.

Now he took her by the arm. She felt in a daze, at once devoured with curiosity and repelled by some unknown apprehension. He piloted her along the wall, following the man in evening clothes.

The air was thick with cigarette smoke. Before they had gone a few steps they found it difficult to proceed. Dancing couples seemed not to notice them, and to strive to dance right through them.

Imogen's feet were stamped on again and again. Finally they reached a tiny alcove and a much tinier table, barely big enough for two, but vacant.

"Thanks, Tony," said Darcy. "And now what will you have?" He turned to Imogen as she sank into the farthest seat, striving to press herself out of sight against the wall.

"Oh! Nothing at all!"

Darcy spoke to the man addressed as Tony. "Bring me," he said, "caviar, chicken aspic, some lettuce with that special dressing you know how to make, and a biscuit tortoni."

"Coffee, *monsieur?*"

"Certainly."

Darcy turned, beaming upon Imogen. The blood had gone from her face. She sat scared, all but breathless. She could see only the benevolent countenance of Uncle Isaiah, but it seemed to be mantling with a species of shocked horror.

"That will refresh us after the ride," Darcy was saying.

"I don't want anything," she repeated. She was hugging the metal box of candy rather spasmodically, but tried to smile bravely.

"You will surely have a biscuit tortoni." She shook her head blankly.

"What! No ice cream?"

Slowly a smile came to Imogen's cheeks; "Perhaps," she admitted; "perhaps a little ice cream."

14

THE LONG DRIVE HOME

IMOGEN'S PLIGHT WAS obvious to every one who glanced her way. She had shoved her chair tight back against the wall, and was all but plastered against it. One leg was curled up under the rungs to which a prehensile toe grabbed and clung. And she clasped the metal box of candy tightly to her bosom.

Her underlip was held between her teeth, and little scarlet spots appeared at the top of each cheek. She looked out with avidity on the scene.

This was a commonplace of New York night life, yet to her it was like Shadrach looking on Babylon shaggy-haired from the desert.

The dancing space was small; no larger than an ordinary room, but so thick with couples they jostled each other. And new ones were joining each moment. No one held back for lack of space.

The dancers were so crowded that they brushed her as they passed. Again and again a swishing skirt would slash over her knees, and she would clasp her chair more tightly, as if fearful she would be brushed off and lost in the mêlée, like a piece of driftwood in a seething stream.

The dancing favor wandered from Charleston to

Chicago, with a preference for the stabler mid continent, because it was the easier style.

Darcy watched his companion narrowly. He did not fail to note her gangling tensity, the startled width of her fawn-like eyes, the dilation of her sensitive nostrils.

"Too close for you?" he asked solicitously.

"No! No!" she protested, but grasped the metal box even more tightly.

"You like this, then?" He laughed.

"Oh, yes!" she gasped. "I never saw anything like it before."

"Not like the country club, eh? Or the school?"

"It's like it—only more so."

A wisp of a smile spread upward from the corners of her taut mouth. He began to realize that her brain was keen, though in experience she was palpably an ingenue. "The kind," he said to himself, "that will knock you out with the ease in which she will take a sensation—a thoroughbred."

Lenly had said to him, "She's nothing but a country urchin."

He had replied, "Maybe, but a Killigrew—and that's all the difference."

As he watched her he could think of but one word—"Killigrew." It sang through his brain like a refrain. He approved everything she said and did, mentally interpreting it as the characteristic attitude of a Killigrew, too well bred to be shocked, even though every physical sense was tingling in protest.

"Come!" he suggested gently. "Put your box of candy down, and try that caviar."

A little mound of black specks lay on the plate before

her. She tested it with her fork. It was like jelly. "Caviar?" she asked. "What is it?"

"The eggs of the sturgeon. Tony gets this direct from Moscow, via Warsaw, Vienna, and Havre. It comes from the Volga."

He did not add that it cost three dollars a portion. Imogen ate about fifty cents' worth, or half a teaspoonful. "It's salty," was her only comment.

"But appetizing. Don't you like it?"

"I suppose I would if I were accustomed to it. Caviar must be an acquired taste."

"Surely you have had it served before—at the Towers?"

"No," said Imogen, dropping her eyes.

He thought he noted a chagrin due to the fact that she lacked experience with caviar, but the chagrin was due to her feeling that she was in honor bound to tell him the truth, and now.

She tried to. "We never have anything that is not grown on the farm," she explained simply.

"What! No imported delicacies?"

She shook her head.

"Nor at Mrs. Morton's?"

She smiled, relieved to think she had told some of the truth without sacrificing his interest. "Not caviar," she smiled.

"That's strange."

"Uncle Isaiah says I am not to have any until I am grown up."

"Who is Uncle Isaiah?"

"Mr. Scroggins."

"Ah? A relative of Mr. Killigrew?"

"Oh, not a blood relative."

Another partial truth, which eased her conscience. She became immediately reserved, withdrawing into herself.

Jennifer respected this reserve. The essential snob in him was rebuffed. He felt he must not push his inquiries too fast. He must not let her imagine his interest was in anything but herself.

Her manner completely forbade further inquiry. He concentrated on chicken, which was being served. She indulged in several mouthfuls, and quite devoured the salad with its rich Russian dressing. And the flaky tortoni!

The very recent three-dollar-a-week clerk in Perkins's Grocery, at Dobbs's Corners, had a fair appetite. Darcy Jennifer thought it characteristic for a Killigrew heiress.

He offered a cigarette.

When she refused, he said: "Don't tell me you never smoke."

She did not want to appear too priggish, so she replied: "I never started. I suppose it makes one ill when one starts."

"Not necessarily. They have a brand here that is especially mild—the Nakara, a Japanese variety. Let me order some."

"No, no," she protested.

But he did. They proved to be two-thirds paper holder, with a scant half inch of tobacco.

"A couple of puffs—and extra mild. Try one," Darcy urged.

Finally she submitted, and took a puff—two puffs. And put the long holder down.

"Well, I'm not sick!" she laughed gayly.

"If you go no further than you have gone to-night, you

will end up as you began—a girl from the country—right from the wilds of Westchester."

He leaned forward earnestly and placed a hand over hers.

"I have no fear of your going too far—not with your antecedents," he said.

She dropped her eyes. She felt very wicked.

"Do you believe in love at first sight?"

She opened her eyes widely, astonished. "I hadn't thought of it," she gasped. "Do you?"

"I never did before, but—"

He dwelt on her longingly. She dabbed the burned end of the cigarette, and looked up at him whimsically, saying:

"And now don't you think you had better take me home—after I have smoked and been out to a night club?"

"Not yet. Look!"

It was time for the chief number of the supper show. The little room had been cleared, and from behind the curtains at the end came a creeping figure all concealed in long draperies. The music began a lullaby, and the figure danced. As she passed a table a laughing youth reached out his arms. The dancer whirled off, unperturbed, and disappeared behind the curtain.

Imogen was looking at her plate—or wasn't she? Darcy could not be sure. He felt he must apologize. "That wasn't on the program," he explained.

She looked up guilelessly.

"Didn't you see? Why—"

"See what?"

He didn't tell her.

Then they danced, and he shielded her from the mob. Once a girl with flushed face shouted:

"Hello, Darc, you old bear! Why don't you call a fellow up?"

But he shook his head gravely, and winked—over Imogen's shoulder.

"We must go—now," she pleaded.

They left a little after two. His bill was $86.75, but she did not know that.

On the way up the Drive, in the moonlight, still vivid, he reached his hand down and let it fall over hers. "What a night for love!" he said.

She withdrew her hand. "It does make one sentimental," she admitted.

"It makes one know how foolish it is to stay single."

"Oh, I don't know!" she ruminated, withdrawing to her side of the seat. She was watching the car closely. To her surprise it did not wabble.

"How well you drive!" she commented.

"That's only long practice, but I feel wonderful to-night—with you. Have you had a good time?"

"Of course, but I begin to regret."

"Smoking, I suppose?"

"It has been the wildest night of my life!"

"What a blameless life!" he laughed. "But don't try it with any one else."

"Why?"

"It might not be safe."

"Then I must dine and smoke only with you?"

"If with any one."

"That's right—reform me."

He reached again for her hand, but could not find it. She had withdrawn to the far end of the seat.

"I feel," said he, "very serious—as if I had found my fate!"

"Really?"

"Yes. I have found you!"

"Now I will have to do some reforming. And perhaps I will have a real job—bigger than yours, Mr. Jennifer."

"Nothing to speak of."

The chatter went on like this as they passed through White Plains, and on up the Elmsford road, and off toward Tarrytown. He was ever at a loss to know if she were really an ingenue, whether she was seventeen or seventy, as guileless as she seemed, or as deceptive as any Eve.

Just as the great entrance to the Towers loomed up, he halted the phaeton by the side of the road, and faced her. Her chin and lips became suddenly taut in the moonlight. Then he was sure she was quite inexperienced.

"Miss Nelson," he gravely began, "I know it's very sudden, but I want to tell you something."

He placed an arm on the back of the seat, as if to embrace her.

"It's terribly late," she muttered. "I am going to have a dreadful lot to explain. Please let us go on. There's the Towers straight ahead."

"I must see you soon again," he persisted.

"Of course."

"How soon?"

"Whenever you like, but please—please take me home now—at once, Mr. Jennifer."

They stopped before the Lodge at twenty minutes to four.

Scroggins was waiting in the lower hall, fully dressed. He had a revolver in his pocket.

When Imogen came up the steps he folded her in his arms without a word. Behind, from under her nightcap, Maria looked on apprehensively.

15

DARCY'S AMBITION

SCROGGINS HAD VERY little to say. He accepted the explanation of the impromptu visit to New York quietly, asked no questions, and concluded a moment later, curtly:

"Very well, Imogen, but I'd not advise you to do it again. Go to bed now."

"All right. Uncle Isaiah. Kiss me."

He kissed her good night. After she had gone up the stairs he whispered to Maria: "Go in and find out all about it. She'll tell you now—before she goes to sleep."

In the big room over the porte-cochère Mrs. Scroggins got the full confession, trying to say as little as possible, striving not to look forbidding.

Imogen related all that had occurred—everything— with the fresh enthusiasm of a girl elated with her first taste of high life. She omitted nothing—neither the cigarette, including the second puff, nor the caviar, nor the exhibition dancing.

To prove it all there was the metal box, with its bright colors on top. She insisted on opening it and thrusting the embossed chocolates toward Maria and forcing her to take one. She confided in Maria just as if she were one of the girls at the school. Appreciating it, Mrs. Scroggins was possessed with fear that she might do something to dissipate the spell. Eagerly she consumed the details of the lark.

"Now, go on, deary," she continued, munching the chocolate, "and how did he make love?"

Imogen blushed a little, but she told, that, too, just as frankly as she had the other—repeated every word that had been said, giving the inflections to increase the verisimilitude.

It was five o'clock before Maria could hear it all, and when she reached her own room there was Scroggins waiting for her, and she had to repeat it, while he listened patiently, without comment at first, just as he would have listened patiently to a report from the farm foreman or from Verhens about the conservatory.

"Hum!" he said when she had finished.

"I told you it would be all right!" Maria exclaimed. "He treated her like a lady, and he was a perfect gentleman."

"Hum!" Scroggins stroked his long blue chin reflectively. "Don't look that way to me!"

"But he was most respectful."

"That's the catch in it."

"What do you mean, Isaiah?"

"I mean these johnnies don't go to night clubs to be respectful. Why, Carl tells me it takes a hundred-dollar bill to go in and turn around and come right out again—five dollars a plate before you sit down."

"But I believe Imogen. He was respectful!"

"Then he is up to something very serious."

"Explain, Isaiah—please!"

"First, tell me what effect it has had on Imogen?"

Maria smiled, replying: "She's a darling. Jumped up and

kissed me good night after she'd ' 'fessed up,' as she said, and cried: 'Now they can't laugh at me at the school any more; I'm a woman of the world; I've been to a night club and smoked and dined!'"

Scroggins became more thoughtful.

"She must promise never to do it again," he announced.

In the morning Imogen promised, and when Carl took her back to school on Monday she left them assured she would never go to New York again without their express consent.

"I think we handled that pretty well," said Maria.

"This Jennifer is bad medicine—I feel it," Scroggins glowered.

On Tuesday Imogen got a love letter—her first. It said:

> I can think only of you, you are the one girl in the world. I am miserable that you did not let me tell you what was in my mind the other night. You make me think only of beautiful things, and I want to be always near you, and to look at you, and to hear you say those sweet, brilliant things you say so well, and to tell what I didn't dare tell you before—that I am mad about you, and love only you.
>
> Yours only,
> DARCY.

Imogen read it through breathlessly, and then hugged it to her bosom. After all, it was a love letter, and she had never had one before. This was her first suitor, the first man who ever had paid any attention to her—except Scroggins and Mr. Perkins.

She read it again—and again. She made a dozen

attempts to answer it, but tore them all up. What could she say? She didn't love him, but—well, it was very exciting.

While in this dilemma, not knowing what to say or do, Selene Henton came to her room. She was on the verge of showing the letter to Selene, but a sense of caution restrained her. But when Selene remarked that she had been to dinner with the Jennifers, Imogen blurted out:

"Oh, yes—and what do you think of Darcy Jennifer? Isn't he a dear?"

"He's a scamp and a bounder!"

"Oh, my! Why do you say that?"

"Because of the way he acted at my house when you were there."

Imogen was crestfallen. "I didn't see anything wrong," she protested.

"And my father says he is no good; he is in bad down town, owes everybody—would be bankrupt if his father hadn't saved him. Why, only yesterday the police came and took his car for a fine he hadn't paid—speeding through Rye the other night."

Imogen gasped, restraining herself from comment. "The other night! Rye!" The night they had skylarked to New York and the Toasted Cheese. The policeman had handed him the blue ticket.

She asked aloud: "Didn't he have the money?"

"No," Selene sneered; "always broke. They say he just lives at one of those disreputable speak-easies in New York, squanders there every cent he can get."

"And the police got his car?"

"Would have, except that his father paid the fine as they were taking it from the garage."

Imogen was exceedingly depressed. She felt as if she were guilty. She had his love letter there. What could she do? She dared say nothing.

Selene was rattling on: "A wretched little fortune hunter, too. Tried to run off with June Raymond last year. Lucky her father nipped that. June had half a million in her own name, from her grandmother."

"Oh, my!"

Imogen could say no more; but when she was alone she read the letter again, for the third time, and was more touched by it than at first. He had permitted himself an extravagance just to give her a pleasant evening, when he couldn't afford it. She felt a kind of pity for him. Perhaps he was too young to understand. A mature character like hers might be a restraining influence.

So the stage of her regard was all set the following day—Wednesday—when, it being callers' afternoon, she was bidden to the visitors' room to meet Lenly Jennifer. Lenly appeared, so she confided, as love's ambassador. Her coupé was parked on the lawn. Wouldn't Imogen take a run with her, and meet some one dying for a sight of her?

"Where?"

"I left him over on the Post Road."

"I'll have to have permission to leave the school grounds."

"Get it—just for an hour."

Mrs. Morton granted the permission. A few minutes later Imogen and Lenly entered a roadhouse a mile away, on the Post Road. Darcy, debonair—pert, even—seized both of Imogen's hands in his.

"What a brick you are to come!" he cried, and turned to Lenly; "Ta-ta, sis! Now, on your way!"

But Lenly said they needed a chaperon; and Imogen protested she must return to the school in an hour. Darcy declared he had asked her for dinner, and insisted she go to the phone and get Mrs. Morton's permission to remain out for dinner. She said she had promised not to go to New York again.

He assured her he knew a "duck of a roadhouse" over on the Hudson. "Can drive there in forty minutes."

Imogen went to the booth to phone. The waiter directed her to the next room, and the door was far from the table where they sat. She got the quick connection with Mrs. Morton, secured the necessary permission, hung up, and started up, when the voice of Darcy halted her.

She looked up, and saw that the telephone booth was evidently placed only a few feet from the table where he sat with his sister, but separated by a partition that did not go to the ceiling. She could hear every word that was said, and it was so startling that she could not resist listening.

"I'll marry her to-day—to-night—the first moment possible."

It was Darcy's voice, only it was high-pitched now.

Lenly's—lower—objected: "But, Darce, you are insane! She's not of age."

"Makes no difference. If she's my wife Killigrew will let up on me."

"Oh, pop'll help you out."

"Never again. Gave me my last chance."

"But go and see Mr. Killigrew personally."

"Can't get to him. Won't see anybody. And he's savage. But once this ward of his is my wife he'll change his tune. Watch!"

"But if he doesn't, Darc! Stop—think! I can't let you go on with this. And it's a crime against the girl. Why—

"Don't worry about her—little simp! Ought to have seen her disgrace me at the Toasted Cheese. She'll never be anything but the stingy relative of the world's prize miser. Just give me the chance and I'll show her how to spend some of his money!"

Imogen sat down in a chair for a few moments to gain control of herself. Her first impulse was to rush from the place hail the first passing car, and beg to be taken to the Towers.

The letter he had written her—her first love letter— seemed to be burning the spot over her heart where she had it hidden. She took it out and tore it to tiny bits, then looked for a place to throw them. She imagined some one finding them and piecing them together and learning of her ignominy. She dropped them down inside the heel of her shoes, half in each. Later, as she walked, she felt a glow of satisfaction in the realization that she was grinding his letter under her heels.

By that time she had determined what to do. She would go on for her own satisfaction, and see just how far he would go. And what was it he had said about difficulty with Mr. Killigrew? That puzzled her. Perhaps she might learn about it. Yes, she would go on.

Imogen reappeared, and said Mrs. Morton had given her permission to stay out to dinner, only it must not be at a roadhouse. This was her own addition; she felt just a little insecure.

Darcy looked to his sister.

"Then you invite her to our house, Len," he said.

A little later they were at the Larches. Mr. Jennifer was held down town for something that night, and so did not come home to dinner. Mrs. Jennifer presided. It seemed to Imogen a dreadfully awkward affair, and she hid her confusion under her natural shyness; but every one deferred to her, and with each renewed evidence of deference she burned with shame. His words rang through her memory: "Little simp! Ought to have seen her disgrace me!" She could not forget them.

Outwardly, Darcy was the soul of chivalry. He waited on her with devoted attention; stood behind her chair when she sat at table, was quickly there to pull it out when she arose, hung on every word she uttered, as if it were priceless.

Afterward, Mrs. Jennifer left the "children" alone, and soon Lenly withdrew. Imogen felt more excited than the night she had glided down the Pelham hill for her first descent to New York—and more wicked. Her feelings were mingled of a vague desire to know how a man would propose, to learn something more about an obscure injury to Mr. Killigrew, and the smarting eagerness to administer a lesson. But she was wearing her only frock, and she looked just as she had before—how had he put it?—"the stingy relative of the world's prize miser!"

Mr. Killigrew a miser! Hum! She was surprised to find herself defending the master of the Towers, he who also had spurned her, though without seeing her, as had Darcy. She did not reflect on the contrariety of this.

They walked on the terrace, but it was too cold for love making, though Darcy did try to place his arm through hers. Before she had rather liked this; now she thought it impudent—but, remembering she had suffered it before, she did not object now. She must lead him on. For she planned a splendidly dramatic climax of telling him to his face what she thought of his impudence. Not before he had declared himself, however.

"Did you get my letter?" he asked.

"Yes."

"Where is it?"

"Very close to me."

"With you?"

"Yes. Right next to me!" She dug her heels in the terrace.

"What did you think of it?"

"I don't know how to tell you."

He slipped an arm around her.

She moved to the door. "It's cold. Let's go in," she said.

He took both her shoulders in his hands, and looked at her squarely.

"Listen, Imogen," he pleaded. "I love you. I am mad about you."

She looked up at him coldly. "What a deceiver!" she thought. "It's hard to believe," she said.

He made to kiss her, but the kiss landed on her shoulder. Her hand was on the door, ready to open.

"Wait," said he. "I must tell you something. You must listen."

"Well."

"I want you to marry me."

So this was all there was to it!

"Oh!" said Imogen, sinking against the door. She was unable to recall any of the dramatic things she had planned to say.

He stood over her with such a queer look on his face, so

uncertain, so pleading, she felt sorry for him; but she knew
it would not do to encourage him. After all, however, he
was her first suitor, and he had proposed marriage.

"Listen, Imogen," he pleaded. "Won't you marry me?"

She gasped, "No! Of course not!" and rushed into the
house.

She expected to find some one. No one was there. He
cornered her in the library, where she flopped into a divan,
a little scared and with all her carefully thought-up phrases
evading her.

"But you must, Imogen, you must marry me."

She turned on him to find out the answers to her questions. "Why—why, Darcy?" she queried, earnestly.

He took this for encouragement and seized her hand.
"Because I—because—" He bowed his head. "Because I
love you."

And the way he said it shook her confidence in the verity
of her own ears back in the road house on the Post Road.

"Won't you?" He looked at her imploringly.

She shook her head, but he thought there was an impish
"come-on" in her eye. He took it for encouragement and
leaned toward her, reaching out his arms, crying, "Oh!
Imogen! I love you so!"

She held him just as he was about to kiss her. "Nonsense!"
she said; but cudgeled her brains to recollect those fine
phrases of dramatic response she had fashioned.

Then she demanded she be taken home, and all the way
tried to remember what it was she wanted to say to him.

When he deposited her before the school he seemed
to take it for granted she had accepted him; for he called
softly, "You will, Imogen; you will marry me. I know it!"

"Nonsense!" she laughed and ran inside. She thought later that Lenly must be right. He was insane. But she told nothing of this to any one.

16

SELENE ON THE WAR PATH

AS SHE THOUGHT it all over by herself in her room at the dormitory Imogen realized her mistakes very clearly. She should not have gone to the island with Darcy Jennifer, should not have ridden to New York with him, should never have seen him again, should not have gone out with Lenly to meet him at the road house, should not have let him propose, should not—

Should not; Should not! Should not! She spent half the night upraiding herself, and then she recalled that long dramatic speech she had expected to make when he did propose—"Ah! Darcy Jennifer, I see through your game at last. There is no true love in you! It is only the Killigrew money that you think you can secure through me! You have been nice to me only for material reasons! You are only a fortune hunter! But I have seen through you from the very first. You thought to deceive an innocent girl; but I am a woman of the world, Darcy Jennifer. I understand all! I am not to be deceived, Darcy Jennifer, by your kind of man! Begone!"

She rehearsed this speech in several ways. She should have delivered it the night before, when she had her chance. No matter. She *thought* it. Then when she felt she had it down pat, and was about to sleep, a contrary thought came to her.

Was she not indulging in a bit of deception herself? What had she to do with the Killigrew money, with her last cent paid down for this year's tuition with Mrs. Morton, existing on the precarious bounty of two servants.

Looking at it that way was she not just as bad as Darcy Jennifer—and a little worse, considering that she had no financial necessity driving her on?

She collapsed and wept bitterly, sobbing for her father.

Finally she slept, and when dawn came she crept to the mirror and eagerly scanned her reflection. Nothing there but the same smooth oval—not a line, not a wrinkle, not even dark lines under her eyes—and she had suffered enough to make her look like an old woman!

Waiting for the breakfast bell, she suddenly came to a new decision. Why not tell Darcy the truth? That would be better than denouncing him—more honest. Then he would drop her and leave her alone—easily enough.

She smiled wryly at this. It wasn't so dramatic as the other. But it would be easier, and more honest. She felt a little relieved at this decision, and went to breakfast and early classes a bit refreshed, though she still needed sleep dreadfully.

At four she was called to the telephone. It was Darcy. He said he must see her, and right away. She was very curt with him. Didn't he know that no one in the school could receive callers except on Wednesday?

"You will be going home to-morrow," he asserted. "I must see you then."

"No. I'll be busy."

"Saturday, then."

"Busy then, too."

"I must see you Saturday. Early. Please."

Again she hesitated, considering that would be the chance to tell him the truth, and to finish it up.

"Well," she said, "maybe—Saturday, but you mustn't come to the Towers."

"Then where will I see you?"

She thought a moment. It would be her first definite evasion of the benevolent care of Scroggins, but also the last. Did not the circumstances warrant it?

"By the grove of big trees, the oaks," she said, "at the edge of the estate."

"Where the road from White Plains makes its first turn?"

"Yes."

"Early, please? What time?"

"Ten o'clock."

"Good. I'll be waiting. Now sure, darling. Everything depends on it. I'm dying to see you!"

"I'll be there! Good-by!"

He would not be dying to see her as soon as she told him about Dobbs's Corners, and the will of Patrick Henry Nelson—and what Mr. Killigrew had said about her, and which she had overheard. No. That would end it—finish her little romance, but it was the best way, the only way. And fair to Darcy Jennifer. She owed him something, didn't she? Had he not spent a lot on her "education" at the Toasted Cheese—when he hadn't enough to pay his fine for speeding? She really felt sorry for him.

SELENE HENTON HAD not been asleep for ten days. Not

Selene. Life had a purpose for her, and a very distinct one, and she did not lose a single day in advancing toward its accomplishment. Getting Peter Killigrew before an altar figured as the most important step in this purpose.

A laudible ambition in Selene, for she intended to be quite worthy of the honor, and was watching her step very carefully with that object in view. And who could say she was a fortune hunter, when her father had many millions of his own, and doubtless would settle a few of them on her? She could meet Peter on his own ground, not as thickly carpeted with millions perhaps, but then, what is a few millions when they are all in the same family?

The problem had been to meet Peter on any ground.

She had been trying for fully five years, since long before she had entered Mrs. Morton's school, and now she was nearing graduation, with no better prospect than ever.

Peter would not attend any social functions. He avoided all clubs except those exclusively of males. He never called except at a few houses of very old friends of the family, and none but these very old friends of the family ever called on him.

The summer before Selene had discovered that Peter was booked to sail for Europe on the Balaklava. Promptly she induced her mother to book passage with her on the same ship. But Peter did not sail. He changed his mind at the last minute and crossed on the Tumbleweed, for Selene was only one of seven young ladies, accompanied by their appropriate mammas, booked for the Balaklava.

That was why she had been so eager to cultivate "a ward of Mr. Killigrew." Yet experience had taught her to be fore-warned and forehanded. The very day following Imogen's visit at Harbor View, Selene had traced the Rawlins family—the maiden name of Imogen's mother—without finding any relationship to the Killigrews.

There proved to be hundreds of Rawlinses scattered through the United States, and several score in the State of New York. Just on a chance she searched for the one nearest the Towers, in the Town of Far View, County of Westchester, and lit on Dobbs's Corners. But the Rawlinses had been extinct there for some time.

The next day Selene said casually to Imogen: "Have you ever been in Dobbs's Corners?" and watched her narrowly.

"Born and lived there—always—nearly," Imogen did not evade. "Why?"

"Oh! Some one said you came from there!"

"Who?"

"I've forgotten who. Does it make any difference?"

"No. Only—"

"Are you ashamed of Dobbs's Corners?" Selene asked coldly.

"No." Imogen flushed. "It's the dearest place in the world!"

Imogen marveled at this, but it was the day she was going to the Jennifers' for dinner, and she was so absorbed in this contemplation she quickly forgot the slight embarrassment Selene had caused her.

On her way home that Friday Selene had her chauffeur go around by Dobbs's Corners. She called first at the grocery Store, the only public place open, and saw Mr. Perkins.

The storekeeper yawned when she asked about Imogen Nelson.

"Know 'Geeny Nelson," he replied. "Ought t' when she clerked right t' this store four year, an' two months. I used t' say her paw was cracked an' 'Geeny, too, but mebby not—mebby not—time 'll tell."

"Her father? Who was her father?"

"Ol' Pat Nelson—kep' books f'r Mullins t' the hairpin fact'ry over yonder-closed several years now. Sly ol' bird, Pat Nelson, ups an' wills 'Geeny t' Peter Killigrew. Haw! Haw! A slick one. Willin' a girl daughter like that! Slipped her out o' th' big end o' th' horn too. Purty smart!"

"What do you mean, Mr. Perkins, by willing her?"

The beady eyes of the groceryman suddenly became suspicious, and his lantern jaws snapped tight. "Who be you?" he demanded.

"Miss Henton from Harbor View."

"Harbor View? Where's that?"

"In Connecticut—on the Sound."

"Huh! Connecticut!" Mr. Perkins's method of saying it indicated he looked upon the neighboring State as a far country, quite beyond his ken. He became very glum. Selene could get no more from him.

However, she had what she was looking for. The next day she instructed one of her father's attorneys to search the records and bring her a copy of the will of a Mr. Nelson late of Dobbs's Corners. Before she returned to school the next Monday she possessed a copy of the original document. At the same time, acting under her instructions to unearth all known facts about Imogen Nelson, he learned about the auction sale of the Nelson bed.

By this time, her suspicions being partially confirmed, and her anxiety being whetted by the fear that she had made another mistake, and was wasting time and effort in cultivating Imogen in the hope of meeting Peter Killigrew through her, she was ready to stop at nothing to know the whole truth.

Therefore she caused her attorney to make inquiry of Reginald McKenna, Mr. Killigrew's secretary, concerning the "ward" of Mr. Killigrew enrolled at the Morton school. The word came back that Mr. Killigrew had no "ward," that he had given a trifling sum only for the education of a penniless orphan, Miss Nelson, but that his responsibility and knowledge ended there.

When, at last, her worst suspicions were confirmed, Selene was in a very bad state indeed. She had been barking up the wrong tree—up two wrong trees, in fact.

For her quick and well-adjusted social mind saw the double danger in the situation. Not only had she made a mistake of cultivating a girl for whom Mr. Killigrew had no regard, and who doubtless could never further her desire to meet the reigning master, but she had disclosed an even more serious possibility.

If the thing were exposed and it became public property that Mrs. Morton had also been imposed upon, the Morton school would suffer irreparably, and while Selene had no love or veneration for Angela Morton, still the prestige of the school was now her chief social armor.

Destroy that, and she would be destroyed.

Distressing, very—until Selene's resourceful mind saw a marvelous way to utilize for her own advantage the very *contretemps* which, she felt, had all but ruined her.

When she saw this way out she came suddenly into a great peace. Here was a way to go cross lots to her objective. It would take a field marshal in the game of social climbing to outwit Peter Killigrew. But who better than Selene Henton was equal to the task. She was elated at her new prospect.

The first step was to call up Billy Van Pelt and get him to come to her that Wednesday—the very Wednesday Darcy Jennifer had fixed on for his proposal.

Darcy was not worthy of the success which Selene felt within her grasp. He did not investigate before jumping at the shadow of the Killigrew name.

Selene, in very different fettle, was sure she was on the right track at last, and one of which not one girl in a million would think.

Billy Van Pelt took Selene to tea at the Brinywood that afternoon. For a long time now he had done his best to fix it so that Selene might meet Peter Killigrew, but it seemed a hopeless task.

Selene came right to the point. "Billy," she said, "I'm coming to town Friday afternoon, about three—my trig is through at two thirty, and that's my last lesson of the week—and I want you to meet me and take me to Mr. Killigrew's office."

"His office, Selene? What's the idea?"

"I have some business with him."

"Business? What kind of business?"

"Never mind. Take me to him. It's very important—to him. You tell him he must see me—in his own interest. That's all. Now be a good fellow, Billy. No more questions. Do as I say."

17

SELENE MAKES A CALL

THE NEW YORK office of the Killigrew estate is a one-story building on a side street in the Thirties, just off Madison Avenue. A thirty-two story skyscraper rises next door, and one of thirty-five stories is planned for the opposite corner—business everywhere.

There is one residence left in the immediate neighborhood, the house two blocks away, where Peter Killigrew III lived. It has been unoccupied, except by a caretaker, for over thirty years; that is, by a caretaker and dogs.

Many efforts had been made to buy that old residence from the Killigrew estate. Even the year before the price offered for it was nearly two hundred dollars a square foot. While nowhere else was it a Killigrew policy not to take advantage of the rise in real estate values, this former home resisted all golden blandishments. It could not be a blanket sentimentality for Killigrew homes; for other former Killigrew residences, both uptown and down town, had always been sold, whenever the market seemed right in the opinion of the reigning Killigrew.

The Murray Hill residence defied the real estate market because Peter Killigrew III, grandfather of the present Peter, had a passionate fondness for dogs—especially for his mastiff, a savage but devoted beast, who had been his sole and constant companion during the last years of his life. Its name was Belle.

The third Peter died thirty-odd years ago, comparatively young, only fifty-some years, of what they called "la grippe." "Flu" it would have been later. Among his last words to Peter the Fourth was an injunction not to take Belle from the yard she loved as long as her blood was alive to seek shelter there.

This dying admonition operated more strongly than a legal will on his descendants. Belle lived only three or four years after her master, but when she passed out she left a litter of puppies.

There were the puppies, nine, mongrel, without pedigrees; but most lusty little things—at least eight of them. The ninth was a runt, half the size of the others, but seemingly as vigorous.

Thereupon the fourth Peter closed up the house, retaining as caretaker a former coachman of his father's, a middle-aged man named Nick Rainey, who moved in with his wife to occupy the place.

All Nick had to do was to punch a clock six times a day, look out for fires, and feed the dogs—a snap, the neighbors called it.

The fourth Peter thought the dogs might live twelve or, at the most, fourteen years. Meanwhile the increase in value of the property would be such as to well repay the hire of the caretaker and the payment of the taxes on the unused land and buildings.

But the dogs multiplied. There were forty-six of the second generation, and a hundred and eighteen of the third. Nick built kennels on four sides of the yard in the rear.

He had extended the walls several feet, and had stretched chicken wire over the top to keep out stray dogs from the neighborhood.

The breed was self-sustaining by this time, and apparently would be perpetual. At one time it seemed that if the third Peter's deathbed injunction was literally obeyed and the yard, kept there as long as any of Belle's blood was alive, the old residence would never get on the real estate market.

Belle's blood had defied the skyscrapers for a maritime generation.

Nature's inexorable law, however, was slowly defeating the dogs. The second generation of Belle's offspring was only two-thirds the size of the lusty first generation. The third generation was half the size of the second, and the fourth much smaller yet.

The numbers dropped off, too. A hundred and eighteen was the peak. They dropped back rapidly after that until the seventh generation of dogs after Belle produced only two miserable little Cretins about four inches high, and not much better than imbeciles.

These stunted, half-witted Cretin mongrels, utterly worthless, were now more than eleven years old, and were giving unmistakable signs of wearing out, despite the lavish care of old Nick and his estimable wife.

When those dogs died Nick and his wife would be without jobs, and they were both well over seventy.

Perhaps there was just a little regard for the value of the unearned increment on the island of Manhattan in the Killigrew policy as carried on in respect to the residence of the third Peter—as well as literal respect for its owner's dying request—for that part of Murray Hill had doubled and quadrupled in value of late years.

It was estimated in real estate offices which knew the secret that those dogs had been the cause of adding about a million and a half of value to the Killigrew estate, for if the residence had been sold shortly after the third Peter's death it would have brought that much less than it would now.

Plainly, the time was approaching when it could be sold. Monthly, even weekly, reports were submitted to real estate experts, sub rosa, on the health of the Killigrew Cretins.

On the Friday afternoon when Selene Henton went to the offices of the Killigrew estate with Billy Van Pelt to be properly introduced, a very important message had just been delivered there from old Nick himself, in the form of a penciled note, saying, "One of them dogs has died, Master Peter.—Nick Rainey."

Peter put on his hat and walked two blocks up the street to the city residence of his grandfather, and penetrated to the back yard and to the graveyard of Belle and her progeny. Nick had planted them all under the grapevine, and the vine had prospered so abundantly that the resultant concords supplied Nick and his wife with all the grapes and jelly they could use, and sell.

Peter wanted to see the last dog—the last living descendant of Belle. Old Nick led him to the kennel facing south-southwest, the largest and best of the many, now deserted and neglected. He pointed down to a muddy streak of fur lying on a mat in the door of the kennel.

Peter reached down, and patted the animal. It opened a

weak eye, closed it again, and wheezed, a decrepit, half-developed, over-fat dog, aged before its time.

"How long, Nick?" he asked.

The old man sighed. "I'm afraid he won't last out the winter, Master Peter."

"Too bad." Peter rose, adding, as if to himself: "Belle did pretty well to live over thirty years—well for a dog!"

"Yes, sir," assented Old Nick, "but the livin' ain't bin much lately, sir. Jus' breathin', y' might say. It's a lesson, sir, in them dogs."

"Lesson? What sort of lesson?"

Peter was looking up and around at the neighbors of the old kennel yard. Beyond, extended over twenty floors of a bustling department store on the avenue. To the right loomed the twenty-five floors of an office building. The other way, across the street, the new steel skeleton was climbing above the thirtieth floor.

All could look down on this strange relic of a former day. Trade was crying loudly for the kennels of Belle's progeny, so loudly that Peter had that day received an offer of two hundred and fifty dollars a square foot for the ground on which the old residence stood, including, of course, the yard and kennels.

"Th' lesson of new blood, sir. It takes new blood t' keep life up an' hustlin'."

"Just what do you mean, Nick?"

"I mean them dawgs, sir. I've tended 'em now over thutty year, an' a duller man'n Nick Rainey would've seen how they went t' pieces, year after year, f'r th' lack o' new blood."

"The dogs did degenerate woefully," Peter admitted. For years he had disliked looking at them. He had only carried on the policy of housing them until they died through natural causes out of deference to his father's wish, as taken from *his* father.

"You don't remember Belle, like I do, Belle, y'r grand-paw's houn'. A great dawg, sir. Remember her well. Big an' proud, an' fine-lookin', an' full o' pep as they make 'em. A dawg fit fer a Killigrew, sir, an' no mistake.

"An' her pups went her one better, leastways three er four on 'em did. Great snakes! Them dawgs were a sight, t' see in them days. An' why? Cause they daddy could leap a twelve-foot fence. Yessir! That's why them pups was real dawgs!

"Some o' them pups could 'a' done th' same thing. I allus 'lowed, only y'r paw made me build that wire nettin' acrost the top. Couldn't get out.

"That finished 'em—after about thutty year! Yes, sir. Y' gotta git new blood. An' go after it, too. Sure! Don't stop 't fences er nothin'."

Peter listened quite carefully. Toward the end he smiled. "Is that philosophy only for dogs, Nick?" he asked.

The old man answered quickly: "Dawgs is not so much differ'nt fr'm humans in lots o' ways, believe me."

Peter was executive again. "Keep me informed about the last one," he admonished. And went back to the office.

As he reentered the low building two blocks away he ran into Billy Van Pelt coming out. With Billy was a girl evidently not more than twenty, in a strictly tailored suit.

A thin-faced girl, and clean-cut, with a direct look in her eye that seemed to say she would always get what she wanted—or know the reason why, rather businesslike.

Peter's only thought of her, if he gave her any thought, was that she was in some business. One met women in business everywhere nowadays, despite the fact that in the Killigrew offices only men were employed. But Peter realized that was due to his own peculiarities. He disliked to have women about, though occasionally he was obliged to deal with them.

"I want to introduce Miss Henton," said Billy, turning to her. "Selene," he spoke with a mixture of gallantry and familiarity, "may I introduce Peter Killigrew?"

Peter bowed rather stiffly.

"Peter, Selene Henton. She has a bit of information she thinks you ought to share with her." Billy smiled broadly, tipped his hat and was off, calling: "See you later."

It was a very important moment for Selene, but no one observing her would have thought so. She treated it rather casually, apparently.

There was a pause in which both seemed ill at ease. But she forced Peter to speak first, through sheer waiting.

"Yes, Miss Henton. What is it?" he asked, not moving. They were standing on the step of the Killigrew offices.

She looked inside. "I want to speak to you privately," she said.

He stepped to a little fence, opened the gate, and motioned her inside. Then he followed her. She looked around.

There was a rather large room, with broad plate windows, and desks on all sides, seven or perhaps eight men working, not a machine, no sign of typewriter or other mechanical apparatus, not a private office, not even a screen.

Could this be the business home of the master of many millions? She had imagined heavy carpets, embossed woods, labyrinthine offices, with the master concealed in the far center in some inaccessible inner room.

He led the way to a broad double desk in the corner, a flat-topped affair covered with glass, and bare of papers. On one side sat a young man, looking through a bundle of reports.

"Miss Henton, my secretary, Mr. McKenna. He is entirely in my confidence. Now, what is it, please?"

She felt strangely depressed. This was no place to vamp a man. Still, she had no such idea when she sought this interview; but what could you do—out there in the open, surrounded by men? It was not encouraging.

She plunged into her errand, however. "It is a delicate matter, Mr. Killigrew, and I have come to you personally and directly because I thought that was the only straightforward thing to do. I could not write or telephone what I had to say, and Billy was good enough to want to see that you knew all about me, and to bring me to you in this fashion. You see, Mr. Killigrew, my mother was at the Towers once when she was a little girl, and—"

Selene felt tangled in her words. It was very hard to say what she had come to say, and she feared she might never get another chance to impress Peter with her social importance, and her mother had been at the Towers once to a New Year's reception of Peter IV.

Evidently Peter lacked a sense of humor. He, too, was puzzled. "Yes, Miss Henton," he admitted. "That is very nice, but why did you seek me now?"

"Because—" She wiped the perspiration from her brow. "Oh! It's about that Miss Nelson—the girl who says she is your ward!"

Peter frowned. He looked at McKenna, on the corners of whose mouth there was the ghost of a grin. "Some one telephoned about her yesterday. What do you know about her?"

Selene's hands were clasping and unclasping. She felt nervous with fear that perhaps she had made a mistake after all. "Is she your ward or not, Mr. Killigrew?" she blurted out. "That is what I wanted to know."

"But I thought you said you had some information for me."

"Oh! I have! I have!"

"Well—what is it?"

The worst seemed over. Selene went on more steadily. "It's just this, Mr. Killigrew. This girl—this Miss Nelson from Dobbs's Corners—is matriculated at the Morton School up in Westchester, as your ward. She is a freshman; I am a senior. And it has become known to me—oh, in roundabout ways—that she is really not your ward at all. That is what I came to see you about!"

"Yes," Peter commented.

Selene rattled on. "And I thought you ought to know she is trading on your name; and I thought if I told you about it face to face a scandal might be avoided, for I am sure you would dislike that just as heartily as I.

"You understand, Mr. Killigrew, I am sure, my interest is at one with yours, for I know how an old and honored name like yours is so often abused and used. My father finds it difficult with the Hentons. Oh! Yes, people do impose even on the Hentons. It is a dreadful thing for people of position to have to stand, Mr. Killigrew, and I sympathize with you."

She came to an abrupt halt. Peter had not helped her. He was looking at her dispassionately, like a scientist studying a new bug.

There was a long, painful silence before Selene exclaimed; "But she is not your ward, is she, Mr. Killigrew?"

Peter looked toward his secretary. "What would you say about that, McKenna?" he asked, in a detached manner.

Mac replied rather flippantly, Selene thought, "Technically, yes, one might call her your ward."

There was a swift intake of Selene's breath.

A humane impulse came to Peter at this juncture. "Of course," he offered, as if striving to soothe his caller, "I hardly expected her to trade on the fact that this technicality exists."

"But she does—she does, Mr. Killigrew, I assure you." Selene was vehement. She felt her ground returning.

Peter looked off into space. "I merely advanced a trifling sum for her needs which my superintendent was to disburse. That is all. You may tell those who inquire, from me, if you wish, Miss Henton."

His air now was of finality, as if there was no further purpose in an interview.

"Oh! Thank you! Thank you, Mr. Killigrew!" Selene gushed with a sudden warmth of feeling, as if everything had been won when all was dark. "You may be assured I will be discreet—most discreet. And I sympathize with you deeply, most deeply. I know how these charitable cases will presume. My father has often been pestered in that way, Mr. Killigrew. You have no idea."

Peter looked toward Mac helplessly, as if asking him how to get rid of her.

"I will go, now, Mr. Killigrew, but I want you to prom-ise to call on me at your very earliest convenience, and I promise to keep a close watch on this Miss Nelson, and to keep you well-informed, and to see that no very untoward imposition is made on your good heart. You will call, won't you, Mr. Killigrew?"

"Yes," gasped Peter.

She seized his hand fervently. "Oh! Thank you! Thank you!"

"If I can," he weakly added.

"But you have promised, Mr. Killigrew, and I will count on you. I know the value of your word. Good-by!"

And she was gone.

Mac winked broadly. "They think up a new one every day," he said, *sotto voce* to his employer, while Selene was passing through the door.

18

UP IN THE AIR!

THAT WAS FRIDAY afternoon, late.

Saturday morning the Killigrew offices were open only three hours—nine to twelve. Peter invariably came in for the last hour to sign checks, and see if McKenna had anything pressing. Sometimes he stayed on after the clerks were gone. He liked to sit at that desk where his father and his grandfather sat, and look out into the tiny rear yard, where a grass plot was religiously kept alive, despite the high buildings all around.

This Saturday, at ten minutes to twelve, just as the clerk on the high stool in the rear had begun to close his ledgers and get them ready for the safe, the phone that stood between Mac and Peter rang.

Mac answered, as usual; then passed the receiver to his employer. "Scroggins, sir," he said.

Peter listened, saying, "Well, Scroggins."

The superintendent's voice seemed shaky. "Master Peter," it seemed to plead, "I am on my way down to see you, but I'm afraid I won't get there by twelve. I must see you—at once. It's very, very important!"

"Where are you now?"

"At the north end of Van Cortlandt Park, in the roadster.

I drove in. Couldn't wait for the train. It will take me forty minutes, at least, to reach you."

"What is it you want to see me about?" Peter spoke in his accustomed voice, a level, severe tone.

"I can't tell you, sir; not over the phone. I must see you. Can't you wait—or else make an appointment to see me later?"

"I'll wait," said Peter, and hung up.

"Wonder what's got into Scroggins," he remarked to Mac.

"Maybe Verhens has really quit—at last. He wants a new sunken greenhouse this winter, and a place in Jersey has offered one, so he told me yesterday on the phone, after you left. Tried to bully me a bit."

"H-m!" was Peter's only comment. It was a principle with him—inherited, like most of his principles—never to let a servant get the upper hand, no matter how valued. He had been willing to build the new sunken greenhouse at the Towers, but this attitude of the obstinate Dutch gardener changed the prospect.

"In that case," said Peter, his mouth growing more compressed, "there will be no new greenhouse this winter. Let Verhens go if he likes."

At twelve the clerks left, promptly to the second. Mac sat before a clean desk, idling for a few minutes. Peter, the tips of his hands placed together, had turned his chair and was looking out contemplating the grass plot.

The Killigrew office was as quiet as a country church on week days. Central storehouse for many millions it seemed like a tomb. The secretary waited, from time to time looking up a trifle nervously toward his employer. He made it a rule, however, never to ask to be let off. It was not necessary with a man whose routine was as exact as Peter Killigrew's.

At a quarter past the hour, Peter said: "You may go, McKenna. I'll lock up."

"I'd be glad to save you the bother, sir," Mac disingenuously replied. He was really itching to be off.

"Never mind. Run along."

"Very well, sir. Good day."

"Good day!"

Peter was alone. Not a sound, even the clock was tickless. The one ray of sun that peeked past the corner of the twenty-two story building in the rear—above the second set-back—had gone since a quarter past eleven. It lasted only forty minutes at this time of year.

The Killigrew offices were getting darker and darker with the passing years—and the rising neighbors. Sunny all day in the time of his grandfather, who had located them there, they now had but forty minutes a day sunlight—and then in one corner only.

Peter shivered, though the office was well warmed. He became glummer and more glum. The vast height and weight of Manhattan began to oppress him. He looked impatiently at his watch. Would Scroggins never come? What had held him?

He walked over to the window, and looked out on the grass plot. He seldom waited, seldom gave himself time to think; but now unplumbed depths inside him began to waken, and ask him questions. Was this oppression he felt the terrific slow weight of those accumulated millions, guarded from generation to generation and now solely in his care? What friend had he? To whom could he turn?

He had faithful servants, yes—Mac and Scroggins, and many others, but servants! He had club friends—Billy Van Pelt, and a few others, constantly begging him to step out; but he felt the lurking object behind all these invitations, just as he felt the seductive, insinuating object behind every woman who approached him, down to this last feminine creature from the Morton School. What was her name—Serene? Yes, serene in longing to lick up the monetary accumulations of his forefathers.

He looked at himself in the mirror. His face was thin; his waist was thin; his head a little held forward; a bit of a worried look on his long countenance. He was fit physically, yes, competent to hold his own at tennis, and in the North Sea he had slung a harpoon against an old whaler and found himself not shamelessly second best. Did he lack health? Or courage? Or what was it? The admonitions of his ancestors to cling to their money? Was that it?

As he gazed at the yard a transformation—curious effect—seemed to come there. He was looking into a series of deserted dog kennels, most of them dusty with long disuse. Only one was furnished. Lolling in its door, wheezing, lay a miserable, exhausted, lonely, over-fed, half-imbecile dying dog—the last expiring end of a long line of lustier ancestors.

He blinked, and the scene changed to the clipped grass plot he knew much better. It was only a trick of the imagination—taking him two blocks away to the backyard of his grandfather's mansion and the wheezing little Cretin waiting there for death.

Peter swallowed very hard.

Was he anything like that dog? Last of a line, lonely, kept

alive by servants whose jobs depended on his dragging out his miserable existence?

What was it Old Nick had said? "Takes new blood to keep a line alive. The daddy was a *dawg*—leaped a twelve-foot fence and back again. And humans are not unlike—"

Nonsense! That was the sort of fool stuff the movies suggested. Better come out of it.

A sharp ring brought him to reality. He had forgotten the outer door was locked. He went to it, and opened. Scroggins was there. Peter let in the superintendent. They faced one another across the desk.

The old man was deeply agitated. That was plain to see. Peter reassured him. "Take it easy, Scroggins, and tell me—what is it?"

"I'll have to begin at the beginning, Master Peter. I have a confession to make." He faltered.

A wisp of a smile came to Peter's lips. If there was any servant he trusted, this was he; if there was any employee he loved, Scroggins was the man. "Grafting again, I suppose," he said, referring to that classic time so beloved of his father when Scroggins had entered in the books, "To graft, two hundred and twenty-five dollars." There were few enough jokes in the Killigrew ledger. This one was seldom allowed to slumber.

"Oh!" groaned Scroggins. "It's worse than that."

"Worse than grafting?"

"Yes, Master Peter. Man and boy, sir, all my life, I've served you and your father, and now, for the first time, I come to you in humiliation. I have abused the confidence you have placed in me. I, pardon, me—" He stopped to regain control of himself.

Peter said nothing. Emotion had been almost drilled out of him. He looked at Scroggins judicially, but with kindly intent. He was thinking of his boyhood, and of the many times he had ridden on Scroggins's knee. Of course he would not deal harshly with the old man. However, it was a well-established principle, learned from his father, to hold all stewards strictly to account, without exception.

"It's about Miss Nelson—Imogen—from Dobbs's Corners, Master Peter," Scroggins went on after a moment. "She has been living with me at the Lodge. Mrs. Scroggins and I have insisted on it. She is an orphan girl, and most adorable. We love her. Indeed we do love her, but I don't know how to tell you, why—I—"

The superintendent, usually so straightforward, stumbled. This was very unlike him.

Peter scowled. "What are you driving at, Scroggins? Do you mean to tell me you have entered this girl at an exclusive boarding school as my ward? Is that it?"

Scroggins's jaw fell. "How did you know?" he exclaimed.

"Did you expect to get away with a thing like that, and not have me find it out?"

"No. No, sir. Well, I—I—"

"Is this your 'confession'?"

"Why—yes—yes—part of it?"

"Oh! Part of it? What is the rest?"

"Isn't that bad enough?"

"It is, though hardly a crime," Peter tried to soften any possible asperity. He already felt this was another "mare's-nest," but it was well to maintain discipline.

Scroggins breathed more easily. From now on he spoke more confidently. "Then you don't object?" he asked.

"I didn't say that. Of course I object, but you may have the benefit of the doubt. If you have entered the girl as my ward, let the entrance remain, though do not enter into any further contracts concerning her in my name. Is that all?" Peter rose.

"No. That's not the worst of it!" Scroggins cried. "The worst is she is gone—has disappeared—been kidnaped, I fear!"

"How do you know? Has the school notified you?"

"Not from the school. From the Lodge!"

"Well, notify the police. Why come to me?"

"It's a strange case, Master Peter. I had to come to you. I need your help."

"How?"

"To get her back. You have no idea how she has grown into my heart, Master Peter. I—" His lip trembled. "I love her!" The old man looked down, abashed.

Now Peter could smile without its being seen. "For shame, Scroggins," he replied, "and at your age! And a married man!"

Fire came into the eyes of the superintendent until he saw the smile. "As a father, I mean, of course, sir. I adore her! She is the breath of my life. A flower, Master Peter. A girl in a million!"

"Tell me about it. 'Kidnaped,' you say? How?"

"This morning I was in the lower meadow down by the State road, a mile and a half from the Lodge. Some transplantings of pine seedlings were being made there, and I wanted to look over the job before the ground froze too hard. There is a row of Lombardy poplars there, very thick, and a hedge of Norway spruce behind. You can't see through from the road. Just beyond is that group of oaks where the fork turns off toward White Plains. Beyond that is a triangle of about three acres, bare, of county land.

"Just as I reached there an airplane came whizzing up from the east. At first I thought it was the daily mail from Mitchel Field flying over on the way to Chicago, but I looked at my watch. It was ten o'clock. The mail goes over at six in the morning and three in the afternoon. Next thing I knew the plane dropped in the bare spot. Accident, I thought, but a second look proved this not true, for the aviator—there was only one—stepped out and began adjusting things quite coolly.

"Then I saw it was a hydro-airplane—two little boats on the skids, and wheels below. The aviator looked at his watch and crossed to the corner under the oaks, where he waited. In a few minutes down the road came Imogen. That's Miss Nelson's name, sir—Imogen! A lovely name, I think.

"I was not more than ten paces off, and could see and hear everything, though they never guessed any one was near. It was plain, she had sneaked away from the Lodge to meet him by appointment, but equally plain that he had put one over on her with the hydroplane. He wanted her to go up in it with him. At first she refused. But he overcame her objections by promising her to get back in ten minutes. That was very clear—both her demand and his promise.

"Finally she got in the basket, or the cockpit, or whatever it is you call it—the tonneau, and the last word I heard him say was: 'What a beautiful day to get married!' Then they were off."

"Flew away?" Peter commented.

"Yes. And didn't come back—not in ten minutes, nor in

an hour. It was then I started for you. I could not tell you over the phone about it, and I wanted your authority to hire a plane and go after them."

"But why chase them?"

"Why, Master Peter!" Scroggins was aghast. "I must save her."

"Who is this aviator?"

" 'Mr. Jennifer,' she called him."

The name struck Peter familiarly. "Jennifer—Darcy Jennifer?"

"Exactly," said Scroggins, "Darcy Jennifer."

The reigning Killigrew in the absence of his secretary went to a steel filing cabinet and drew forth a dossier, which he carried to the table. After examining it for a few minutes he remarked: "I think I know that aviator—a bit of a scamp. Call up the Noonday Club and see if Mac is there. He may be in for lunch. Get him for me."

In a few minutes Scroggins handed the receiver to his employer. "How long did we give that fellow Jennifer to settle, Mac?" Peter asked.

"Until Wednesday," Mac replied.

"And then what?"

"The district attorney, I told him. But he ought to come across and make good. His father is well fixed, though overextended."

Peter hung up.

"If it is the same man," he remarked to Scroggins, "I have good reason to know him. He sold me some shares in a rubber plantation, that never existed. Twenty thousand dollars. Mac got on to him, and threatened him with both Federal and local authorities. He used the government mails, it seems, though he came to me personally. Walked into the office—plenty of cheek. I gave him until next Wednesday to refund the money. Promised no prosecution if he made good before noon the middle of next week."

Scroggins was becoming highly excited. "I see now," he cried, "what it is all about! It's a terrible thing, Master Peter."

"He'll probably get the money—not a very large sum, after all. If not, I may give him a few days more."

"I wasn't thinking of the money—but of Imogen!"

"Don't worry about her—a little adventuress like that can look after herself, no doubt. You told me she had been looking after herself for several years."

At first this was like a personal wound to Scroggins. He sank back, deeply hurt. Then his face flushed and he replied, almost in anger: " 'Adventuress,' Master Peter! If there ever was an innocent girl in this world it is Imogen—bland as a baby!"

"They usually are! She'll take care of herself!"

Fire darted from the old eyes of the superintendent. He demanded: "Did you look out for yourself when this wolf fastened his fangs on you?"

Peter's jaw dropped now. Scroggins had hit him for the first time. He made no reply. Scroggins saw his advantage.

"And you're an experienced man, accustomed to dealing with fake schemes every day—and with a competent secretary like Mac to back you up and keep you out of trouble. Why—" He choked for utterance.

"I'd hardly call him a wolf—just a weasel. A sneak. I make it a rule not to suspect club friends, and his father and I belong to the Morris Hunt."

"And doubtless Imogen wouldn't suspect a guest at an exclusive school like Mrs. Morton's."

Scroggins had the best of the argument. That was plain, for Peter made no reply. He put the dossier back in its cabinet.

"Well," he concluded, "we can't do anything about it to-day. When you return home you may find she has returned."

Scroggins was thinking deeply. "No," he asserted, "and I begin to see what was in that devil's mind. 'A beautiful day to get married,' he said. Promised to get her back in ten minutes. Failed to bring her back. Flew north.

"Why, don't you see, Master Peter?"

"See what?"

"The plot of this worthless scamp?"

"Out for a holiday, I suppose, Saturday afternoon— trifling with a poor girl."

" 'Poor girl!' She is entered at Mrs. Morton's as 'the ward of Peter Killigrew.' That's how he knows her. And Peter Killigrew threatens him with jail if he does not give up twenty thousand dollars, which doubtless he has not got, by next Wednesday. But if he can marry the ward of Peter Killigrew before then don't you see that he can have a mighty good hope of escaping any penalty, and probably of getting a substantial wedding present into the bargain."

"Then the joke will be on him," said Peter.

Scroggins was wild. "But he will have married Imogen!" he cried. "And what a terrible thing for that marvelous girl!"

"Marvelous! How marvelous?" Peter was evincing a strange interest; but neither of them seemed to note it.

"Marvelous because she is unlike any other girl I ever

knew—the essence of purity, of innocence, of intelligence, and poetic—a dream of happy spring!"

Peter laughed. "I forgot. You are in love with her."

"And so would you be if you saw her!" Scroggins replied hotly. Then, seeing the frown come to the Killigrew brow at so bold an expression, added hastily: "I beg your pardon, sir."

By this time Peter had led the way to the outer walk, and they stood there before the roadster. Peter looked at his watch. It was one o'clock, time the fellows would be getting in to the club for lunch. "Sorry, Scroggins, but what can I do?" he asked.

"Authorize me to hire an airplane and go after her—to save her."

"Very well, go ahead—but keep it out of the papers—and don't let me in too deep."

"Thank you, thank you, sir!"

When Scroggins arrived at the Lodge he found Maria in intensified distress. A phone message had come from Poughkeepsie just after Scroggins had gone, saying Imogen had asked them not to worry-she might not be home for two days. But not from Imogen, from some one else. Very suspicious.

As Scroggins turned to the phone to look up aviation stations the front door opened, without the bell. Strange. Who would dare enter like that? He turned to face Peter Killigrew.

"I came up in my car," the master of the estate explained, almost casually, although in all his lifetime of service with the Killigrews Scroggins had never known of anything impulsive like this to happen before to any of his employers. "Nothing doing in town Saturday, and the Tumble-weed is in dry dock. Thought I'd take a look at this girl of yours. Where is she?"

"Not back yet!" said Scroggins, tragically.

"Then let's go find her," said Peter.

Scroggins began poring over the numbers of the aviation stations. "Yes, Master Peter," he responded, "at once!"

19

A DEEP-LAID SCHEME

SCROGGINS WAS NOT very far wrong. He had made a shrewd guess on insufficient evidence.

To understand fully the complex passions which were hastening this affair to a climax, while they hurled Imogen across the wintry face of the State of New York, it will be necessary to retrace slightly the recent adventures of Darcy Jennifer.

On the previous Wednesday—preceding the night of his first proposal—Darcy had been summoned to the Killigrew offices early in the morning to face McKenna. Peter was not there.

Mac confronted him with an affidavit, sworn to before a notary, and signed by a registered civil engineer, declaring that the lands of the so-called "Liberty Rubber Company" in Liberia were practically worthless, being in a dense swamp, inaccessible, and with no prospect of development.

A month before Darcy had sold bonds in this company to Peter Killigrew, and had taken therefor his personal check for twenty thousand dollars. He had represented, first by letter, and then orally, that the lands were rich with rubber trees, and had added a few other vivid details, such as a description of a crude rubber refinery, a godown, a railway, and a terminal. Pure fiction, or rather, impure fiction; criminal, to be exact; criminal in the eyes of the County of New York, where the lies had been told to get money; and criminal in the courts of the United States, whose mails had carried the lies for the same sordid purpose.

Jennifer blubbered, and begged for a chance to see Mr. Killigrew. Mac was not affected by the tears in the eyes of the young man. He said, however, Mr. Killigrew would be lenient if the money was returned immediately.

"How can I return it," cried Jennifer, "when I got only eight thousand of it?"

"Ah," said Mac, "forty per cent commission for selling. Pretty steep, I'd say."

"I never was in Liberia," Darcy protested.

"Evidently not," Mac admitted.

"I thought the rubber trees were there, and the godown, and everything!"

"You 'hoped' it—for forty per cent commission."

"Selling those bonds is worth forty per cent. A salesman has to keep up a lot; it costs money."

"I have no doubt. But if you want to escape the Tombs you will have to return the full amount at once."

Jennifer pleaded for time. Mac gave him twenty-four hours. As a parting shot he made a slip—very unusual for Mac—in saying, "It is only Mr. Killigrew's desire to avoid publicity for your father and himself that induces him to be as lenient to that extent with you."

That word "publicity" stuck in Darcy's mind. Until now, and in the presence of most serious consequences as the result of his unsound methods of making a living, he had not considered how he could play on this "desire to avoid

publicity." It took several hours to make up his mind—and extremity. He was really desperate before he seized on Mac's chance words, meant only to emphasize the acuteness of his peril. Before long, however, they presented to him the idea of a way out of his trouble.

First, he made one more effort to locate his "principals," the Messrs Creinsky and Dovekin, who had engaged him, because of his entree to exclusive clubs, his personal front, and his father's name, to sell the rubber bonds—and to pocket forty per cent of the gross.

The offices they had maintained in a Fifth Avenue building had not been opened for four days. He induced the superintendent to let him in. The desks were in disarray, every evidence that they had departed.

As a matter of fact, Creinsky and Dovekin had known for four days the jig was up. At the first hint of investigation they had destroyed all written evidence of their activities, taken their available cash, and lit out.

Jennifer in disgust and despair upbraided himself, though silently, of course. "What a boob!" he said. "To let them get away with sixty per cent!"

To his credit it must be added that he began to calculate that if he had the sixty per cent he might square himself, for his only sale had been to Peter Killigrew, and he still had nearly four thousand dollars of the eight he got for his single sale.

He might possibly have raised four thousand—but twenty! That was a stiff sum, especially for a young man who had previously exhausted his credit and his financial standing.

Jennifer went straight to his father's office, however. The elder Jennifer, his secretary told him, had gone to Cleveland and Toledo for a ten-day trip. Darcy got the Cleveland hotel address, and managed to locate his father on long distance. He did not dare go into details over the phone. He merely stated that he was obliged to have sixteen thousand, five hundred dollars by the next noon.

"I couldn't produce that much cash for you by to-morrow noon to save you from the penitentiary," shouted Jennifer, senior, just to make it strong.

"That's what it will mean if I don't get the money," gasped Darcy.

"Don't be an ass! And don't call me on long distance again—not on my own phone bill," came the sharp rejoinder, as the phone was disconnected.

Jennifer, senior, evidently did not take the penitentiary threat seriously. Darcy went outside to a booth, and tried to get him again, but failed. He asked that a call be left, and waited in his father's office to have it honored, but no reply came. Darcy considered taking the train for Cleveland, but he immediately had a lively vision of what would happen the following day if he did not appear at the Killigrew offices, and he did not want to further arouse suspicion of his honest intention by leaving town.

It was only then, while waiting vainly for a long distance from Cleveland, that he thought of Imogen at the Morton School. When he first met her at the Henton home he had started in to cultivate her solely because she was "the ward" of Peter Killigrew, and it was part of his instinct as a "go-getter" salesman of securities to the gilded rich to neglect no avenue to their better acquaintance. He had fortunately laid the foundation for a campaign which circumstances might compel him to quicken.

Now that word "publicity" dropped so glibly by Mac sprang to his cornered and harassed mind.

Leaving word to have his father held for him if he called, and to keep that wire clear, he went downstairs and called up the school, and made the date for the afternoon tea at the road house.

When he went back his sister Lenly was there in his father's office. This was annoying, for if his father should call back, as requested, from Cleveland, he would not want to go into any further details before Lenly. But he really had little hope his father would ring him again.

Lenly, however, presented assistance in another direction. She could help him with Imogen. To accomplish this he felt he had to tell her something of his dilemma, though he glossed over its more sinister aspects. He neglected to mention the possibilities of the Tombs and Atlanta. If he had confided this very definite menace Lenly might not have said he was "insane" when he told her he wanted to marry Imogen, and without delay.

Before that Lenly had offered to let him have her jewels.

"A bag of shucks," said Darcy. "Couldn't raise a thousand on them. Need over sixteen thousand."

So Lenly invited Imogen to dine at the Jennifer home that night, and when Darcy made his rather impromptu proposal later, she was deeply concerned to know all about it. She seemed to be relieved to learn Darcy had not been successful.

"It would be a stupid thing to do," she assured him, "and I hope you forget it."

"Don't you like the kid?" Darcy asked.

"Oh! She's nice enough—rather a shy little kitten—but you ought to remember the old adage, 'Marry in haste and repent at leisure.'"

"They said that in the old days—before they brought the divorce courts up to snuff. Who is going to let a little thing like a mistake in marriage stop him these days?"

"But it's not nice to think of divorce before you're married."

"It's not sensible not to recognize a way out before you go in. Besides, I may like her—she's an intelligent little thing. She may brush up."

"But you are not settled enough to get married, Darcy."

"When I am settled, will you guarantee me a chance to marry into the Killigrews?"

She did not reply.

"I'll take my chance when I have it," Darcy hotly added.

He dashed away from the Larches that morning—Thursday—without going into further detail with his sister. A plan was already coming to life in his brain. And it would require a deal of working out. He drove in, and before he crossed the Harlem River, he had perfected the chief details.

Time was essential. He would have to get more time. So he drove straight to the Killigrew offices, which he reached even before Mac's arrival, at his accustomed nine thirty.

"I have come early, Mr. McKenna," he said, "to tell you I can't possibly raise that money to-day. I must have more time."

"I have no authority to grant that, Mr. Jennifer."

"Will you ask Mr. Killigrew?"

"Won't do any good."

"But I haven't the money, and if I had a little time I am sure I could get it for you."

"How much time do you want?"

"A week."

"I'll put the proposition up to Mr. Killigrew. Call me at noon and I will let you know."

At noon Mac told him Mr. Killigrew had consented to give him until the following Wednesday at noon, practically a week.

"Thanks," said Jennifer. "That's all I need."

Then he got Imogen on the phone and made the appointment for Saturday morning. Just where and how he would accomplish the rest of his design was not clear. Chance dictated it.

While waiting for noon and the assurance from Mac he had studied the "want ads" in a morning paper, until he found something that seemed to be just what he was looking for. It read:

FOR RENT—Adirondack cabin, fully equipped for

winter; three master rooms, three baths; larder stocked with
staples; fishing, hunting near by; reasonable to reliable tenant;
near head of Schroon Lake. Phone Owner, Caledonia 10005.

As soon as he was sure of meeting Imogen Saturday
morning, he called the Calendonia number, and found the
owner of the Adirondack cabin to be a bachelor who had
usually occupied it in the winter, as well as in the summer,
but who was prevented this season from making his accustomed sojourn. He was more eager to have it occupied and
cared for than to secure the rent. In a short half hour, Darcy
was able to convince him of his desirability, and had paid
down an advance, and had the keys.

The location of the cabin was some miles south of Elizabethtown. One could take the night train, go straight
through, get off at Westport in the morning, and engage
a conveyance to get to the cabin early that day by way of
Elizabethtown.

About twelve hours from New York, was the best one
could make of it, the owner said. Of course, you could do
the trip in a similar lapse by motor, but at that time of year,
the middle of November, one might encounter bad roads
and be delayed.

Darcy feared twelve hours was too long for the purpose
he contemplated. And the seclusion of the Adirondacks
seemed essential for another phase of his purpose.

He got in touch with a commercial airplane station,
and tried to rent a plane. They had none for immediate
delivery. He would have to put in an order and wait for a
month or six weeks.

He wasted the rest of that afternoon—Thursday—

going to the Government hangars, at Mitchell Field and on Governor's Island, to see if there was not some way in which he could secure a plane. But without avail.

On the island, however, he got a tip. "There's a guy in Bayonne, over in Jersey," confided one of the mechanics, "who has got a boat-bird he wants to sell. She's a two-decker, and flops up in a gale of wind; but she's a plane, and in straightaway, clear weather not too high up, you can get away with her."

This was after dark. Too late to go to Jersey that night. Fortunately, he still had Friday.

Bright and early Friday morning, Jennifer was in Bayonne. He found the airship—a bi-hydroaeroplane, rather battered, but apparently sea and air worthy. The owner showed him she could do sixty miles an hour easily, and even ninety or a hundred. Darcy had studied aviation during the war, and proved he could operate.

The price was eighteen hundred dollars. He bought it for fifteen hundred dollars cash, nearly half his remaining capital, and arranged for its delivery in a field north of White Plains Saturday morning at eight o'clock. He spent the early part of Friday taking finishing lessons in its operation from its former owner.

Returning to Manhattan in the afternoon he secured a pilot's license when he cited his experience as an aviator's apprentice in the war. Then he sought a fellow he had employed on former occasions, sometimes a race-track tout, at others a rubber for prizefighters, Marty Bing.

"Now, listen, Marty," said he, slipping him a roll of bills, and a railway ticket to Westport. "You're leaving the Grand Central to-night, and you get off up there in the morning early. Get your breakfast and hire a flivver, or anything else you fancy, and beat it down the cement State road to a little town called New Russia. You'll make it in less than an hour. Get the local justice of the peace. Put him in your flivver, and beat it as fast as you can for the cabin."

Jennifer gave Marty a copy of the map loaned him by the owner of the leased cabin.

"When you get there," he went on, "walk right up and knock. If I don't answer right off, wait until I come out. I'll be there."

"Then, I suppose," Marty winked, "the dirty work begins. What is it, a murder or somethin'?"

"No murder!" Darcy assured him.

"That's a shame," Marty replied. "Nothin' I like better'n a murder, specially on Sunday mornin' in th' woods. Gives y' a good appetite f'r breakfas'."

"You'll have plenty enough appetite, and I promise you something to satisfy it, too."

Jennifer's final preparation was to hire another follower, one of Marty's pals, to ride up to Poughkeepsie the next morning, Saturday, and wait until he saw an airship sailing above the Hudson.

"That will be me," said Jennifer, "and to make sure, watch for me to drop a handkerchief. When you see the handkerchief drop, take this letter, open it, call up the number inside, and deliver the message, over the long distance phone, just as you see it written down there."

"Maybe I can't read it."

"It's typewritten."

Whereupon, he handed over a sealed envelope.

That night, Darcy rested securely, though he did not go

home. He did not want to face his sister, Lenly. She might have too many questions. He regretted having taken her into his confidence about Imogen.

On the whole, however, he was quite gratified with his preparations. If Imogen kept her word and met him, as agreed, he did not see how anything could prevent his being able to "talk turkey" to Peter Killigrew on the following Wednesday.

20

FLYING AWAY

DARCY SPENT FRIDAY night in a road house on the Armonk road a little north of White Plains. He wanted to be on hand for the delivery of the plane. He had held out half the purchase price to insure a conscientious arrival.

The sky was dark, a few stars still out, and the sun not at all visible when he took his station in the field by the roadside which he had described. It was only five thirty. He wondered if he had not made a terrific mistake. How could an aviator make out this field—and in the dark—among so many?

As agreed, he turned on all the lights of his roadster, in which he had made the journey, and which it had been agreed the aviator was to pilot back to its garage at the Larches. Then he attached his searchlight to the sunshield and tilted it up, full force. Every five minutes, he described an arc with it across the whole heavens.

Three-quarters of an hour passed that way and he was numb with the cold, when a *put-put-put* along the road made him wary. It was a motor-cycle cop. When he reached the bars Darcy had taken down in the near-by fence, he stopped and turned in.

"What's the idea?" demanded the uniformed man in

leather puttees, as he dismounted and took in the traveling arc of the searchlight. "A message to Mars?"

"Not exactly," said Darcy, anxiously scanning the air toward the south where lay White Plains, and, beyond, the greater city.

"Signalin' Canada, is it, then?"

"Another guess, officer."

A luminous edge had appeared along the eastern horizon, first sign of the sun.

"Come, bucko! What's doin'? Don't tell me you're dotty!"

"Whoopee! Here! Here!" Darcy suddenly became frantic with enthusiasm. He waved his hat and yelled fiercely.

Following the direction of his yelling, the cop saw a dark mass with four bright eyes, winging away from the southwest, lazily, like a huge billy goat with flapping paddle wheels.

"It's my bird-boat! See! Not so late!" Darcy yelled again.

The yelling evidently was not necessary, for the searchlight on the roof of the roadster was powerful enough. In a few minutes, the plane glided to a safe stop a hundred yards away, on the brown turf. A man in sheepskin and leather dismounted.

After looking at his watch he said: "Twenty-two minutes late. That's because I turned off the river at Yonkers—thought she was Tarrytown—fool mistake, for they don't look alike at night. But I counted the ferries 'stead of the lights. Didn't like to make that mistake, either, for I like to keep over the river long's I can. That's good advice to you, Mr. Jennifer. Keep over the river whenever you can—or any considerable body of water. That's where a hydroaeroplane has it on any other sky flyer."

Meanwhile Darcy was examining his new purchase with intense satisfaction. The twenty-two minutes made no difference. He had figured on more than that, for he was only ten miles from his trysting place and with three and a half hours yet to wait.

In a few minutes, the motor-cycle officer went his way. Darcy made sure again he could rise and light without mishap, and understood the particular tricks of the plane.

"I'm going to name her Honeymoon," he said.

"Queer name for a bird-boat," commented the man from Bayonne. "Nobody'd have time for a honeymoon aboard her; she's too fast and too tricky."

"That," Darcy replied, half to himself, "is just the idea, fast and tricky. My idea of a honeymoon."

"Well," said the man from Bayonne, "so long. Take care of yourself." He buttoned the second seven hundred and fifty dollars inside his inner vest, and went his way to the Larches in Darcy's roadster.

A few minutes before ten, Darcy landed in the field outside the far meadow of the Towers and near the grove of oaks. Scroggins had seen this. He had also seen and reported to Peter Killigrew the prompt appearance at ten of Imogen. He thought he had overheard what was said between them, but he missed much of it.

Especially the talk about marriage. Imogen had come with one purpose only, she thought—to tell Mr. Jennifer the facts about herself and thus be rid of him. She had no doubt that he would again ask her to marry him, and that would afford her her chance.

At the same time Nature could not ignore the fact that she was a girl just turned seventeen, and that this was her first suitor. No man before had ever made love to her, much less asked her to marry him. She might have been more short with Darcy Jennifer. She meant to be. But somehow—

When he said: "This is a beautiful day to get married"— casually almost, she immediately replied: "That's what I want to talk about."

"Fine. Then we are of the same mind! Couldn't be better! Come on!" He led her toward the field where lay the hydroaeroplane.

To answer, she had to pass beyond a huge oak, where he had led the way. Thus she passed beyond the hearing of Scroggins. No other words they spoke actually reached his ears, though he could still see them plainly.

As she came to the other side of the oak, she saw the hydro-aeroplane lying on the brown turf. The heavy frost of the night before was melting in a strong sun. The engine of the machine was throbbing softly.

"My!" Imogen exclaimed. "Who left that here?"

"It's yours!"

"Mine!" She laughed queerly, with a twisted smile. Just for a moment, a brief second perhaps, she forgot the line of conversation about marriage.

Conversation about marriage is likely to be started by the man in the case, anyway. At least, Imogen felt that was the etiquette. However, perhaps no breach of etiquette was required to take her mind from her determination just for the first moment of her surprise at seeing an airplane lying there in the field by the side of the road she had traveled oo often—and hers!

An absurdity, of course, but requiring explanation.

"I brought it to you—as a present," Darcy went on, stepping to the side of the cockpit, where two steps of a tiny ladder extended down over the basket.

"But—but!" Imogen gasped. "What could I do with it? Why, I can't even run a motor car!"

"This is easier than a motor car. Step in. I'll show you!"

The surprise had been shrewdly prepared. It accomplished its purpose, though the girl still hesitated—for just a moment—trembled on the brink of her great adventure as a little fly reaching out its feet on the edge of a vast web might tremble and hesitate, unable to see or to imagine the spider at the far center.

"But—I'm—afraid." While she said she was afraid, neither her manner nor her voice indicated fear. Indeed, for the moment, curiosity and surprise had mastered her.

"Nonsense!" He reached forth his hand to her, from the side of the car. His smile seemed most engaging.

"But," she objected, while reaching forward to look at the curious little boats that lay a few inches from the ground, just above the sulky wheels with their pneumatic tires, "I thought you wanted to talk."

"Surely—after we've had a little ride—or during it!"

"My! I couldn't talk while I was riding in that!" she gasped.

"Very well, then, when we get back."

Of course, she knew perfectly well that once she had had her talk with him, she would never see him again, this strangely attractive young man in whose villainy it was hard to believe, having heard only so much of it as came from accidental overhearing from behind the partition of a dining room in a road house, this smiling young man who

had been so respectful when inducting her into the mysteries of New York night clubs, this young man who planned
such an unbelievable surprise as this totally unexpected
airplane set down here by exotic chance in this far meadow!

Moreover, she had never been in an airplane. What harm
could there be that bright November morning, with the
sun just beginning a healthy climb into the great blue skies
above, in rising away with him—and then in telling him
the truth, if need be?

A quick dropping of her eyelashes indicated that his
preliminary battle was won. "You won't go toward New
York?" she asked.

"No," he assured her, heartily, "in just the opposite direction. Come!"

She took his hand, and permitted him to assist her into
the cockpit. After all, if she kept her promise to Aunt
Maria not to go again to New York without permission,
and her promise to herself to tell him the truth as soon as
he asked her again, what harm could there be in this?

Indeed, what harm?

He had to give the plane a good shove and run along
the ground with it for many yards, and try several times,
pushing buttons and turning cranks, before the unwieldy
thing did rise. But it did, and took them up with a rhythmic
long swish, and before she could draw in a hasty little gasp
there they were gliding along over the tops of the trees, and
rising higher, and ever higher.

It was like a spectroscope, or going through a tunnel, or
getting into "high" suddenly in the Deisel-Mascisti, but
nicer than any of those. Strangely quieting, not fearful at
all.

And there was the Towers down below, spread out like a drawing in a book, dull and huge on the brownish-green turf!

And the Lodge! A stately consort of the elder and more mighty parapets in the wider lawns beyond.

And the brick farm office, square and tiny, almost; and the granite garage, with its second story of plate-glass windows, all overgrown with ivy. She could see the roof where Cel's wife was hanging out the washing. She laughed. Aunt Maria did not know that.

And the meadow below—a team, with two workmen, and another man, all looking up. Why, the other man was Uncle Isaiah!

She leaned over the basket and looked down toward him. He was waving his hands and shouting frantically. She tried to hear what he said, but the noise of the motor cut out every other sound.

She hoped he would recognize her. She took out her handkerchief and waved to him.

The men grew smaller. Presently they were the size of dogs. Still she waved her handkerchief, shouting greetings, hoping she would be heard.

Now they were very tiny—the size of rabbits. Still she waved.

Before long the men were no larger than bees, than flies, than distant ants crawling on a spear of grass.

"Uncle Isaiah!" she suddenly wailed. It seemed as if a terrifically poignant longing had come over her as she saw the last of him, and of the squat Lodge, now no bigger than a thimble on the far landscape.

She turned and grasped Darcy's arm. "Please—please,"

she demanded, "turn around and go back. I've gone far enough."

For a moment he said nothing. His face was tense and set straight ahead. Again she tugged at his arm, imploring him to return.

After a moment more of silence he replied, rather irrelevantly, "See that smoke over there! That's Poughkeepsie, I think."

"But I want to go back!"

"Yes. It's Poughkeepsie!"

"Please! Please!" She tugged at his arm. He seemed not to hear her. She looked at him closely for the first time since they had come into the basket together. Then she saw the leather head-dress pulled down over his ears. That was why he could not hear.

She leaned close to his ear and called, "Let's go back now!"

He nodded as if he heard, and answered, "Yes, it's the Hudson!" He pointed to the left ahead. "See! That's Kingston!"

She subsided, not sure that he hadn't heard, and not sure that he had. Anyway, she reflected, he had been respectful that night in New York at the Toasted Cheese.

And the Hudson was fascinating from above. Now she looked down and back on it—and ahead—a lazy, winding, ribbon of azure blue, with flecks of ice in the coves.

She smiled at the sheer momentum. He turned for the last time and looked at her, reassured by her smile. "Great—eh?" he said.

"Yes; but isn't it time to go back?"

He heard this—strangely—and replied, "Wait a bit."

They came directly over the river now, and seemed to rest above it, a bird whose wings reached from shore to shore. Of course, the plane wasn't that wide, but it seemed so.

What bigness, what power, what suspense. Imogen was buoyed with exultant feelings. Whatever fear she had left her! Her eyes dilated marvelously.

With an occasional sly glance Darcy noted her awakening to the sheer momentum of his dashing escapade. "Young Lochinvar," he said to himself, "out of the east!"

Poughkeepsie lay before them—smoky, big; a large, black, irregular patch on the brown fields.

At this point, he dropped a handkerchief. It trailed aft, fluttering slowly to earth. She did not see it.

Just beyond they came to the first patches of snow, below Kingston. Further beyond, in the fringes of the Catskills, the snow became heavier. They could see it lying in deep ravines in the mountains, but with the summits still bare.

She tugged again at his arm, and spoke close to his ear. "Listen!" she said.

"What is it?"

"When are we going back?"

"Why be in a hurry? We've got all day."

"They'll be worried about me."

"Didn't you see the message I dropped at Poughkeepsie?"

"What message?"

"An envelope, with a message to the Towers."

"No, I didn't see it. What did it say?"

"Not to worry. That you would be back later."

This was not entirely a lie. He had dropped a handkerchief as they passed Poughkeepsie. Monty's pal, waiting for the signal, had seen, had opened the sealed envelope, reading inside: "Phone Farview, number 11, get the super-intendent, or his wife, deliver this message: 'Safe away on a trip over Sunday. Back next week. Don't worry.—Imogen.'"

Monty's pal had followed instructions, so that when Scroggins returned from the city he had found fuel to fan his anxiety, which was not exactly the effect Darcy had desired. That message from Poughkeepsie he had planned to stop pursuit over the week-end, which was all the time required for the operation of his plan.

However, he did not know that Scroggins would be behind that hedge of Norway spruce, beyond the Lombardy poplars, just before he flew away with the Honeymoon express.

"Really?" Imogen was surprised, partially reassured, but puzzled. She wanted to ask more questions. She did ask several, but it was very difficult to talk in that machine, buzzing up there so queerly, part of the time in the clouds; at times, it seemed, in the tree tops. Mr. Jennifer evidently had difficulty with his hearing.

But not with his speech. Before long he was saying, "Look! I believe that is Albany—beyond! See the long bridge! It's the Albany bridge!"

The significance of the name, not anything she saw, gave her a sudden fright. "Why, Albany's nearly a hundred miles from the Towers!"

He looked at his wrist watch, calmly saying, "We've been up just one hour."

"Oh, my! Please let us go back now, Mr. Jennifer!"

"Hungry?" he asked, reaching under his seat and bring-ing out a paper of sandwiches, which he followed with a vacuum bottle containing hot coffee. "Here's a bit of lunch."

She resisted the food. "I can't eat unless you turn back," she said.

"Very well!" He turned the nose of the bird-boat to the left. It began describing a long, long circle, slowly, majestically, like a vagrant eagle. "We'll go back, but eat—this air makes one hungry!"

She ate a sandwich and drank some coffee. She watched them draw away from the river, and kept her gaze carefully on that landmark. She felt as if the Hudson was a guide, an anchor. She was no longer enjoying the ride. Something about it seemed sinister. The man beside her—this Mr. Jennifer—seemed to forbode evil. Yet she was determined to keep a stiff upper lip. All must still be well. The day was clear and sunny.

If they had come that far in an hour why not return in an hour. Perhaps her fears were groundless.

After a time she asked, "You are going back now, aren't you?"

"Sure."

"But the river is way off there. I can hardly see it any more."

"We are returning inland."

"But there is a big city. What is that?"

"Pittsfield, Massachusetts. We'll circle home that way." He lied glibly, for they were directly over Schenectady then.

As they passed Balston Spa he told her it was Lenox. "Ever been there?" he asked.

"No." She didn't add that she had been nowhere. But she knew that Lenox was nearer the Towers than Albany, and was reassured.

He was encouraged to lie some more. Over Saratoga he

called out, "Sharon Springs." That was a hundred and fifty miles away, back to the east and the south, and almost that much nearer the Towers.

Then a body of water loomed ahead. As they came nearer it seemed bigger and bigger. "My!" cried Imogen. "Is that the ocean? How quickly we got there. You'll have to go inland more to reach the Towers, won't you? But what are those mountains around it? And it's not the ocean? Why, the land is on both sides. What is it?"

"Long Island Sound, I guess," said Jennifer.

They were passing above Lake George.

"Hope I'm not lost," he said casually. "I'll turn here. No need to worry yet, though. It's the shank of the day."

She had grown very pale. Something ominous seemed all about them. Was it the water below? He assured her that they were safer over water than over land, due to the little boats on their shafts. It must be the mountains that oppressed her, those mountains rising on the left—rising, rising, higher and higher, with the taller and taller trees, and deeper and deeper ravines. Snow entirely covered them. They were not like the Catskills, with only the gullies white; here everything was white, beautiful, awe-inspiring—but disquieting.

Was he in truth lost? She saw how intent he was, peering down constantly, studying, guiding the wheel carefully. They came to another large body of water, and crossed its tip.

"What is that?" she asked timidly.

"Don't know." He knew it was Schroon Lake, but could think of nothing that looked plausibly like it in the southern part of the State.

Finally his eyes lit up. He had seen the gap through the mountains with the cement road lying there, like a silver tape, and, nestled in the pass near the summit, the settlement that spilled through a gorge—Elizabethtown.

He consulted a map pasted before him on the board, and turned left again. In a few minutes he gave a sharp exclamation.

"Gee!" he said. "I felt something crack. Hope it's not my radiator. We've been going pretty fast."

She was too frightened to speak.

"I'll have to alight," he announced, seeing a cleared space ahead, "and see what's the matter."

They slid safely into a long snow bank. Ahead of them was a rambling log cabin, the walks cleared, evidently inhabited.

Jennifer sighed with relief. So far his plan had worked admirably.

21

THEY INSPECT THE CABIN

HE HELPED HER out of the cockpit. She collapsed on the lower step of the outer ladder. She drew up and away, fearful to antagonize him. Here they were lost in the wilderness. He seemed to be her sole hope of escaping. Moreover, what had he done as yet to alarm her?

Reason argued thus in her, but instinct rebelled. At last she was thoroughly awake to her danger. She could not define it, could not see it; she could only surmise it.

He saw the fright in her face. All color was gone. Her skin was pale as tallow; her eyes lustrous, dilated, but sunk deep in her head. Her teeth were clenched tight and her arms held rigidly to her sides.

Then she began to shiver and shake, trembling all over. He quickly took off his overcoat and threw it around her, and she did not protest, not daring to trust herself to open her mouth, fearful she would faint.

"It is cold," he said. "Sorry! Here, take a drink. You need it up here in the snow with only that thin coat."

She had on a light fall wrap with a narrow collar of fur, but thin stockings and low shoes. She looked at him steadily, still shivering; then managed to say quietly: "No, thank you."

He found the vacuum bottle. "There's a little coffee left. Drink that!"

She drained the coffee bottle, and felt better.

She managed to look around and take in their surroundings, an accomplishment impossible at first through her absorption in realizing that they were many, many miles from the Towers, and far up in the mountains.

Now that they were on the ground these mountains seemed so much bigger than when aloft in the plane. They went right up, up in all directions; ravine after ravine, crag on crag, climbing endlessly to far horizons.

She had never seen such mountains. All her life accustomed to the hills and dales of middle Westchester, with their gentle slopes and cultivated rondures, these stark cliffs and forest-clad slopes bore in on her terrifically.

They seemed to suggest something violent, something startling like this flashing change which had precipitated her there.

Now a noise made itself felt. A constant crashing, smashing noise, steadily ripping, roaring, tumbling, dashing, crackling! She looked in the direction whence it proceeded, and saw sparkling wisps of feathery water.

It was a stream, but what a stream, with force enough there in the snow to rip through any attempt at the formation of ice! The gentle brook flowing past the hairpin factory only sighed and gurgled. This was a wilderness, stream, savage.

Her afflicted eyes sought the comfort of the cabin just ahead. That was the one relief in the terrific expanse.

There were curtains in the windows, dainty yellow curtains. Somehow she took courage at the sight of those curtains. They seemed to say that all was not lost—that there was still a way out—that perhaps this was only a nightmare, after all.

She rubbed her eyes. Was it a nightmare? No. There stood the log cabin, yellow curtains and all. Very small curtains, it appeared on second glance.

Meanwhile, Jennifer was examining the plane. He was down on his back, easing up under the engine. He came out, rueful-looking.

"Just as I feared," he said. "The radiator isn't working!"

Somehow she knew he was lying. But it hardly seemed wise to say so, little as she knew of engines and radiators.

She jumped to an earlier deception, now struggling in her memory along with the others.

"That couldn't have been Long Island Sound," she protested.

"No," he admitted, making a show of virtuous concession. "Must have been Lake George!"

She knew Lake George was nearly two hundred miles from the Towers. She looked at him in silent misery. What could she think but that he had done this deliberately?

He jumped to denial of her unspoken accusation.

"I thought we went the other way from Albany," he asserted boldly. "Really I did. Must have turned around without knowing it. I'm not used to driving a plane."

These mountains, then," she said, "are the Adirondacks!" She knew her geography well enough for that.

"Must be," he admitted. "Rather stunning, eh—in the snow?"

She tried to make the best of it and smiled, asking:

"Hadn't you better fix the radiator quickly so we can get back before dark?"

"Oh, I couldn't fix it," he blithely responded. "It'll take solder and a real mechanic."

She looked toward the cabin. "Maybe there's one in there," she suggested.

"Maybe. Let's see." He led the way.

No response came to his knock.

Meanwhile she stood in the path looking around. She noted wires leading from under the eaves and proceeding to the tops of near-by trees.

"Looks like a telephone," she suggested. "If you can only get in, you can call up somebody."

"Good! You wait here. I'll go to the back and see what I can do."

In a moment he was inside and had unlocked the front door, standing aside and bidding her enter, with quite an air—gayly.

She walked in cautiously and looked around. The cabin was furnished inside. Opposite the door was a huge stone fireplace, with logs laid and kindling wood, all ready for a match. Bookshelves packed with books stretched on either side. There was a long oak table and a number of comfortable rustic chairs. Portieres concealed an entryway beyond, apparently leading to a kitchen. At the right were two doors—to bedrooms, possibly.

Then her heart suddenly leaped with joy. Just behind the door she saw a telephone, one of the wall-bracket variety, with a long-armed receiver.

"There's a telephone!" she exclaimed.

"I thought there'd be one."

"Yes." He seemed to admit this grudgingly. It offered an unforeseen complication.

"Let me call the Towers first," she pleaded, jumping toward the wall, seizing the handle and turning it vigorously. To her fierce joy the bell rang.

Instantly the oppression of the mountains faded. She was back under the gentle protection of the ivy-colored porte-cochère of the Lodge.

"Then you can get some one to fix the radiator," she smiled gratefully over her shoulder while waiting for the answer.

"All right," he assented, and went outdoors.

A wave of forgiveness toward him surged over her. His leaving her alone like that for her message home was so thoughtful, a simple reassurance of his respect and concern, and of his breeding. It flashed across her mind that perhaps she had suspected him unjustly. More than half her apprehensions had been worry about what Aunt Maria and Uncle Isaiah would say. And now in just a moment she would be able to speak to them, to tell them, to explain. Then she would not feel so far away—as if marooned in another world.

"Number, please?" came the voice from Central.

The blood surged to her face. She felt she was blushing furiously.

"Fairview 11," she called glibly. "Fairview 11—I mean in Westchester."

"Long distance?"

"Of course. Fairview 11. Oh, hurry, hurry—please!"

"Wait. I'll connect you with long distance. What is your number?"

"I don't know. Do you have to have my number?"

"Certainly. Wait a moment."

She waited, bland, content. But the wait was long. She called, "Hello, hello!" several times, but there was no further answer.

She rang the bell, at first easily, for it seemed strangely dead; and then furiously. No response. She looked up. There in the doorway stood Jennifer, watching her silently.

"What's the trouble?" he questioned casually. "Long distance hard to get?"

Again her face was as tallow. "This is funny," she said in a hollow voice. "They answered and then they stopped. Here—see if you can get them." She held out the receiver.

He rang and listened, rang and listened again and again. Finally he hung up and said: "Nothing doing. Disconnected for the winter, evidently."

"It's not disconnected—it wasn't a minute ago," she protested hotly.

"You may have overheard a neighbor on a party wire," he suggested.

She felt ready to cry. She passed outdoors and looked again at the wire leading to the tree. It was sagging now. She examined it more closely, and saw it nipped off close to the eaves of the cabin, just where it came from inside. She followed the loose end into the snow and picked it up. Freshly cut, no doubt about it.

She walked back into the cabin and closed the door and looked at him steadily, though his back was to her; for he was kneeling before the fireplace busily coaxing a blaze to start under the prepared logs.

A strange little chuckle rose inside from the depths of

her consciousness. The sight of the cut wire seemed to refresh her, seemed to dispel all her haziness.

There could be no doubt about the situation now. He had deliberately trapped her. Then everything had been a lie from the very beginning—the promise to be gone ten minutes only, the assurance he would turn back home from Albany, the confusion of Lake George with Long Island Sound. Probably the radiator was not hurt any more than the telephone wire had been before he tampered with it.

Being sure of all this helped wonderfully. She began to feel more cheerful right away. After all, the situation had its novelty and its thrill. And let Mr. Jennifer beware. She would match her wits against his.

She remembered the curious delight with which she had related to Aunt Maria the episodes of her trip to the Toasted Cheese, and her final cry: "Now I am a woman of the world!"

This might be no idle boast when she got back this time.

The fire, which soon sparkled and roared, helped reassure her, as it soon filled the cabin with a glow, and there seemed no dearth of knotty pine and spruce sticks in the huge bin just outside the kitchen door.

Jennifer faced her cheerfully, and, now that she was sure of his deliberate deceptions, she found she could estimate him more coolly. She was almost ashamed of herself for not detesting him more roundly. He was so personable, so "nice."

"We had better try to find the road and get some help," she suggested.

He looked out. The sky was getting dull with twilight. His watch said four ten. In those ravines late in November the twilight set in at four in the afternoon and it was dark by four thirty.

"I'm afraid we'd get lost," he objected, "if we started this close to night. Hadn't we better wait here. Looks as if some one ought to turn up here before long. Cabin belongs to some one."

"We can't stay all night!" Imogen protested.

"Suppose we have to?"

"How can we?"

"How can we do anything else?"

"You ought to know. You ought to find a way out."

"I think it's marvelous luck to strike this cabin—just waiting for us, apparently. I'm not disposed to run away from it until morning and there's good daylight ahead of us," he said.

She had been looking at the two closed doors at the end of the big room. She stepped to the lower one, opened it, and entered.

It contained a single bed, bureau, chair, mirror, and a clothes closet. There was one small high window, but no door out.

She returned and went to the other room, the master's room, evidently, in the corner. It had two windows, a three-quarters bed, a dressing table, with a chest of drawers, a full-length mirror, a rocker, and straight chair. But, more important, an outer door leading to the porch; and with a key turned in its lock.

She tried the key. It worked. The door opened on the outside to the porch. She locked it again and slipped the key under a rug. Then she saw the door to the main room of the cabin also held a key. She tried it. Practical. Good.

She returned, and said: "Very well, Mr. Jennifer. I'll take this room," indicating the corner one. "I like it. You see, it's the best. And I'm such a little pig!"

At this her first sign of relenting, he came toward her impulsively, exclaiming: "You little angel!"

She held up her finger. "Beware!" she said. "Or I'll fly away; and I won't take you, for you ought to fly and take me!"

"I will—in the morning. Don't worry. There'll be a village within a few miles, and it'll be easy to get a mechanic up then."

He began nosing around. He called her to see the china closet. It seemed to have all manner of dishes, enough for six or eight people, and glassware. They went together into the kitchen. There were plenty of utensils, pots, pans, a three-burner oil range, with the reservoir full of oil.

"Looks like an acetylene plant," he said, pointing to pipes overhead. By this time the gray dusk filled the cabin. He saw lamps in the wall brackets in the kitchen and living room, and a large central light in the living room. He lit them, and they burned in a waxlike white flame that easily cut out all the shadows. It seemed more illuminant than electricity, though maybe not so brilliant.

"Pretty soft, I'll say—what?" Darcy seemed in high spirits.

Imogen could not help feeling reassured. After all, it was quite an adventure—her first flight in an airplane, itself enough to constitute a high spot in experience, only to be so quickly followed by swift descent in the far Adirondacks; and then, instead of possible cold and exposure here in the snow, to find this marvelous cabin, well lit, finely heated—

Darcy was speaking. "Now, if there's only food, we'll be all set." He had discovered the icebox, but it was empty.

"Too bad," he asserted. "People must have shut down for the winter. See! The lower doors are open for ventilation."

"Yes," she admitted half-heartedly. She had been thinking that possibly the owners were only off somewhere in the woods for the day and would return toward night.

He did not give her time to dwell too long on this thought. "Let's look in the cellar," he suggested, disclosing a door beyond the kitchen in a tiny L.

She let him go ahead, for it was dark. In a moment, however, a soft glow spread up the stairs, and he called: "Come down! It's quite light. And such a find! We're in luck!"

She descended, pausing at each step. As soon as her head came below the beams of the floor she could see it was no ordinary cellar. It had no dark corners apparently. It was all neatly cemented and clean as possible, and stocked with many good things.

She stepped into the middle of the cellar with a little exclamation of delight; for she suddenly became conscious of her hunger. Her appetite quickened, and it was warm, very warm, in comparison with the ground floor above!

He saw the color come into her cheeks, so pale before. "You look a heap better," he commented. "I was scared at you when we first lit; you were white as a sheet."

He stepped in her way, and instantly she became very serious. After all they were in the cellar, and she suddenly realized he stood between her and the stairs. A vast fright consumed her. He seemed to understand, for he moved away from the stairs, leaving her exit clear.

She breathed more freely.

"Look!" he said, and pointed to a ham hanging from a rafter. Three sides of bacon hung beside it. A barrel of flour stood in the corner beyond, and a tub of sugar. There was a big bin of potatoes, and boxes filled with onions, rutabagas, turnips.

"What is this?" he asked, picking up from another box a few small, knobby red vegetables, looking like malformed and highly colored potatoes.

"Jerusalem artichokes," she asserted. "They're awfully good. Father used to raise them. Let's see." She bent over the box to be sure they were not mildewed. No. The cellar was dry and warm.

She rose and a soft creeping thing, like a furred rope, dropped over her neck. She screamed—a terrific yelp—and began pawing and struggling with the seeming engine of destruction.

He rushed to help her, and in a moment she saw what had happened. In coming up from the box of artichokes she had brushed into a string of dried peppers hanging from a rafter.

"What's the matter?" he laughed. "Think some one's trying to murder you?"

She burst into hysterical laughter, and then sank on the lower stair, sobbing violently. She clutched a handful of artichokes tightly to her bosom—just as she had the metal candy box that night in the Toasted Cheese.

22

IMOGEN'S PERIL

TACTFULLY DARCY TURNED his back and began examining the shelves. These contained row after row of glasses, jars, and tins. After a moment, when he heard her sobbing grow less, he spoke aloud. "You ought to see what's here; canned peaches and pears and apricots; tomatoes in glass, and string beans, and peas; and I wonder what these are— look like tiny little carrots. I wonder!"

She heard him and became ashamed of her outbreak. She threw the artichokes back into their box, dabbed a handkerchief at her eyes, and came forward.

"I must be terribly nervous," she said. "I thought that was a snake!" Rather a glib evasion of the fact of her fear that this was where he had lured her. Now she realized how foolish she had been. She was eager to reinstate herself in his eyes—that she might go on fencing with him, and find out what he really intended.

"No snakes in winter," he stated.

"I can see that now," she wryly admitted, "but I didn't stop to reason when that string clutched me." She pointed to the peppers. "Look! It's red, and green, and white—like a snake, isn't it?"

He admitted that a man with the D.T.'s might be justified in thinking it a snake. "Or," he added, "a girl lost in the woods—a young girl."

She was eager now to show her bravery and spirit. "Well," she asked, "what shall it be for dinner?"

They argued the matter for minutes. They decided to get something that could be fixed easily and quickly. They found a tin of tuna, and took up with it glass jars filled with string beans, tomatoes, and what proved to be candied carrots, with a can of peaches for dessert.

It proved to be a rather complete dinner. They could find no coffee, but located a can of tea. Imogen even found a can of soup to begin with. Everything was piping hot in less than half an hour, for the oil stove worked to perfection. She mixed a batter of cakes with flour, tinned milk, and desiccated eggs. They found salt and pepper, and failed only when it came to butter.

After the meal she began to clear away the dishes. She had tried the water tap running into the sink, but no water came.

"Turned off," he said, "for the winter maybe."

"Never mind," Imogen replied. "I'll melt snow. It will be nice and soft."

"Resourceful—eh?" He tapped her under the chin.

She looked at him sharply. "Little minx!" he taunted.

He seemed to be a different man. No one could be more respectful, more tactful at times.

But now he stood there in the kitchen door, his arm on the jamb, blocking the way back to the living room, while she was fixing the gas flame under the bucket of snow he had brought in from the bank just outside.

"Say!" he persisted when she made no reply.

He came toward her.

She saw it would be impossible to get past him to the living room. There were two other doors in the kitchen, one to the L, leading to the cellar—an impasse!—the other leading outside.

She rushed outside, slamming the door behind her.

The night was pitch dark, no moon, a few stars, and quiet. The snow was banked up high around the rear porch. It had blown in from the steep slope which rose far into high timber right beyond.

Hearing him come from behind, frantic, her arms bare to the elbow where she had been getting ready to wash the dishes, she dashed into the snow bank. The snow was light, dry, and fluffy, and dashed over her, covering her as in a cloud of down.

She thought to fight a way through, and went on blindly, head first, thinking she was headed for the side of the cabin, and so would get around to the front. Beyond that she had not thought. Anything to escape the man behind her.

However, she was going directly into the hill, and in a moment she was quite buried in the drift, and spluttering to get out.

She found herself in his arms. He was dragging her back into the kitchen. She was fighting with him, and he was trying to say something; she did not stop to distinguish what it was.

He got her inside, locked the door, put the key in his pocket, and thrust her into the living room. She spun over toward the fire, and stood there, shaking off the snow.

He came and reached out his hands to help her. She

leaped at him in wild fury, and clawed for his face. In a second her nails had dug holes in both cheeks.

He threw his hands into the air, cried: "I surrender!" and dropped into a chair.

She brushed off the snow, and warmed her hands over the fire.

He put his hands to his cheeks and brought them down to examine them. "Blood!" he said. "You baby wild cat! Didn't know you had the spunk! Never mind, baby! Daddy 'll spank you by and by!"

He started to rise. She looked at him calmly.

"Forgive me!" he muttered.

She went to the kitchen and brewed some tea—very strong. And brought it in a thick cup. "Drink that!" she said, placing it before him.

Then she continued with the dishes in the kitchen.

She was busy for half an hour, looking in on him from time to time. He consumed the tea, then went out the front door. She followed to see what he was doing. He was washing his face in the snow.

When he came back his lashes were wet, and the front locks of his hair. There was a red furrow down one cheek and many scratches on the other. From the red furrow the blood was flowing rather freely. He put his hand up and saw it red. He went out and got a handful of snow, and kept it pressed against his cheek for some time.

Imogen said nothing and did not approach him.

"Little wild cat!" he muttered over and over. "Spunky as the devil!"

She accepted this as a soliloquy

After a few minutes the action of the snow seemed to

stop the flow of blood, but when he sat down again and came within range of the fire the tiny red drops oozed out once more.

"Severed my jugular vein, maybe," he sputtered. "Fine fix you'd be in if somebody'd come along here and find me dead, and you have to go to the electric chair."

She found a newspaper and handed it to him. "Use the white part of that," she said. "Make a little ball of it, and swab your face with it. That will stop the flow of blood." She restrained an impulse to minister to his wounds personally.

"Thanks!" he murmured, and followed instructions. Then he leaned back and looked at her, one cheek plastered with a blob of paper, its curling edges crimsoned.

She kept the large table between them; and sat on a small chair near the fire, which she watched carefully, every once in awhile placing a fresh stick of wood on it.

Some time elapsed thus before he leaned forward. "Say, kitten," he began.

His eyes appeared less wild than they had been. And the blob of paper was drying, without any more blood oozing from beneath.

"Imogen!" he added.

"Well?"

"The tea cured me—or the snow—or maybe those clever little claws of yours. Ha! Ha! Clawed sensible! How's that?"

She regarded him calmly, without response.

"I apologize," he pleaded. "Come on! Be a sport! Be a good fellow: Forgive me! You got me wrong! I meant nothing! I wouldn't hurt you for the world. Why, you ought to know me by this time—after the Toasted Cheese and everything. You're just nervous—unstrung. I don't blame you—being lifted away from home like this. Lots of things to get on a girl's nerves—and you've got the proper spirit, too. Like to see it in you; but you've got Darcy Jennifer wrong. Won't you forgive me?"

She lowered her eyes. "Certainly," she replied, "I forgive you, and now I'll—" She started to rise to say she would retire, when he got to his feet.

He was still emphasizing his good intentions. "Why!" he exclaimed. "How could you think I'd take any advantage of you? Don't you know we're going to be married—soon's we can find a preacher?"

This gave her extreme satisfaction. It was the thing she had come out with him that morning to hear, so that she could have her chance to tell him—and they had come through all this journey and travail and danger and hardship for what she had expected to finish in ten minutes.

"I'm not going to marry you," she began.

"Guess again, Imogen."

"I am not going to marry you," she repeated. There was something else she had intended to say, something about him.

"Thought we understood each other about that," he continued.

"It's not me you want," she found her voice to assert. "It's money—I have seen through you from the start, Darcy Jennifer." This was it! She was on the track of her previously prepared dramatic speech.

He laughed loudly. His brain seemed quite clear, and she seemed so small and ridiculous over there, one side of her face lit by the firelight—her little oval face, so serious, so saucer-eyed, her reddish hair tantalizing. "A sweet little thing," he said to himself, "spunky and ignorant!"

He said aloud: "Money? You have money, Imogen? I am delighted to hear it. Money is always a good thing to have."

"It's not my money!" she cried. "It's Mr. Killigrew's money. I know. I heard you tell your sister, Lenly. In the road house that afternoon you invited me from the school. I'm ashamed of myself for letting you get me up here—and you lied about the radiator—and cut the telephone wire. Oh, what a liar you are!"

She leaned back wanly against the stone side of the fireplace. A large tear slowly trickled down her face, but she felt vastly relieved. She had it out of her system. Now she was not hiding anything any longer.

He started toward her and she went around the table, keeping it between them. "Don't touch me," she warned him, and brought out a little knife she had been hiding. It was one from the kitchen.

Again he laughed. "Put that away. I wouldn't harm you. I mean it. For I do intend to marry you, Imogen. Really!"

"Not when you find out I am not a ward of Mr. Killigrew's!"

To her own surprise she said it in a more direct, a more telling way than she had dared hope she might achieve. She flushed with satisfaction as she saw him start.

"What's that you say?"

"I am not Mr. Killigrew's ward."

"Nonsense! You are entered at Mrs. Morton's school that way."

"It's a mistake. Mr. Killigrew never—never—" She faltered, unable to say what she had intended. It seemed a reflection on Scroggins, toward whom now her whole heart and soul seemed leaning.

"No matter," Darcy went on. "You live at the Towers."

"At the Lodge," she corrected.

"The same thing."

"It's not the same thing. The Lodge is—" She intended to say that was the residence of Mr. and Mrs. Scroggins. Again she was prevented from expressing, by her own reflection that this might be a disloyalty to the old man who had befriended her, whose love she could not doubt, whom she loved like a foster father.

"Oh, well," he shrugged his shoulders, "what's the difference? I'm not marrying you because of where you live."

"But Mr. Killigrew hasn't anything to do with me. I'm not his ward, I tell you."

He put a hand over his mouth and looked at her intently. The depth of her feeling, her aroused anger had intensified her ethereal beauty. Her eyes glowed appealingly there beyond the lowered fire. He could see her quivering.

The strain of the days he had gone through, the long trip, the food he had had, their lonely cabin in the wilderness, urged him on. He was not going to cavil at a whim or two now, or take the word of a cornered girl.

He suddenly concluded she was far cleverer than he had ever thought. "Might not make a bad wife," he reflected, "just as I told Lenly."

As proof of her cleverness she had thought of that lie about not being Killigrew's ward—to stop him. He chuckled deeply. What if she really knew his real situation, and the shadow of the penitentiary looming ahead of him for the coming Wednesday?

Time to tell her later.

Now there she stood alone, quivering, red and mauve in the firelight. He advanced toward her.

"Imogen!" he murmured softly, across the table which she circled, keeping just out of his reach. "You misjudged me cruelly. Whether or not you are Mr. Killigrew's ward makes not the slightest difference to me. I love you for yourself alone—you—just you—you adorable little bundle of sweet spice! Your claws only add to the wild flavor of you!"

He jumped the table and had her in his arms.

Then the knife came from behind her back, and she stabbed him. He felt the blade go into the fleshy part of his right arm.

He seized her hand, and twisted it. The knife clattered to the floor. At the same moment she slipped from his grasp. He bounded after her.

In a second—it seemed—she was beyond the door to the corner room. It slammed in his face, and he heard the key turn in the lock. He hurled himself against it, but it stood firmly. The cabin was well built.

He called again and again. He hammered on the door.

There was no response.

23

KEEPING EVERLASTINGLY GOING

THE NOON BEFORE, Scroggins discovered over the telephone what Darcy Jennifer had spent the better part of one of his precious days to learn, that an airplane was not so easy to buy as an automobile, for instance, even when one was sinewed with the Killigrew name and money.

Outside of the government service none would be available inside of twenty-four hours. And this was not yet a case for the government, Peter decided, at least not the military branch.

Peter sent word to Carl to get out his line eight Pershing, a new racing roadster. "She'll do about as well on the ground as a plane can do in the air," he assured Scroggins.

About one o'clock they started north, Peter at the wheel. He seemed more alert, more alive than Scroggins had seen him for years.

"Hydro-aeroplane—eh?" Peter commented as they rode into Katonah. "Then he'll make straight for the river, and our job won't be so hard. He'll want to keep over water. I know those birds. Scouted on one during the war."

They crossed the Albany Post Road, and drove down to Garrison. Until then they had asked no one if a plane had been seen. Here they found a watch tower of the New

York Central. The flagman looked from out his octago-
nal windowed viewpoint, and took his cob pipe from his
mouth.

"Sure," he said in reply to the question. "I saw the feller—
just before the ten fifty-two went down. Started to cross
the river, then changed his mind and turned north, kept
on right over the water. I saw his boats after he turned."

It was then five minutes of two, and a ferry would cross
to West Point at two. "We'll wait and take it," said Peter,
"for the road goes nearer the river on the other side, and
we'll have to keep close to the water to find people who
saw him."

"I believe we are better off in a road car than we would
be in an airplane," Scroggins offered.

"I foresaw that while you were phoning for a plane,"
Peter replied. "On the ground you can ask people for the
trail. Aloft you can only look down for your quarry, and it's
almost like hunting a needle in a haystack. I don't think it
will be hard to find him.

"Luckily, he's headed up the river and there are few
planes in operation here this time of year. Now, if he had
chosen the cross-country route, he would be in the path
of a great deal of regular plane travel—mail planes go by
twice a day—and people would have paid little attention to
him. Here, it's probably been months since a plane passed.
Nearly every one will remember him and be glad to tell
about it."

The ferry pulled out of its slip, and a moment later they
were crossing the river to West Point.

"You seem a natural born sleuth," Scroggins suggested.

Peter smiled. "I'm a deputy sheriff of Westchester

County, and don't you forget it," he replied. "I have to get something out of being a grand juror, and being drawn to White Plains every winter and paying a hundred dollars a plate for the annual dinner in town."

A few minutes later they were on the Storm King trail. Peter stepped on the gas. The Pershing line eight acted as if it wanted to be in Canada for tea. Before long, the needle pointed to 84. A motorcycle cop trailed in after them, and they left him as if he had been standing still.

The needle pointed to 87. "She can hit ninety!" Peter asserted.

"Better slow up, Master Peter," Scroggins urged. The chassis was weaving as if in a terrific gale. "That cop will phone ahead and have us pinched."

Sure enough, three miles south of Newburgh, a phalanx of motor cycles appeared. They covered the road, and held up their hands in unison.

Peter put on the brakes, but they had to part to let him through, then wheeled and overtook him. The chief grunted: "Are you birds hijackers or just regular bootleggers?"

"We haven't time to stop," Scroggins began.

Peter was removing his goggles, and fumbling in his clothes.

"Never mind the fixing. Keep going until you come to the station. We'll pilot you. They phoned us about you from the foot of the trail; snapped your time, and we snapped it; you were doing around, ninety. What do you think this is? A speed course?"

"No. But I—" Peter was having difficulty in locating something in his pocket.

"Save it for the judge, kid. And step along."

By this time, Peter had located the thing he wanted, a leather case. He reached it over the side of the car to the officer.

The chief looked at it. "Deputy sheriff of Westchester. What's that got to do with it?"

"I'm after a man—escaped, officer."

"Oh!" The three seemed suspicious.

The second examined the engraved pass more carefully. "See!" he said to the chief. "This is one of them millionaire passes—hundred-dollar dinner plate souvenirs. And look at the name this bird's put into it—Peter Killigrew. That's going some!"

The chief looked up, more suspicious than ever. "Peter Killigrew, eh?" he gruffly accused. "You've got a nerve to flash that on me."

"Don't you believe this is Mr. Killigrew?" Scroggins interfered, for Peter could not quite see the drift of the episode yet.

The chief grinned at his subordinates. "Step along, bo," he shouted, "and mind you keep her under thirty—straight to the station."

"But he *is* Mr. Killigrew!" Scroggins loudly proclaimed.

"And I suppose you're Piermore Bilton."

The superintendent rose in his full dignity and said: "I am Scroggins, Isaiah Scroggins, the superintendent of his estate in Far View, Westchester County."

The chief bowed low, mockingly.

"If you hold us any longer—" Scroggins was furious.

"On your way—on your way—and hold her to thirty—"

"But—" Scroggins spluttered.

"Aw! Tell it to the judge."

Twenty minutes later in the municipal court in Newburg, the magistrate received them. In three minutes they were released, with apologies to Mr. Killigrew.

Peter gave the chief a cigar, and a packet of cigarettes each to his two assistants.

"Now," he said, "if you want to make good, get down to the water front and locate some one who has seen a hydro-aeroplane going up the river earlier to-day."

The chief salaamed. "You bet your life, Mr. Killigrew. And if there's anything else you want, just push my button."

Perhaps it was lucky for them they had been stopped in that manner, for the motorcycle chief got their news for them, and from twenty miles up the river, in a few minutes by phone, from his outlying stations.

Yes, the plane had been seen. Nearly all the watchmen noted it, and apparently two figures in it, going along easily at seventy to eighty miles an hour—nearly three hours before. They passed Kingston sure of their way.

Again at Saugerties, they found the trail warm, and at West Camp, and at Catskill. At Coxsackie, there was no one to be found who had seen the plane, but they pushed on and at Ravenna, only a few miles below Albany, they found a riverman who had seen the plane.

At Albany, a dozen people they asked remembered the big "bird," and they disquietingly agreed on the fact that it had turned left, leaving the river and sailing to the west.

"Making for Canada," said Scroggins, "it's nearer that way."

"It's about the same straight north, and there's water,

too, that way, Lakes George and Champlain. Queer. I don't understand it."

Peter was puzzled for the moment.

Finally, he suggested they keep on the main highway to Schenectady, and make further inquiries there. If necessary, they could retrace their steps. "This fellow Jennifer," he soliloquized aloud, "was not an experienced aviator. He would want to keep near a main traveled road that he could see from above, in case of accident. So if he left the water he'll keep to the State highway."

This reasoning proved sound, for at Schenectady they picked up the trail again. A gasoline station man had seen the plane come up from the south, on a wide circle, and strike straight north along the line of the State road to Ballston Spa.

The Pershing pushed on. "Only an hour and a half of daylight left," said Peter. "I am afraid we will not get him to-night, unless he stopped long before this."

The trail was clear through Saratoga and Glens Falls and into the little town of Lake George, almost deserted now for the winter. Again they found a gasoline man who had seen the plane, headed still due north. They toiled it until it had left Lake George, and then they had to come back on their road to get the highway to Pottersville. At Schroon Lake again they got word of the plane.

By this time it was four o'clock and the dusk was beginning to fall. They pushed on, up along the creek bed, where a dozen bridges crossed and recrossed the winding stream.

Darkness found them in this ravine, with the rushing stream breaking through the snow that lined its banks. Twice they had passed through stretches of road where the snow threatened to hinder them, but the wide traction of the Pershing's balloon tires enabled them to make it.

The tires were practically new, but Peter several times lamented the fact he had come without chains. Now they came to a deserted stretch of road where the wind had a good sweep and where the snow had not been permitted to stay, but had been blown aside.

Instead, there was a long glassy stretch of ice. While rounding a corner on this stretch, going nearly fifty miles an hour, the roadster began to skid. The four brakes stopped the wheels but not the car. It collided with a fence and nearly toppled on into the bed of the stream.

"That's the end of speeding for this day," Peter announced, "until we reach a garage where we can get chains."

They had not seen a human being for twenty miles. A little later, about five o'clock, they passed the sign of a post office and stopped to read. "New Russia" it said, but there was no one visible. Boards were nailed over the windows and doors. Even the post office was closed for the winter. This was a summerland.

Something, however, a sixth sense perhaps, caused them to pause there at New Russia, and go from house to house looking for news. Not one house could they find occupied. There seemed nothing to do but push on until they found some one.

Later they were to know that if they had pushed up an almost buried road, from New Russia, they would have penetrated the clearing where lay the cabin sheltering Jennifer and Imogen—only eight miles away.

But it was after dark, and the road was not visible. They proceeded along the main highway.

An hour later they drove into Elizabethtown at a very sober pace, about thirty miles an hour. Scroggins bought chains at a garage, and Peter found accommodations at the Eagle House. Acting under his instructions, Scroggins signed the register "I. Scroggins and friend, New York."

It would have been a fine piece of news for Elizabethtown if the local paper had found out that Peter Killigrew spent the night in a two-dollar room like any drummer on his mountain rounds. But they never found it out.

NOT MORE THAN fifteen minutes' ride away—by the plane or the Pershing, if the impassable mountains had been crossed by a good highway—Imogen had locked herself in the corner room of the cabin about the time Peter and Scroggins had made up their minds to retire for the night and wait for daylight to permit them to decide which way to go next.

Jennifer soon grew bold enough before long to arm himself with a chisel and hammer found in the cellar. With these tools he went outside on the porch and proceeded to try lifting the window to Imogen's room.

She could hear plainly what he was doing. Making sure that the window was fast, but still fearful he might break it any moment, she unlocked the door to the living room, took out the key, and then closed the outer door. A strong cross-bar slipped easily into place.

Quickly, she made sure that the kitchen door in the rear was safely locked.

Now she was safe in the warm cabin, with plenty of food and fuel and drink; and Jennifer was outside in the snow.

He soon made it plain, however, that this would not last. He hammered on the window pane until she was fearful it would be broken. She put out the light so he could not see in.

She could hear him shouting, and went close to the window.

"What is it?" she called out.

"Let me in or I'll smash the window!" he cried, tapping it smartly with his hammer.

She knew that with one blow he could come through. For a moment she contemplated running out the rear and into the night, and striving to make her way out through the drifts.

But she had done that once. It seemed certain suicide.

Where else could she go?

The other room! She had passed it up in the beginning because it had no second door. The window, she remembered, was high. She wondered if it was too high to be easily reached from outside.

He was pounding and pounding, threatening to crash the glass at any moment. She would have to think and act quickly, or he would be in on her through a broken window.

"Wait!" she called, "I'll let you in." He stopped and went to the door.

She unbarred the door and then rushed to the smaller bedroom, hurled herself in, and locked it just in time to escape him. He hurled his shoulders against it vainly. She heard him curse.

She saw the light come on, through the keyhole.

A long silence. Then he knocked—gently—courteously. "Imogen!" he called.

She replied cautiously: "Well!"

"Sleep well, and don't worry, for I'm not worrying! You can't get out of that room except by this door. And when you do come out—make up your mind to meet your new husband! What's that you say?"

She made no reply.

"You say you can get out the window?" he called.

She had not said it, but she had been thinking it.

Another silence. Then she heard him outside the house, dragging heavy things. Then hammer and nails began working over the single window. She rushed to the sole opening of her chamber.

He was boarding her in, and nailing the boards on tightly. Again his voice sounded outside her door, from the living room. "Aw, Imogen!" he pleaded. "Come on out—this is the only way!"

She offered no sound.

"You could make this a peach of a honeymoon!" he called.

She looked through the keyhole. She could see him sprawled in front of the fireplace.

After awhile he called again: "Aw! Imogen! Come and kiss a fellow good night!"

After that, his words became less and less distinct. The fire died down. She began to suffer from the cold, and took a comforter and a blanket from the bed.

Drawing a chair up so she could look through the keyhole from time to time, she wrapped herself in the blanket and the downy comforter, and soon felt cozy.

She began nodding. Then, every once in awhile, she would bite her lip to keep herself from sleeping.

24

AT THE END OF THE ROAD

MARTY BING FOUND the same condition at New Russia that Scroggins and Peter had found—a preference of the inhabitants for other climes toward the end of November. Post office closed, houses closed, hotels closed; he had to journey seven miles to find a store open.

It was a little crossroads country store, on the road to Keene Valley, a place for hunters and woodsmen to trade. Marty found it just after noon, in the flivver he had hired at Elizabethtown. He asked for the justice of the peace.

"Hain't no jestice 'round here," the storeman replied to his query, "but if hits a constable y' want, why I guess we kin fit y' out. 'S somebody got th' law onto ye?"

"No, I want the law on somebody."

"Take me, then. I'm th' constable."

"I want a justice of the peace."

The storekeeper glumly shook his head. "Y'll have to go to Keene Valley fer Jedge Dolliver. That's fourteen mile, only th' road's snowed in. Better take th' State road down t' Schroon Lake—twenty-six mile—an' mebbe Jedge Truex'll do. Only come to think on it, Jedge Truex has went t' Albany t' th' legislature. Yer best ticket's 'Lizabethtown."

"Just came from there."

"There's two on 'em there. Jedge Cook an' Jedge Vilas."

"That's about the same distance as Keene Valley."

"Six o' one; half dozen t'other."

Marty discussed it with his driver. There seemed no better way than to go back whence they had started in Elizabethtown.

While they were on the road, however, they located the trail, turning off into the hills just below New Russia, the trail clearly indicated on the map Jennifer had given Marty, a copy of the one he had obtained from the owner of the cabin.

They found the trail just before three o'clock in the afternoon, and started back, retracing their route up the gorge toward their starting point. Marty felt he was safely set now for his final play of the coming morning.

About an hour later, Jennifer flew over in the hydro-aeroplane. Three hours later, Peter and Scroggins thundered past the same spot in the Pershing, but it was quite dark then, and they could not have seen the trail, even if they had been looking for it.

Marty found Judge Cook in his office on High Street, Elizabethtown, and willing to make a deal for a little trip the following morning for what seemed a liberal fee.

The appointment was made to get away by eight o'clock.

The flivver had been hired from the principal garage in town, the one near the Eagle House. That night, there rolled in next to it a rakish, underslung, high-powered roadster, the type seen thereabouts in the summer time, but seldom in the winter.

It was Peter's Pershing, which spent the night touching fenders with the town flivver.

IMOGEN MUST HAVE fallen asleep, though she could not tell how long she had been in the chair wrapped in the clothes taken from the bed, for when she looked through the keyhole again, she could not see any sign of life. The lamps were burning down low, almost ready to go out. The fire was dead, only charred sticks and ashes in the fireplace.

The cold waked her. It was still pitch dark, might be evening, might be early morning, or any time between.

She wrapped herself again in the blanket and comforter, but she still felt cold. She did not dare lie down in the bed. She felt safer sitting up.

To keep awake, she tried all sorts of maneuvers to see through the keyhole, a difficult proceeding. Jennifer not being visible, she concluded that he had gone to bed in the other room. In that event, it would be safe to venture outside, especially as she had kept the key to the other room and could lock him in if he was there.

Slowly and softly she went about unlocking her door. She turned the key with hardly a sound, but as she opened the door it creaked. She stopped for minutes. Still no sign of life. He was doubtless sleeping soundly.

She opened the door with greater courage and stepped into the living room. A sound behind her startled her, as she jumped toward the outer door in a panic.

She looked back and there, right beside the door she had opened, he lay, on a couch, covered with clothes taken from the other bedroom. His mouth was open. It was a low snore she had heard.

From the floor near the fireplace she picked up the kitchen knife with which she had stabbed him. Holding this tightly in her hand, she stood over him and watched his deep, disturbed breathing. She thought what a good brow he had, what a fine nose, what a loose mouth—and baggy pouches under his eyes—so young!

Pulling aside the tiny yellow curtains, she looked out. It was still night, but a late half moon was visible above the tree tops, lovely and clear. By its visibility, she could see the dark frame of the plane lying off in the clearing, on top of the snow, like a huge moth dropped on a white counterpane.

And their tracks leading to the cabin door. From the woods beyond, there seemed to proceed a cleared space, like a road. She felt encouraged. Once it was really light, she would not hesitate to try to make her way along that road alone. There must be some one near a nice cabin like this, and so well stocked.

Then she went back and took another look at Jennifer, with his mouth open and breathing with an occasional low snore. He looked so weak—almost pitiful, she thought—and her fear began to go.

She examined the fire, shoving the ashes aside. Underneath were live coals. Out of the woodbox she chose a few splinters and began coaxing the fire to life—but silently, glancing every moment to the couch to see if he stirred, ready to run if necessary.

This time, she concluded, she would go straight for the road.

In fifteen or twenty minutes she had a good blaze going. She went to the kitchen and lit a fire from a burning splinter, which avoided the striking of a match. She placed on the fire a kettle of snow taken from outside the back door.

When she came back from this he was sitting on the

edge of the couch, blinking, looking dully at her, and holding his head in his hands.

"Morning, Imogen," he moaned. "Oh, what a head!"

She stood at a safe distance near the door and asked, "Are you sick?"

"Awful! Better'n being dead, though."

He flopped back to the couch, and pulled the covers about him.

She piled more logs on the fire.

"Fire's great!" he commented. "Thanks! You're a game little sport. Awful glad you forgave me, but that's right. You took me wrong. I didn't mean you any harm."

Physical fear of him was rapidly passing, but she carefully concealed and secured the knife inside her bodice. She watched the kettle until the water began to simmer.

A little later she noticed a few streaks of gray light coming over the timbered slope beyond the kitchen door. Was it dawn?

"What time is it?" she called in to him.

He looked at his wrist watch, replying, "Twenty minutes to seven." And then he held his head again, moaning, "I'd give a right leg for a cup of hot coffee!"

She was rummaging through the kitchen cabinet, where she had found a bag of oatmeal. She prepared some of this in a skillet, and placed it to cook. Then she further examined the cabinet. It had several little patented devices, and curious reversible drawers.

Pressing on one of these springs out popped a coffee grinder. Just below was a covered box. Opening it she found several cupfuls of roasted coffee beans. She put them in the grinder and turned the crank. Presently the aroma spread through the cabin. She found a coffee pot and filled it.

"Am I looney, or is that coffee?" cried Jennifer, rising from his couch and crossing weakly to the door of the kitchen. She turned to see him standing there, swaying against the jamb, where he leaned for support.

"Yes. It's coffee!"

She had no fear of him now. Daylight was at hand. And the way to the road was clear. Before long they would be out of this.

"You're a brick," he mumbled; "dead game little sport. I'm going to treat you square for this."

"At last?" she asked.

"Look here! What do you mean?"

"Nothing."

"You aren't holding it against me for last night, are you, Imogen?"

She looked down and away, as if shaking her head.

She went on with the breakfast preparation, while he carried in some wood from the shed outside to the wood-box by the fireplace.

She served the peaches left from the can opened the night before in two saucers placed on the table in the living room. He ate his without waiting for her, and apologized. "My head is splitting. You don't mind if I don't wait, eh?"

"Eat!" she commanded.

Then she placed the oatmeal before him, He devoured a portion. "Come along," he insisted. "Aren't you hungry?"

"Yes," she admitted, taking her peaches to the kitchen, where she was browning some cakes left from the night before.

"When'll that coffee be ready?" he demanded, standing behind her.

"In two minutes."

"I can't wait. Head's better already, though."

"You want it strong, don't you?"

"Sure!" he admitted.

While she stood over the coffee he said, from the doorway, "Say, Imogen, this is the best thing ever happened to me—getting to know you like this—makes me think you're the real thing to be Mrs. Darcy Jennifer."

She looked blackly at him, but her eyes stopped on the upper part of his right sleeve. "What's that on your coat?" she asked.

He looked. "That!" He pulled the sleeve and it stuck. He winced. "Must be where you plugged me with that knife."

"Oh! Let me see!" She went to him, and helped him remove his coat and roll up his sleeve. The knife had entered the flesh. Blood had oozed out, but was dried. She got a basin and filled it with warm water, then stepped inside the L and tore a piece from her petticoat.

Leading him back to the living room, now quite light from the sun's rays, which began to struggle in through the yellow curtains, she bathed and bandaged his wound.

As she finished, but without touching her with his hands, he bent swiftly down and implanted a kiss on the back of her hand. She affected not to notice this, saying only, "I hope there's no infection now."

She served the coffee and the cakes. After he had ravenously eaten three-quarters of the supply he appeared to have entirely regained his spirits. Even his loose mouth seemed strong again.

She started to take out the dishes.

"Don't bother about that," he protested. "I'm going out and see if I can't fix that radiator myself. If not we'll walk down that road until we come to a garage or a parson."

She paid no attention to the remark, but went on with the dishes. "Great day for a wedding," he added. "Sunday, too!"

Still she made no reply.

It seemed useless to repeat what she had said to him the night before. She had already said what she intended to say—if not in just the dramatic form she had imagined.

It wouldn't do, however, to give him any inch of further assurance. She was not out of the woods yet.

So she replied, "You don't know much about the Morton school, do you?"

"Very strict with the girls."

She turned her back to avoid his seeing her blushes.

"Ha! Ha!" He took it as a joke, and went out to his plane, though, in reality, he wanted to look for Marty Bing. He located the road. Then, to kill time against the arrival of his confederate, he melted several gallons of water in an old boiler.

He started the engine and was relieved to hear it purr again. They could travel whenever they liked now. He turned from the plane to see her standing on the porch.

"What do you think!" he said blandly, rejoining her. "The radiator's in shape again." He smiled ingratiatingly.

"Then we could have gone back home last night?"

"Only I lost the way. It's daylight now. We can inquire, soon's we get out where there are people. Come, let's get warm."

He led the way back into the cabin. His watch had just told him it was a few minutes to nine. Where was Marty Bing?

A voice from the woods answered his thought. "Hello!" A long call.

Both rushed to the door. A flivver was grinding through six inches of snow.

"Help at last! Well, isn't this great!" Jennifer was all smiles. He rushed forward to meet two men who presently dismounted in the clearing. In a moment he was back, leading them—one a rat-faced city type, the other a rotund, amiable man in a great coonskin coat.

"Miss Nelson," he called to Imogen, as she stood before the fire, "here are the Heaven sent helpers of two young fools. Let me introduce Mr. Bing of New York, and Judge Cook of Elizabethtown. Judge, Miss Imogen Nelson of Westchester County. Mr. Bing, Miss Nelson. Well, well! What a jolly party. How about a little coffee, gentlemen? Imogen, is there any more coffee?"

"No," she blithely consented, "but I can make some."

In a few minutes there was steaming hot coffee for the newcomers.

While they drank Jennifer said to her, so all could hear: "Isn't it a piece of luck the judge here is a regular justice of the peace? Saves us a search."

Imogen started guiltily. She had felt so secure in the presence of the strangers, and now suddenly her edifice of confidence began to crumble.

"How?" she asked dully.

"Why, the judge can marry us."

She looked to the judge. He was beaming expansively.

The coffee had been very good, and the sharp November air bracing indeed.

"Quite the ticket for me, folks. I'm just as good as a parson—and quick to oblige. I like to encourage sentiment whenever I see it. Nothing more romantic than a marriage in the woods!" He looked from one to the other in the essence of good nature.

Imogen felt her body grow like steel, and her brain began to work deftly. "I'd like to ask you a question first, judge?" she began, very softly, with the properly demure hesitance of a bride.

"Sure, ma'am. Many as you like. Shoot. We got the full day."

She drew in her breath as she inquired, most innocently, surveying the three from her saucerlike eyes, above which her reddish hair was brushed negligently:

"When you marry any one, do both parties have to consent?"

The judge slapped his knee and roared with laughter.

"It's one of the essentials provided by the statutes," he exclaimed. "Fair enough, too, I always say."

Jennifer winked at him. "She means she's not sure about my consent, judge, but that's all right. I guess we understand each other."

He grinned at Imogen and stood beside her, though not venturing to touch her. He did not believe she would dare rebel.

"Come on, judge," he insisted. "Say the word, and get it over with."

The judge rose slowly as became a man of dignity and

poise, not to say avoirdupois. As he reached his feet he was astounded to hear Imogen say coldly, definitely, decisively:

"Then you can't have any wedding, for I refuse to give my consent."

Jennifer looked at Imogen forbiddingly, and then motioned to the judge and Marty to go outside.

"Little lovers' quarrel," he explained.

"I'll call you in a minute."

The two went out. Jennifer turned on her explosively. "He really is a justice of the peace, Imogen!" he cried. "I told you I'd make good—and I will. And we must be married now before we go back. And I love you!"

He went toward her, hands outstretched. She turned and fled into the smaller bedroom and locked the door in his face. He joined the judge on the porch.

"A little fool," he hotly asserted. "I'm going to protect her against herself. Judge, I'm going in there and hold her, and you come in and read the ceremony."

"You mean without her voluntary consent?"

"Sure. It's only a lovers' quarrel, I tell you. She wants to marry me. Didn't she come up here with me last night? Well, you know what that means. I'm not going to let her outrage herself in this way."

The judge was troubled; he shook his head.

"Too bad," he said, "but you'll have to do your own love-making. That's not my business."

"But you can perform the ceremony. Here!" Darcy produced a roll of bills and peeled off one with a big numeral.

The judge waved it aside. "Fifty dollars is enough for a

proper ceremony. I've married many for less. But against the girl's consent—no, sir-ee!"

"Here's two hundred!"

"Never!"

"Five hundred!"

"Not for a million!"

The rotund man, scowling now, began waddling back toward his flivver, his coonskin brushing the snow indignantly.

"Wait!" yelled Darcy. "I'll get her consent."

At that moment, and before anything further could be done, a steadily increasing rhythmic swish through the woods became audible.

Marty Bing was the first to see what it meant.

"Some one coming, boss!" he called. "A sporty roadster—two men!"

The roadster, however, was not having the easy time of it the flivver had enjoyed. The road was not wide enough for such a wide chassis. Again and again saplings had brushed the sides of the car as it went on, at a very stiff pace, too, for that rough wilderness. Now it was brought to a standstill while still a few hundred yards from the clearing. Its front fender was caught in a two-inch tree, which held it against all persuasion of the benevolent old gentleman who seemed to be the passenger, while the driver sat and fumed at him to hasten in prying it loose.

Taking a good look, Darcy Jennifer recognized the driver.

"Good Lord!" he exclaimed under his breath to Marty Bing. "It's Peter Killigrew. Good night!"

He ran for the plane, calling to Marty. As he climbed

into the cockpit he said to Marty: "Get back to New York, see my father, and get him to fix me up before next Wednesday. And tell him I'm in Montreal. I'm taking no chances on being nabbed."

Marty helped him run the plane off the ground. A moment later the big boat-bird lifted away above the trees, skimming the edges of the clearing, and headed north.

About the same time Scroggins pried the Pershing loose. Peter, looking up, saw the plane get away, and noted Jennifer was alone in her.

"He left the girl behind," Peter said to the superintendent. "You look for her. I'll keep after the crook!"

And he turned the roadster and was off back along the trail.

Imogen came out of the room at the sound of Scroggins's voice. They embraced silently with intense feeling. Marty and the judge took them to Elizabethtown in the flivver. There they hired a car to take them to the railroad station at Westport. They took the night train for New York, and reached the Lodge the next morning. Master Peter drove into the plaza at the Towers that afternoon. Scroggins sought him at once.

"The plane came down at South Plattsburg," he said. "Ran out of gas. Jennifer swears he did not harm the girl."

"I don't believe he did."

"Good!" said Peter. "Then I'll keep my word with him. I agreed if it proved the girl was O.K. he could have until the end of the week to settle. He's gone to Cleveland to see his father."

That seemed to close the interview. Scroggins waited for Peter to ask something more about Imogen, for it seemed that at last he was about to accomplish his long nurtured object of making his employer acquainted with his "angelic child." He had always believed that if Peter would only see her, her destiny would be settled—and most favorably.

"Shall I call her up to see you?" he suggested.

The master of millions scowled; The flavor of the adventure, which he had seemed to enjoy while they were having it, had passed, evidently. The glow in his eye had faded. The stoop came back into his shoulders, wrinkles into his forehead.

The weight of responsibilities seemed upon him again; the caution required to steel himself against all sorts of adventurers, male and female, came into his voice.

"I never want to see her!" he replied levelly. His voice was very hard.

Scroggins felt as if he had been struck.

"Women mean nothing but trouble," Peter went on listlessly. "I didn't go up there to rescue your girl, but to land a crook."

Scroggins smiled at this, for Peter had landed the crook only to let him go—and with more rope. But he said nothing. He had learned it was wiser to wait a more propitious occasion when the wind of disfavor was not blowing so strong.

Peter evidently wanted to emphasize his unnecessary affront. "A little outcast like that is bound to stir up mischief," he persisted. "Tell her she will have to marry the next scoundrel who tries to get her. I wash my hands of her and of all her escapades!"

25

TOBOGGANING THRILLS

PETER HAD SAID that "the little outcast" would have to marry "the next scoundrel who gets her." Scroggins reminded him of this, with his tongue in his cheek, a long, long time afterward.

Meanwhile, after her return from the north woods, Imogen seemed unlikely, if left to her own devices, ever to meet any young man again, scoundrel or otherwise. She seemed strangely listless and uninterested in anybody.

Scroggins had noticed this when he took her away from the cabin in the flivver. It had not seemed to strike her as peculiar that he did not have a Killigrew car. She asked no questions about it. Which made things easier for him, because he did not want to tell her about Master Peter—not yet.

Scroggins feared Imogen in one way, as much as she feared his employer in another. She always kept him on the *qui vive* because of her inaccessibility. She made him feel that she was not a fixture at the Lodge, but a mere transient, likely to migrate at any moment.

He didn't like this. He wanted her there always.

This feeling was not engendered through any reticence on her part. On the contrary, she was attractively frank. For instance, she told him and Aunt Maria everything that had happened to her while with Darcy Jennifer, even to the use of the knife and the binding of the wound.

She worried about the difference it might make if the girls at school heard the news. Perhaps not with Clare and Gwen and the gold plate crowd, but with the solid gold crowd—well, she would hate to have the puritanical Selene Henton know it.

Not telling this worry absolved her from discussing the problems that grew out of it in her own mind, so that Scroggins and Aunt Maria remained in ignorance of what really ailed her.

What they saw was a girl naturally reticent, and very shy, suddenly thrown back into herself, and rendered twice as shy, much more reticent than before.

She got back to the Towers the Monday morning before Thanksgiving. After breakfast Carl drove around in the Deisel-Mascisti to take her to school, but she begged Aunt Maria to phone and have her excused for the day. She said she felt too fatigued, what with the Pullman the night before, and almost no sleep the night before that.

She was excused from school that day. Tuesday she begged off, also, and then asked to wait until after the holiday.

There was a truly Thanksgiving feast in the Lodge the following day, with the prize turkey from the farm, and dressing made of chestnuts grown on the place. Scroggins and his wife were vocal with their rejoicing. Imogen wept.

Scroggins and Maria solaced her as best they could. Alone, later, Scroggins demanded, "What's up with her,

Maria? Do you think that scamp really harmed her, and she's not telling, to protect him?"

"No, I don't think so."

"What is it, then?"

"She's a very high-strung girl, and oversensitive. That's all. Most girls would think that was fun. She's taken it to heart."

"Don't seem natural," Scroggins justifiedly protested.

Monday morning Carl drove up again in the Deisel-Mascisti, and Maria sent the maid to call Imogen, who had been allowed to sleep late and have her breakfast served in bed, although she had specifically before this refused all such pampering.

The maid came down in fright, crying, "She's gone, Mrs. Scroggins!"

The room over the porte-cochère, the room dedicated to Imogen, with its lovely expanses looking over the broad lawns and down to the very distant Hudson, was deserted. The bed had not been slept in that night.

Scroggins was called in and a hasty conference disclosed nothing.

After a little thought, however, Scroggins said he saw light. "I know where to find her," he announced.

"Where?" Maria demanded.

"Wait! I'll have her here in an hour or two!" He dashed off in the Deisel, straight for Dobbs's Corners.

He found her in the old garden, clearing up the frosted shrubs and fallen leaves in her hardy chrysanthemum bed.

"Why, Imogen," he protested, as she went into his arms and buried her head on his paternal breast, "how could you run away and distress your Aunt Maria like this?"

"Didn't *you* worry any?"

He tweaked her nose for this saucy remark. "Not when I thought of your old garden," he replied. "You see, I know you better than you think."

"Then why don't you know I hate that school!"

Scroggins whistled. "Is that it? You don't want to go to school?"

She shook her head vigorously.

"And will you come back if you don't have to go to school any more?"

She smiled wanly. "If you want me to."

"Can't live without you. Come. Carl's waiting."

So she returned in the Deisel-Mascisti, but not to Mrs. Morton's. That exclusive resort at Pumice Bay knew her no more. And Scroggins had the devil's own time to get back any of the five thousand paid for the year's tuition, though less than a third of a year had been used.

Mrs. Morton finally gave back five hundred—"board

allowance," she said. The balance was liquidating damages for "preventing the matriculation of another pupil."

Selene Henton came to call during the second weekend in December. She wanted to be sure that Imogen really did live at the Lodge and not at the Towers, and to quiz her about Mr. Killigrew. But whenever his name was mentioned Imogen changed the subject, difficult though that was with an experienced girl like Selene.

"What did you do to Darcy Jennifer?" Selene asked before she went.

"Nothing. Why?"

"His sister, Lenly, says you have hypnotized him—that he is desperately in love with you."

Imogen changed the subject.

Selene went away miffed, but she had succeeded in setting up in Imogen's mind another source of worry to prey on her, and to render her even more shy and reticent.

She began to think about Darcy in retrospect with more tolerance. Had he really loved her? His whole action had been so strange, so compounded of respectful attention and wild abandon, such an extreme of vicious youth and gentle bearing!

She wondered if some devil had not driven him on to offend her as he had. She thought only of excuses for his conduct, never of accusations.

Not that she cared for him. No. She couldn't care for him. But if he was desperate with love for her! Still, if so, why did he not try to see her again? There had been no effort.

Of course, Imogen would not have seen him if he had, still— Selene must have been exaggerating, though rather a precise girl, and striving to give the impression that she did not gossip.

These were her only thoughts, except those she gave her flowers, for Scroggins had sent a gardener over to Dobbs's Corners to transplant all the roots that would bear it at that time of year. The ground was not yet frozen hard, and he managed to get up her giant artichoke, her peonies, and iris, and the Circassian lilies.

Scroggins had a bed prepared for her own bulbs in the corner of the garden. She spent much of her time there early in December. Then came a snow which covered the ground, and drove her into the greenhouse with Verhens, who had always been her friend.

The holidays came and went. Shortly after the first of the year Scroggins got a check for five hundred dollars from Mrs. Morton. He told Imogen of it rather boastingly, saying he had deposited it to her account.

"Can I do what I want to with it?" she asked.

"Certainly."

"Then I want to go on a holiday."

This seemed queer. Scroggins looked at Maria. She was as nonplused as he.

"Where do you want to go?" he asked.

"To Lake Placid," Imogen said without hesitation, "to see the winter sports."

After a moment's thought Scroggins smiled. "I see," he replied; "your last visit to the Adirondacks was so pleasant you must go again."

Immediately he was sorry he had said it, for she blushed furiously. She insisted, however, she wanted to go to Lake Placid.

There was no particular reason. She just wanted to go. Alone?—they asked. Not necessarily, she said. In fact, it would be better if she had some one to be with—a woman, of course.

Mrs. Scroggins, who had suffered unmentioned pangs at Imogen's withdrawal from Mrs. Morton's school, having had the slenderest opportunity to avail herself of the social prerogatives belonging to the guardian of a pupil there, could see no charm in Lake Placid.

"In the wintertime the mountains must be awful cold," said Aunt Maria. "Why don't you go to Florida—or California—or the West Indies?"

"It's not just—just a pleasure trip," Imogen modestly asserted. "It's something I don't know how to explain, couldn't explain it to myself. I just want to go there and— and toboggan!"

Scroggins insisted that she be humored. He did not want to have her leave the Lodge; but she seemed pining for this trip, and he wanted to indulge her. Master Peter had gone back to the city for his winter residence in the town house, and there was little to do on the farm, so Scroggins would miss Imogen. Nevertheless, she must go.

They secured a governess through an acquaintance who was superintendent of an estate in Purchase, a woman of middle age just over from Scotland, formerly governess to the children of a peer on an estate in Northumberland; Miss Petrie, a serious-minded, competent, trustworthy person.

Imogen seemed to like Miss Petrie immensely. She expressed herself as extremely grateful to Scroggins for finding her.

They prepared to go to Lake Placid the middle of January for two weeks, and, if they liked, to stay another week, or even longer. They outfitted in knickers, sweaters, woolen jackets, short skirts, leggings, and furs.

Scroggins told Imogen her five hundred paid for the clothes, the governess, and the trip, together with the hotel expenses for two or three weeks. Maria protested vigorously to him, in private, for he had dug into his savings to foot the bill, which was a whole lot more than five hundred.

"Makes no difference," he replied to his wife. "It's the only thing Imogen's ever really wanted, and she's going to have it. Mrs. Morton's school was your idea. She didn't want that—didn't need it. So this is really coming out of her money."

"I wash my hands of it!" Maria cried. "You'll ruin us for that girl if you don't call a halt!"

Of this, of course, Imogen knew nothing.

She went, accompanied by Miss Petrie, on a Sunday night. Monday morning they breakfasted on the glassed-in portico of the casino, and looked out to see the early morning enthusiasts skating on the ice.

An hour later, having joined a group formed from the hotel desk, under a guide, they trudged the way to the top of a long hill, and a little later were sliding down the fairway, high-banked with walls of snow so steep they seemed to be going through a white tunnel.

On the jump the toboggan turned slightly and Imogen was plunged into a snow bank. Miss Petrie rushed to her assistance, greatly alarmed. Instead of finding an upset girl, she discovered one radiant with a joy somewhat more than just physical reaction to the robust sport.

Imogen fairly beamed with delight. "Now!" she cried. "I know why I wanted to come to Lake Placid!"

"Why?"

"Oh!" Imogen tried to speak, and gave it up, concluding rather lamely with "Oh! Because!"

But she, herself, knew why. It was for the exhilaration of that douse in the snowbank, the sharp stimulation of that snow on her delicate skin, the icy tang of the whole winter experience.

And for something more that it symbolized—something deeper, something spiritual—the springs of her life!

It took her back to that dash into the snowbank behind the deserted cabin a few short weeks before when pursued by Darcy Jennifer. She flushed with latent shame when she began to reflect that possibly she had enjoyed that experience, after all.

Was it not the time she could remember most vividly? Peril survived! What more stimulating!

When the realization of this came to her, she was at first puzzled, then ashamed, and then riotously pleased. After all, it proved—did it not?—that she was a normal girl—and was not satisfied alone with flowers and to be a recluse.

Yet, to whom could she tell this? Not to Miss Petrie. Not to Aunt Maria. To Uncle Isaiah? Maybe—but not quite.

The days sped on wings. The snow, the rarefied air, the exhilarating sports filled her with ecstasy.

But she avoided personal contacts. Except for Miss Petrie and the guide they employed from the hotel, she spoke to no one.

Until one day when she was out skiing. Her indefatigable energy had tired Miss Petrie out, and she lay down after lunch. Imogen proceeded alone up the seven-mile trail, to the east and north of the hotel. At the top of a peak she paused to survey the grandeur of the rugged landscape, with its evergreens laced in white.

Over beyond, not so many miles, she said to herself, lay the cabin where she had spent that perilous night. Dangerous? Yes, but exciting. Perhaps the thought made her just a little bit giddy, for when she started to slide down the incline one ski was not straight. She landed at the bottom on her head!

The next moment a young man was at her side, helping her right herself. She thanked him, and passed on, back toward the hotel.

He seemed going in the same direction. He did not ask to join her, nor did she say anything more to him. Of course, she could not help noticing him—just a bit.

His mouth and chin were not loose or weak—like Darcy's. That was the first thing she saw. But she thought maybe his brow was not so broad. Maybe it was, though. He had a rather long face, and seemed very serious, for so young a man.

She wondered if he was lonely. He looked like it. Once or twice she thought he glanced in her direction, but she could not be positive.

They reached the hotel at the same time. By then she was a bit fearful that maybe he had kept on with her for a further chance to speak. She became distrustful of herself, especially after she had just been saying to herself that the real reason she liked the snow was because it reminded her of the time when she had come into dangerous contact with the only villain of her acquaintance.

So, when they reached the hotel, she ran from him for fear he might try to speak again.

The next morning, there he was on the veranda with his skates. She, too, had her skates. He smiled at her. She hardly dared return the smile, and thought she had not done so. But when they reached the hockey ring he spoke to her, saying: "Good morning! I am glad to see you are not injured."

"No, thank you," she said, and hurried on.

That afternoon she was with Miss Petrie, walking along the trail through the woods leading from the toboggan slide, when he suddenly appeared in the path, and lifted his cap.

"Who is that?" asked Miss Petrie, rather suspiciously.

"I don't know," replied Imogen, truthfully and with alarm.

The next day there he was again. This time he would not be refused. He came forward cordially and held out his hand.

"Good morning!" he said. "I think we ought to know each other, don't you?"

"Y-yes," she faltered.

"I also think we should be introduced, don't you?"

This being her thought, she gasped: "Y-yes."

He glanced across to the desk where the manager was leaning over in conversation with a guest. "Pardon me," he said, "just a moment."

Shortly he returned with the manager in tow. She saw him whisper something previously to the hotel man, who now beamed on her most expansively.

"Ah, Miss Nelson," said the manager, "may I present a

very good friend of mine, and of the hotel—Mr. ah—Mr. Peter Jones."

Mr. Jones bowed, rather charmingly. The manager smirked at him, and went away. Imogen disliked the manager. There was something *too* friendly about him.

Then Miss Petrie came up, and Imogen introduced her. Mr. Jones evidently did not relish the presence of the governess, and withdrew shortly, saying he hoped to see Imogen again. She repeated the expression of hope.

"Who is Mr. Jones?" Miss Petrie demanded.

"The man who picked me up when I fell on my skis. Isn't he a perfect dear? His manner! His reserve! What breeding!" Imogen was a bit carried away.

"Jones?" queried Miss Petrie. "A common name. I would not advise you to have much to do with him."

26

A SHOCK

IMOGEN FONDLY IMAGINED that she was having the time of her life on the last remnants of the auction of her father's antique bed. It was the first vacation she had ever had, and, she thought, probably would be the last. Going to the Morton School had been a severe trial, for she was on her mettle there every moment.

Of course, she could not stay on with Scroggins after the spring came. He had taken her bulbs out of the garden at Dobbs's Corners, and she had permitted it, but that was during a weak moment.

Her money would be gone when she got back from Lake Placid, and she could not endure the thought of living on charity. That is what it surely would be if she stayed at the Lodge any longer.

So she entered into the sports with a zest which comes only to those who feel obliged to put everything they have into one extravagance.

Most of the guests at the fashionable hotel were merely enjoying a pleasant interlude in many other expensive diversions. They accepted it in the nature of the lake they patronized   placidly. They dressed for sports, and dressed for dinner, and yawned, and calmly enjoyed themselves without too great an exertion, with plenty of steam heat.

The social atmosphere, therefore, was restrained, languid, and anything but exhilarating.

Early in the week of Imogen's arrival, there descended on the resort a movie company, headed by one of the queens of the silver sheet. She flared everywhere—in yellows and greens and reds, and made up, seemingly, at all times, for the camera or the footlights.

"Plenty of color in her," remarked the manager of the hotel to one of his old patrons.

"Yes," admitted the patron, "as colorful as a scarlet tanager!"

"If you like color," went on the manager, "there is the real thing."

He pointed to a slender girl walking demurely past with her skates under her arm. Her knitted suit was of white, with a slender band of Alice blue. Saucy red curls peeked from under a rakish tarn. Her cheeks glowed with a health which matched the hair.

"If there's art in that make-up," the manager boasted, "it's of a higher order than they produce in the movies."

"Simplicity of nature it looks like. What a little peach! Who is she?"

"A Miss Nelson—sort of a mystery here."

"This her first winter?"

"Yes."

"Where from?"

"Registered from 'Westchester.' That's a village, you know, as well as a county. I wanted to ask her, but didn't like to presume. I have a hunch she is not 'Miss Nelson' at all."

"Who, then?"

"Some well known heiress, perhaps. She has a way about her; carries herself in that self-possessed, strangely shy manner that only girls of the greatest families know how to affect. And—she has a governess."

"Ah! A governess? Does that prove she is an heiress?"

"Doesn't prove it, but it helps."

"Incognito—eh?" the patron ruminated.

"Is that common here?"

"No, but it's done."

"Do you permit it?"

"How can I prevent?" the hotel man asked.

"You require satisfaction of the identities of your patrons, don't you?"

"If they act like ladies and gentlemen, and pay their bills, and have enough luggage to protect us, why—" the manager shrugged his shoulders.

The patron's curiosity was much aroused.

"I wonder who she is. Looking at her now from here, I don't know but that you are right. What an aristocratic profile! And the poise of her head! And look at the little feet and their high arch! And the perfect taste of her clothes—quite without affectation—the simplicity of a grand duchess, or a stenographer!"

The manager laughed. "Where did you get that stenographer?"

"She's an imaginary stenographer."

"Thought so. I never met one like that."

The mysterious "heiress," meanwhile, had been overtaken by Mr. Jones, who asked if he could not accompany her for the morning on the rink.

She seemed quite contented with his companionship, and let him put on her skates. Then they joined hands, cross fashion, and skated for a long while, silently. Imogen's silence was only matched by that of Mr. Jones.

For half an hour neither said a word. The rhythmic *swish-swish* of their sharp skates cutting curlecues in the ice made the only sound. Their pace seemed perfectly matched, their stroke the same. They turned in unison, without the slightest hesitation, with neither asking a question nor making a remark.

"Tired?" he asked at length.

"No."

They skated another half hour in the same way.

"Shall we stop?" he asked.

"If you like."

"I thought you might be tired."

"No," she said simply. "I could go on like this forever!"

"So could I."

"Lets!"

They went another hour—without a smile, without a miss of stroke. She was half a head shorter than he, and yet her stride seemed as long as his. Curious. Yet she did not exert herself, nor did he lessen his stride to accommodate himself to her. Very curious. Unusual.

Yet neither spoke.

When they finally sat down at the landing stage and he knelt to take off her skates it was as if by mutual consent, for still neither spoke. It seemed as if neither wanted to break a strange little spell that enveloped them—a heady, crystal-clear, invigorating spell redolent of pine cones and balsamic perfumes.

Again he was the first to speak. "Sorry to quit," he offered apologetically, "but it's luncheon time."

She sank back on the seat, and sighed. "I'm not hungry!" she said.

He looked into her blue eyes, gazing up at him silently, took in those rakish wisps of red hair racing from under the tam, saw the spread of the blushing pink in her cheeks, and suddenly put his hand to his forehead, and sat down, too.

He felt a bit dizzy. Perhaps the rarefied air.

"Does the altitude affect you?" he asked.

She turned on him, gasping: "Is that it?"

"Then you do feel a little—what shall I say?"

"Yes—" Hesitatingly: "I do!"

"So do I!"

They sat for many minutes in silence, during which he removed his skates.

"Buoyed up, kind of?" She ventured at last, glancing at him timidly. "Sort of like a cork on water."

"Or a balloon!" said he.

"Like being in an airplane!" She began blushing furiously.

He looked at her, and noted her change of color.

"Do you like airplanes?" he asked.

"No, no," she hastily answered, "I—I like this better!"

"Skating, you mean?"

"Yes. S-skating!"

"I think the ice is better to-day than yesterday," he asserted.

"Oh, much better!" she agreed. "It's perfect to-day."

"Quite—perfect!"

Another long pause. Then he suggested: "I suppose we had better go to the hotel—the dining room will be closed."

She sighed. "Yes, I suppose so. But I'm not hungry."

"You will need your luncheon, though." He was regarding her solicitously.

"Often I don't eat any."

"Please, to-day—will you—with me?"

"I'd like to, but—well, Miss Petrie is waiting."

"Can't we give her the slip?"

"I don't know how."

"We'll have luncheon served on the gundeck—up there!" He pointed to the glassed-in sun parlor over the long veranda.

"I didn't know you could."

"Let's see!" he suggested.

So they lunched alone in the sun parlor. The servants seemed most willing to do anything for Mr. Jones.

To record more of their conversation at this time would be repetitional. The most important things they uttered were not conveyed by means of words.

After lunch she felt she was obliged to hunt up Miss Petrie, but the Scotch governess was deep in a book—something about psychology, or was it physiology—and told Imogen not to mind her, to run along and have a good time, and to be sure and get back before dark.

Imogen said nothing about Mr. Jones. By discreet silence she let it be inferred she had lunched alone. She found him waiting up on the trail to the toboggan slide. It was nearly time for the three o'clock slides to begin.

They were ready for the first, and he piloted her to the

front seat, while he was just behind. She looked off down the fairway, with its banked tunnels of glistening snow.

Then he said—and it seemed to her he was extremely timid about it—"If you don't mind I'll hold on—so—" and put his arms around her.

Nothing strange about that, for every one else did it on the toboggan. She looked back over her shoulder into his face, and those blue eyes under the reddish hair, flanked by the glowing cheeks, brought him another feeling of rapid buoyancy.

"The air is rare!" he said.

"Precious!" She snuggled closer, for the guide was pushing off.

Then the descent, the unutterably swift descent down the incline, receptive as a greased hollow to a spear shaft. She thought her heart would lift right out of her bosom. She shrieked, and he begged to know if she was injured, and she muttered, "No—I'm terribly happy—but the wind goes so fast."

But it was over so soon—in a few seconds, it seemed.

Then they climbed the long incline again. That was fun, too, going along slowly, stopping from time to time for a better view of the valley as they rose above it, step by step. And another slide!

The next time he dared say to her, "I wonder if you ever read poetry?"

"Of course—don't you?"

"Did you ever read, 'If I Were King?'"

"You mean Tennyson?"

"No. This is a play—by McCarthy, I think."

"Can't you repeat some of it? I love poetry."

They were arranging themselves again. He had managed, for the third time, to get her the front seat, and was getting fixed behind. It seemed almost natural—quite the proper thing—to have him slip his arms around her—to be secure, of course, for the swift slide.

"It runs like this," he said, while she glanced over her shoulder into his face, " 'The best of all reasons for a woman's loving a man is because her heart is of just the right size to hold in the hollow of his hand.'"

He faltered over the last, adding lamely, "Only that is not the meter, just the idea. I never was good at poetry."

Lucky the guide pushed off at that moment, for she knew not what to say in answer, but the exhilaration of the toboggan's rush was not equaled by the lift in spirit. Was it the poetry or the firm clasp of his long arms which seemed lifting her into the blue sky, above the tops of the tallest trees, over the vast mountains?

Yet he seemed distraught when the toboggan came to a halt, and it was time to help her up. He seemed almost afraid to touch her again.

And he did not propose that they slide again, but started back down the trail toward the hotel. Something had broken the spell—the perfect spell of their playtime. Had he become self-conscious with repeating the line of François Villon?

He was, in fact, thinking to himself at that moment, "Villon was a vagabond, a worthless wanderer," and his mind, working as if pursuant to subconscious directions, began probing something she had said way back at lunch. It was about an airplane.

He went at it bluntly, without the slightest realization of

where it would lead him. He only knew he had a sudden unaccountable antagonism for this reddish-haired ingenue. For a matter of six or seven hours she had held him in utter thrall.

Nothing like it had ever happened before, and surely there must be something very wicked about a girl who could do that to him. "When were you up in an airplane?" he asked, dully.

"Several months ago," she answered quickly. She too felt the passing of the spell, not because she was losing it, but because something had come into his face—something that rendered him suddenly very old, world-weary.

At first she had thought him a very young man, not over twenty-five. Now he seemed aged—fully forty.

"Funny," she added, nervously, at a loss to say something to please him, "it was up here-in the Adirondacks, too. I flew up the Hudson and way up over Lake George, and over a little place they call Elizabethtown, I believe it was."

He turned on her with almost a savage snarl. "You!" he snapped.

It was like a blow in the face.

"Why, yes," she faltered. "Of course.

Why not?"

"What kind of an airplane?"

"One with little boats on—to stay up in water."

"A hydroplane?"

"Yes."

Her wide-set, innocent blue eyes almost unmanned him. He looked away as from forbidden things. "Excuse me," he murmured, and hurriedly walked away.

They had reached the veranda of the hotel. He was so

rude he did not even open the door for her. She was almost as shocked as when Darcy Jennifer leaped the table to reach her that night in the cabin.

He sought the hotel manager without delay. "Who is this Miss Nelson to whom you introduced me?" he demanded.

"I don't know. Registered as Miss Imogen Nelson and governess, Westchester," replied the manager.

"Westchester what?"

"That's the queer part of it. I don't know. Village, I suppose, or county. I believe she's an heiress."

"Why do you think she's an heiress?"

"I don't know."

"Well, why don't you know? What kind of a hostelry are you running?"

His eyes blazing, Mr. Jones talked down further explanation by ordering, very curtly, "Get me a wire to New York, call Midtown 37978, and keep the wire clear."

A few minutes later in his room he said, into the phone: "That you, Mac? I'm in my room at the hotel at Placid. Listen. Get Scroggins on the wire and find out where that girl of his is, and her full name, and other particulars, who she's with, and so on. Get it without delay, and relay it to me here. I'll wait. No. Don't tell any one, especially not Scroggins. Name? Ah, yes. Peter Jones."

Then he sat gloomily in his window and consumed cigarette after cigarette, looking out desperately at the chill winter landscape. The sun had just gone down. He bitterly asked how any one could be fool enough to come to the woods in the winter time.

In half an hour the bell rang. He picked up the receiver. "Yes, Mac," he called.

"Imogen Nelson," the reply came. "She's at Lake Placid, same hotel you're at, with her governess, Miss Petrie. Is that all? Very well. Good night."

Peter Jones checked out that night. He had his dinner in his rooms, and did not see Imogen again.

27

PETER CHANGES HIS PLANS

THE FOLLOWING MORNING Peter Killigrew arrived at the offices of the Killigrew estate just after the clerks were opening for the day, and quite some time before Mac came in. He greeted his force curtly, explaining that he had reached town from a trip in the early morning, and had come straight from the train.

He performed the unusual service for himself of opening his mail. He glanced through it hurriedly. Nothing interesting. He called up the Montauk boathouse and asked how soon they could get the Tumbleweed into commission.

The boat engineer was surprised. "Why, Mr. Killigrew," he exclaimed, "I thought you intended to leave her here until spring!"

"Changed my mind."

"When do you want her?"

"To-day—this afternoon."

"I'm dreadfully sorry, but that's impossible."

"To-morrow, then. I'm starting on a tour of the South Seas at once."

"But, Mr. Killigrew, she's in dry dock, and her stern plates are off. They were buckled, you remember, by that iceberg near Spitsbergen last fall. And the engines are fouled too. They are apart, and we have ordered a new crankshaft for the starboard turbine."

"Don't go into details. When can I get her?"

The boatman was evidently distressed. He could not remember having known Mr. Killigrew in this unreasonable frame of mind ever before. "Really," he pleaded, "it will take a bit of time."

"How much? Quick! Tell me—day after to-morrow?"

"I'm afraid, Mr. Killigrew, the Tumbleweed could not be ready to sail for a fortnight, at the best, and if we could have fully three weeks—why, sir—pardon me, I must say this is sudden!"

The phone had been hung up on him.

Killigrew called to his head clerk. "Look up Atlantic liners," he said sharply, "and make a reservation on the first one that lifts anchor out of this port. I don't care where she is bound for. Only it must be the other side."

"Yes, Mr. Killigrew. At once, sir."

"And reserve a cabin for me—a suite. Be sure it has its own private dining saloon and a private entrance to the officers' deck. Examine the plans yourself. Be sure the suite is situated so I can avoid all passengers. Make no mistake about that."

"Yes, Mr. Killigrew. Thank you, sir."

Every head in the office bent over its task. All felt the tensity, the extreme and unusual tensity in the atmosphere.

"And don't tell any one I'm sailing," the master fired across the room at the clerk, who was already lifting the telephone receiver. "Keep it out of the press. Book me as Peter Jones."

"I understand, sir."

Peter walked to the outer door and looked up the side-walk. There were the usual hurrying few passers-by of an ordinary morning on a side street near Fifth Avenue. But his secretary was not visible.

Peter came back, flexing his fingers, pulling the lobe of his ear, scowling. One clerk had whispered to another that he looked like the devil. So he did, as if he had not slept well. The corners of his mouth sagged.

"What's the matter with Mac?" he demanded.

Having addressed no one in particular no one answered. All bent soberly and industriously, appearing not to notice his mood.

"Answer me, some one. When is Mac due?"

The nearest clerk, the head bookkeeper, a man of middle years, employed in the Killigrew offices since he was a boy, replied, "He comes in about ten, always, Mr. Killigrew."

The clock indicated nine forty-five.

Peter looked at the clerk as if he would like to anni-hilate him, but said nothing. Every one eagerly awaited Mac's arrival. He had been coming in an hour later than the rest of them for too long a time. They hoped he would be brought up standing.

Peter walked around the large desk from his side to Mac's, and stood looking down at the little pile of mail before Mac's place, letters addressed to him personally. He thought he recognized the handwriting on the top letter. He turned it over. On the reverse flap was printed: "The Lodge, Farview Road, corner White Plains Road, West-chester County, New York."

From Scroggins, of course. Must be estate business—the

superintendent of the Towers writing to his secretary. He
turned away and walked to the window and looked out on
the lone grass plot, brown on top, with dull green indis-
tinct below. The snow had melted, except for one little ridge
along the north wall, where the sun never hit.

The view changed, and his mind's eye saw white mountains and evergreens laden with clinging white draperies,
and a long toboggan slide! And an oval, girlish face with
blue eyes and reddish hair. Not red hair, though. There was
blue in it, or mauve. No, dash it—that was her eyes!

He went back to Mac's side of the desk with a savage
exclamation, picked up the top letter absent-mindedly, and
slit it open with a paper cutter.

Inside was a letter from Scroggins, and an inclosure.
The letter said:

Dear Mac:

I inclose the weekly report from the dairy.

See how the Holsteins are picking up. It's old-fashioned
bran mash. I knew they would.

And, say, Mac, you gave me a surprise yesterday phoning
in to know about Imogen. I was rather pleased to think Mr.
Killigrew might want to know about her, because I have
always felt his disapproval of her being here. And, Mac, she's
a mighty nice girl. My wife and I like her very much, and
we're so used to her now we'd not know what to do if she
left us. I only let her go up there to Lake Placid because she
had her heart set on it, and I love her as though she were my
own daughter.

Now I want you to know what a simple little girl she is,
Mac, because the time might come for you to put in a good

word for her, and if I ever had to let her leave the estate it would just about break my heart, and my wife's, too.

So I send you herewith, confidentially, you know, the letter we got from her yesterday. It's just like her—a regular wildflower, I call her. Different from most girls nowadays.

Of course I suppose Mr. Killigrew won't want to know more about her, but if he does and you think it proper and fitting, you can let him see this letter.

Yours very truly,

I. Scroggins, Superintendent.

Peter placed the letter back with its inclosure into the envelope, and left them on Mac's side of the desk. Then he walked to the window again and looked out.

The dirty ridge of nearly melted snow was still there: the skyscrapers were towering above them: and the clerks in the room were working hard, heads bent over their desks.

He looked at his watch. Still five minutes to ten, only. He sat at his own side, and then boldly reached over for Mac's mail, and made a point of opening it all, looking about to see if he was observed. Apparently no one paid any attention.

He drew forth the inclosure from Scroggins's letter, and read in sprawling, unformed, girlish chirography:

Dear Uncle Isaiah:

I am so happy here. The snow is everywhere, not like it is at Far View, melted off in spots like a poor horse with the mange and his hair falling out. The coat of snow on the mountains is rich and without a hole, like that fur coat you wanted to buy me and I wouldn't let you get.

Miss Petrie is a darling, goes with me everywhere, and we have lots of fun. The skates you bought fit so well, and I hired a pair of skis, and the tobogganing is thrilling—you fall and fall, just scared half to death, and then wake up and want to do it all over again.

I am so glad I came, and I haven't met anybody except a young man the manager introduced to me, a Mr. Jones. He picked me up when I fell coming down a slide on my skis. Mr. Jones, I mean. He is very nice and shy, and I only saw him that once. I only tell you about him because I promised to write about everybody I meet, and he is the only one so far.

Lots of love and kisses to Aunt Maria and you—and a great big extra hug for you.

Lovingly,

Imogen.

P.S.—Miss Petrie says Mr. Jones has a common name, but I rather like him just the same. I wonder if it is on account of his name, for I'm afraid I really like common people best.

A step sounded in the entryway. Peter glanced up. Mac was coming in, brisk and efficient, on the minute of his accustomed time; for the hands of the clock pointed just to ten.

Peter thrust the letter back in its envelope and quickly slipped it into the middle of the pack.

Scratching pens ceased. No one moved. The entire force was in suspended animation to listen to the expected blowing up of the chronically late secretary.

"Good morning, McKenna," said Peter absent-mindedly. "I got in a bit early. Opened your mail to kill time There!" He tossed it over.

A sigh of disappointment spread over the office. Was that all Mac would get? Then he could go on getting down at ten, when they had to get down at nine? Huh! Some people have all the luck.

Mac began the day's business briskly, delving into the details of stocks and bonds and real estate. Casually, in the midst of it, he remarked:

"I suppose you saw this letter from Scroggins?"

"Yes. File it."

"Shall I say anything to him?"

Peter tried to be casual about it, but feared he blushed. Finally he ordered curtly:

"Tell him to forward any other letters he gets from that girl—at once!" He thought he noted a sly smile on Mac's lips, so he added hastily: "She's an odd character. If Scroggins's reports continue favorable, we may want to do more for her."

"Yes, sir."

The head clerk came over. "I have engaged the Presidential suite on the Leviathan, Mr. Killigrew," he reported, "sailing to-morrow for Southampton. It has three rooms, bedroom, private dining room, reception room, and bath. There is a private staircase to the hurricane deck, and a private rail down that to the bridge. You may be quite protected from the public, sir."

"Very good."

"The head steward requests information as to the number in your party."

"Only myself—and my valet."

For the next three hours Peter plunged into work. He had been off on a few days' vacation, and he was planning to take another for an indeterminate stay, and he charged Mac to think of everything that might come up while he was away.

The office was accustomed to these erratic movements of the youthful master of millions. To all practical intent McKenna, for a large share of the time, was the head of the estate. Yet they never could tell when Mr. Killigrew would descend on them and demand a strict accounting.

This seemed to be one of these occasions. He studied every item with exacting questions. One after another he had each clerk on the carpet, quizzing him, probing his methods and his accounts with the severe cross-examination of a prosecuting attorney. Peter seemed driven by some devastating force bent on finding trouble. An exact and cautious man, in these respects being advanced far beyond his years, he seemed now on the track of some devious and baffling fraud.

Mac was puzzled, but met the quiet, steely questions with engaging frankness, feeling he had nothing to conceal. But he was grateful for the arrival of one o'clock. He did not want to appear as if he liked to get away, even for the customary noonday respite, and he welcomed Peter's comment that it was time for him to go. The head clerk usually stayed in between one and one thirty, when the chief bookkeeper, who went at twelve thirty, came back. Thus there was always some one in.

This day Peter said to the head clerk as soon as Mac and the others had gone: "You can go to lunch now."

Without comment the head clerk went. That left the Killigrew offices in the sole possession of their proprietor.

The moment he was alone Peter went to the file and

got out the letter from Scroggins, extracting from it the scrawled epistle from the Lake Placid Hotel. Then he sat down in comfort, alone, his back to the door, and read and reread it.

He chuckled and smiled now, for the first time that day. "A common name!" he softly repeated. "I'm afraid I really like common people best."

He must have had plenty of time to memorize it fully, for he did nothing else than look at it from one to one thirty, when the chief bookkeeper came back. Then he thrust it into his pocket guiltily.

A few minutes later he left the offices with word to Mac to call him at his club. He felt indignant at himself that he should be in the position of sneaking into his own files, and of indulging in intrigue to deceive his own clerks—about a trifling letter from a shabby little penniless orphan.

Imogen's letter remained in his pocket. He found it there as he was eating his lunch alone, and seemed pleased. He read it again.

He did not go back that afternoon to his offices. Instead, he played billiards in the club rooms until late, and then went for a sparring lesson to the athletic club. He felt physically keen. Perhaps the air in the woods had been good for him.

The next morning he was in the office again before any one—at eight forty. Mac came early too, but not before Peter had gone through all his mail. There was nothing from Scroggins.

He came back from lunch rather promptly, to see the two o'clock mail. He asked Mac when the other mails came in. There were four more—up until 5:37 P.M. He mumbled something about looking for a government report on oceanography.

At three, the head clerk reported that the suite on the Leviathan was ready for him to go aboard and occupy at any time after five in the afternoon. The ship would weigh anchor at midnight.

"Thanks," said Peter, glumly.

The offices closed usually at five. The clerks that night saw Peter at his desk for the first time in their experience when they were leaving for the night. Mac said he would stay. Peter told him to go, and meet him at his club in two hours.

At five forty-one—a few minutes late—the postman came in with the last mail of the day. He handed Peter a half dozen letters, with the remark: "It's a rare thing to see you here this time of day, Mr. Killigrew!"

Peter could hardly wait for him to leave, for he had seen in the batch of letters one with Scroggins's handwriting. He went to his desk, striving to be casual, but, missing the cutter, tore open the envelope with his finger.

Yes. An inclosure, a fat one. He devoured it.

It said, pathetically, it seemed:

DEAR UNCLE ISAIAH:

Miss Petrie and I have decided to come back the end of this week. It is nice here, but I think it is nicer at the Lodge.

I told you I would tell you everything about any one I met, and so I must tell you about that Mr. Jones. It is awfully queer. I don't seem to have any luck with me. First there was Mr. Jennifer, and now there is Mr. Jones.

I don't mean to compare them, please don't think that,

Uncle Isaiah, because Mr. Jones has a good, firm chin, and I like him very, very much; only he just evaporated like a snowball in the sun, only quicker—more like a duck dropping into a lake in the summer.

I can't understand it at all. You see, we went skating together and then tobogganing. Oh, yes! And we had luncheon on the top of the veranda, where it's all glassed in.

And we had such a good time. He seemed just like a member of the family. Somehow I thought of him as if he might be a son or yours—he was so thoughtful and really nice. You do know what I mean, don't you?

He quoted poetry—dear poetry—but somehow I can't recall the lines—something about a king and a girl who loved him. It wasn't Tennyson, but it sounded like Tennyson. We seemed to be such good friends, and I was just beginning to wonder if I couldn't tell him all about you and Aunt Maria, and maybe ask him to come and call on us.

We were coming to the hotel, and he asked me about riding in an airplane, and I started to tell him about that awful ride—you know, in the one with boats on—when, suddenly, with hardly a word, he turned and left me, and never came back.

I asked Miss Petrie to find out about him, and where he lived; but she said nobody would tell her, and that when she asked a bellboy he laughed and said everybody knew Mr. Jones was not his name. Miss Petrie says she felt sure he was a criminal, but that seems so foolish to me.

Why, Uncle Isaiah, a criminal wouldn't know poetry, would he, and be so *nice?* You have no idea how *nice* he was! Of course I'll never see him again, but it does make me wonder why he ran away that way.

There must be some bad luck about me. So I am coming back in two days. Lots of love and kisses to Aunt Maria, and a great, big hug for you.

Lovingly,

Imogen.

P.S.—I am telling you all about this because I want you to know I didn't really care anything about Mr. Jones, only the queer way he acted made me wonder so much.

Love,

Im.

Peter looked into the January gloom for a few minutes. Then he did some telephoning on his own hook.

At the club at seven Mac came to him. "Your valet," he said, "has all your things on the pier waiting for you."

"Not going," said Peter.

"But Ahrnen paid for the suite; had to buy it away from the Duchess of Nottingshire and her retinue."

"Find the duchess, and tell her she can have it—with my compliments!"

"She may have other plans—"

"Make her a present of it. I'm not going on the Leviathan!"

"Oh!" said Mac. He was not in the habit of asking questions; so he waited for further orders. They came promptly:

"Send my valet to Grand Central," said Peter. "I've changed my mind, and am traveling inland."

That night he occupied a drawing room on the Adirondack Express.

28

NIRVANA

PETER KILLIGREW WAS certainly a lonely soul. He got what he wanted when he wanted it—nearly always. He wanted to be alone—nearly always. That was what he arranged for in reserving the drawing room on the Adirondack Express, just as he had expected to get it when he took the Presidential suite on the Leviathan.

And then when he had what he wanted, he found that was not what he wanted at all. After the train left the Grand Central he sat for some time and watched the ice in the Hudson and the cliffs of the Palisades beyond. It was too early to go to bed. He was afraid he would not sleep anyway.

So he left the seclusion of his drawing room with its mahogany and green velours, and went out into the public smoking room, and sat down moodily in the corner, and looked out. Two drummers were smoking and swapping yarns.

One was saying: "They're all alike. I told her so."

"And what did she say?" queried his companion.

The first drummer leaned closer, and whispered something. Both went into gales of laughter. Without looking at them again, Peter got up and walked out into the sleeping car.

That was worse than loneliness.

The porter was making up the berths. In the first was a woman with a baby, nursing on a bottle. Ordinarily, Peter disliked babies in public, especially little ones, too squally, too messy. And he pitied mothers; such a lot of sordid details to absorb their time. Necessary, maybe, but—

He walked slowly past this mother and her infant, waiting across the aisle while their berth was made ready. The baby looked up into his face and must have noted the scowl of sympathy, or something, for he reached forth and seized one of the buttons on Peter's coat, and started to climb right over the seat.

The mother saw the child's maneuver, and quickly brought it back to her arms, apologizing to Peter. He was forced to accept the apology. As he did so he was overwhelmed with the look on the mother's face! Serenity! Utter content! So far from being annoyed by the baby she was completely immersed in thought for it—and radiant with a strange joy!

Peter got a look at his own face in the mirror of the next compartment. Hollow eyes! Lantern jaw! Lines in his forehead! Bah! A miserable face!

He passed several middle-aged couples, matter-of-fact, easy-going, making themselves comfortable. And then, in the end seat, he came upon a sight that sent an odd wince of pain through him.

A young man about twenty-five and a girl a bit younger holding hands, slipped down in the seat, look-

ing at each other, vacantly. What was that vacuity in their
countenances—ecstasy?

His foot ground on a hard substance in the aisle near by.
He looked down—grains of rice. Then he saw rice in the
girl's hair, and in the coat collar of the young man. And out
of the young man's coat pocket hung an old shoe, tipsily,
while above them, from the rack, hung a cheap suit case,
labeled: "Newlyweds—don't disturb!"

He went back to his drawing room, and closed the door.
There was no place for him out there. He had to be alone
with his thoughts. They were not entirely pleasing.

He had canceled the suite on the Leviathan—unnecessary expense, a violation of the Killigrew principles of
thrift; for the Killigrew fortune was not one of those new
fortunes made overnight in which waste in accommo-
dating the pleasure or convenience of chief executives is
looked upon as legitimate expense. Any wasting of any
Killigrew dollar was always looked upon as a species of
crime.

That, however, did not cause him such anguish as it did
to face the fact, as he must, that he was retracing his steps
to Lake Placid for the distinct purpose of placing himself
again in the atmosphere of temptation.

To subject himself to the spell of a girl! And such a girl!
A nobody! A penniless orphan! The foster child of one of
his own employees!

His father would have been terribly shocked. His grandfather would turn in his grave. His great grandfather would
have disowned him!

Peter Killigrew had been well trained. He was the product of the careful, shrewd, laborious discipline of seven generations of level-headed, clear-thinking ancestors.

They had endowed him with a will like steel, a character proof against most of the blandishments of the world, a shrewd instinct to guard against most of the world's ingenuities. And they had presented him with a complex money machine of many millions.

He was a fit driver for a fit machine.

Only an accident, a misfortune had left him unprotected—the death of Ann Hilary, shortly after that of his father. His father had approved of Ann for his wife, and it was Peter's nature to accept everything his father approved.

But Ann was dead. His father was dead. He was alone—and vulnerable.

This, and much else, ran through his brain to the tune of the grinding wheels on the Adirondack Express.

The much else had to do with red hair and blue eyes. Of course, it was inconceivable that he should take this little outcast seriously. There was a trick in it, surely; some weakness of his mood, or some witchery of the girl; some wickedness of a designing little adventuress luring him on.

The best way to settle it was to expose her—in his own eyes. Lay bare her charms. See enough of her to become positive that she was indeed only a trifling adventuress, a wicked little schemer, willing to grab a scamp like Darcy Jennifer one moment, or flirt with a commonplace idler like Peter Jones the next.

Or did she really know who he was?

The latter thought pleased him. It made him feel he had good reason for going back to Lake Placid. He was going to prove that she was scheming all the while, that she knew he was Peter Killigrew masquerading as one Jones, and pretending innocence for the sake of more effectually charming him.

Let him only prove that and he would be content. He could be through with her, and go on his way and forget her—and keep away from all women thereafter!

On this casuistry he slept—fairly well.

He detrained at Placid in the early morning.

It was very early, barely six o'clock. Too late to go to bed again, not late enough for any of the habitues of the hotel to be about. They breakfasted between eight and nine, and some as late as ten.

A girl like Imogen, of course, he thought, would be apt to sleep late, and be around about ten. What could he do with four hours?

A hike up a seven-mile peak seemed a good way to stretch his legs, and fill in the time. He started out briskly, about six thirty.

A mile from the hotel, he saw a tiny figure in white woolens, with a thin band of Alice blue, trudging ahead.

He hastened along. She stopped to rest, and he overtook her.

"Miss Nelson," he said, "you are up early. It's not seven o'clock."

Daylight was barely in the sky.

"I couldn't sleep very well," she replied casually, listlessly. Not especially glad to see him, he thought.

This annoyed him, though if she had been glad he would have attributed it to the "design" of a "schemer."

Evidently she was going to say no more, for she shortly began trudging along up the path. He felt obliged to go on with her. How would he begin the conversation? Certainly not by apologizing for his behavior in leaving her so abruptly two days before. He felt justified in that—thoroughly justified.

They went on in silence for a mile or more. The sun began to show above the far rims of the mountains by this time, a red sun, without any halation, a little pink above, but mostly a round red sun—honest, direct. A fair day.

She did not stop again until she reached the halfway house, a little rustic shed in a clearing on a plateau jutting out over the long valley. From it one could look down onto the great toboggan slide, deserted now, waiting for another day and its stimulating sports.

She stood looking down the mountain, while he looked at her. He felt indignant at her, such a wee wisp of a nonentity to force him to cancel a trip to Europe and come back to this bleak mountain! And then to snub him!

He longed to make her smart for it!

But what could he say? What could he do? He was not even sure yet that she knew who he was.

"I haven't seen you for two days," he remarked. It annoyed him more to think that he was speaking first.

"Yes, I missed you." She said it simply, as if stating an obvious fact. Nothing yet to put his finger on.

"Had to go back to town—sudden business call." He owed her no explanation, he felt, yet here he was making one.

And she did not even appreciate that he was almost humbling himself. "I see!" she replied casually.

She expressed no further interest in him directly. She did not even ignore him so that he could persist in bringing a personal expression into play. Instead she said, "I'll think I'll go back now. Miss Petrie will be up."

The name "Miss Petrie" annoyed him still more.

"Haven't you had your breakfast?" he asked.

"Only a cup of coffee. I'll have breakfast with Miss Petrie about eight."

"Why not with me?"

There he was pursuing her again, pleading with her. He felt terribly self-conscious, as if she had put something over on him. She looked down abruptly, and he felt his heart bound a trifle, as if he had made a gain. "Why, I don't know!" He thought he saw she was trembling. "If—if you want to—"

"Of course I—"

"Join us."

He gritted his teeth. "Us?" She meant Miss Petrie, too.

"Can't we breakfast alone—on the gundeck?" he persisted.

"I'm afraid Miss Petrie wouldn't like it," Imogen slowly objected.

"She won't mind. Please."

Then, while she still hung back, a resolution he had made—the resolution not to apologize—suddenly became as water, and he impulsively exclaimed, "I acted awfully rude the other day—running off as I did. Won't you please forgive me?"

The blushes mantled up over her neck and cheeks so prettily. He could see plainly now, for the sun was above the horizon. Her long lashes dropped over her blue eyes.

Then she looked at him fully and frankly and held out her hand, saying, "Of course."

And he took the hand and held it for minutes, while neither of them said a word.

Then he felt the altitude again—as if they were up in a great height. And all of his worry and sleeplessness and everything disappeared. Caution and doubt and hesitancy left him.

He thought of the look on the mother's face the night before in the sleeping car, and of the young man and the girl on the front seat, and the chalked sign on the cheap suit case—"Newlyweds—don't disturb."

And as they started down the mountain side—hand in hand, a fact of which both seemed unconscious—he was saying silently to himself, "As pure as this snow, and as guileless as a pine cone!"

A little farther he was saying—still silently, for neither had spoken again, "If this is love let me never wake up!"

And then he began to worry, and to plan how he would prevent her from knowing he was Peter Killigrew.

But how could he prevent that?

Of course he could prevent it. This was only a lark—a wintry interlude. Presently he would be back in town again, in his office or at the opera, or sailing for the South Seas on the Tumbleweed.

Look out! He must not be a ninny and fall to the level of that country clerk, oblivious of the old shoe, and the chalked luggage, and dripping telltale rice.

Yet Nirvana beckoned! Oh, Nirvana!

29

THRILLS AND DOUBTS

PETER HAD A dog, a collie named Nelle, the only creature whom he believed loved him for himself alone. He was devoted to Nelle. Whenever he could he took her on his trips, except by sea. He had tried once to take her on the Tumbleweed, but she became seasick. He feared she might die if kept on board; so, two days out, he put back from a long cruise, just to get her safely ashore, where she would be more comfortable.

Nelle never questioned anything he did, never took offense at anything he did, never showed her teeth to him, and never asked for favors. If he was in bad humor and spoke to her crossly she showed no resentment, and when he spoke to her again kindly she was instantly as grateful as if he had been continuously affectionate.

A perfect companion, the accordion of his moods.

He kept thinking of Nelle as he sat at breakfast with Imogen. Nelle was the only living thing he felt would be the same to him if he were poor.

And there was an unaccountable, an eerie luxury in thinking that this slip of a girl—this nonentity, as he persisted in regarding her—had no thought of his money, did not look upon him as Peter Killigrew, master of millions.

It was a new experience, as fresh to him as the taste of a potato to an Eskimo.

At first he had resented the fact that she had not fawned on him when he reappeared; but her quiet dignity, her unspoken rebuff, now seemed quite appropriate, and convinced him that she had no idea of his identity.

A heavenly human being, of course, yet absolutely sincere. Something to think about there. Especially when he had never known any one like that before—not any one with red hair and blue eyes, and a soft, purry voice, and hands softer than velvet.

He began to tell her about Nelle, how Nelle would lie at his feet while he read, with her head across his instep; how Nelle liked to climb on his desk, but only if there were no papers to disturb; how she never interfered with his work or his eating, but only rejoiced in being near him.

"She must be a great comfort," said Imogen. "I like dogs."

"You have one, I suppose."

She shook her head. "Not now; he died."

"Then you did have one?"

"Yes."

"When was that?"

"Years ago, when I was a little girl. He came running into the garden one day when I was working on the Japanese iris. He had no muzzle on nor a collar, and the dog catchers were out. He seemed to know it."

"Ah! A stray?"

"He didn't belong to anybody near where we lived. So I kept him in the garden and fed him, and the dog catchers didn't get him, and after that he never left me—until he died."

"What breed?" Peter asked.

"I don't know. Just a dog."

"Mongrel, I suppose."

"No. A wonderful dog. Brown and black and white, with straight hair, and big brown eyes."

"You don't know what kind?"

"Father called him a mutt, but he was just like the description of your Nelle—the finest companion. Once he bit a tramp that came to the door and tried to push his way in when I was alone. You should have seen the tramp run."

Peter felt a bit miffed to have his thoroughbred Nelle, four times winner of championships in dog shows compared to a stray "mutt;" but he did not voice this resentment.

He was feeling indulgent now toward Imogen. Proximity to her, close observation had dissipated any previous thought that she was a "siren" or an "adventuress." She was too transparently naive for that.

He came into quite a glow of self-satisfaction. His infatuation, or whatever it was, was wearing off. She was such a simple little creature she could hardly lure a man. He was enjoying his adventure incognito, now that he felt sure there was no danger in it. No reason why he should ever let her know who he was.

"When your dog died," he went on, "why didn't your father get you another?"

"No other dog happened along."

"Why didn't he buy you one—when you were so fond of dogs?"

Imogen laughed. "Father," she said, "spent money only on plants and seeds."

"Ah! Rather strict, eh?"

She flashed instant denial. "The most generous man that ever lived," she asserted. "He gave me everything in the world."

He barely restrained a smile at this. Here would come the amusing part—he would lead her on to embroider with lies a fictional account of her destitute father, the Patrick Henry Nelson who had willed him a worthless estate.

"Very indulgent, was he? Everything you wanted? How fine!"

"Yes!" she sighed. "I lacked for nothing."

"Sent you to Europe, I suppose, and boarding school, and bought you plenty of pretty dresses."

"Oh, no! Not Europe, and not so many dresses. You see, I didn't want that, but—"she seemed abashed—"he did send me to boarding school—for awhile—until I got tired of it."

No direct lie there. He must lead her into one. "If he got you everything you wanted, what was it?" Peter boldly asked.

"He was with me—always," she replied simply, "and read to me, and taught me, and I was never lonely. He had a rare mind; he knew everything, and he was very wise. He taught me all about plants and flowers and nature, and books, too. I always felt I was richer than any one else.

"Every one else knew so little, and such petty things; and he knew so much, and told it all to me. My father was a great man. If he had ever cared to go in for politics or anything like that he would have been as famous as Abraham Lincoln, I am sure. He was just that kind of man—

just like Lincoln, kind and wise and true. But he gave his whole life to me, while Abraham Lincoln had to spread his over a nation, and that is what made me so much richer than any one else."

"I see!" Peter felt a lump in his throat.

He could not fail to think of Peter Killigrew IV, although he loved his son, absorbed in the estate and his money, forever going from one board meeting to another, seldom talking of anything but to give directions to servants; turning over his son to tutors and governesses; talking to him chiefly about methods of conserving the estate, dwelling always on one thought—not to dissipate the accumulations of his forefathers.

Suddenly Peter became prey to a strange, unaccountable jealousy. A species of psychic sneer passed across his mind. He felt he must de-rate this obscure deceased flower hunter who occupied so high a place in the esteem of his chance companion.

"What did he do for a living?" Peter asked rather brusquely.

Imogen's head went up. "He ran the factory!" she asserted with a sort of defiance as if daring any one to deny it.

"Ah! He owned a factory!" Here would be the lie! Peter would be gratified at last.

"No. He didn't own it, but he knew more about it than the owner; and without him it would have failed long before it did."

"Ah! It failed?"

"Because women bobbed their hair so much. You see, it was a hairpin factory."

"And your father managed it! How interesting!"

"Well—no, he didn't manage it. Mr. Mullins did that. He was the owner."

"But how did your father run it if he wasn't the manager?"

Imogen was a trifle vexed for the first time. "Why, he told Mr. Mullins what to do, and kept track of everything for him. Don't you see?"

"But what was his position in the hairpin factory?"

"Mr. Mullins called him the bookkeeper, and he did keep the books; but that was just a sort of way of entering him on the pay roll."

"Oh! The bookkeeper!"

"But he was much more than that," Imogen exclaimed. "He did all the ordering, and all the selling, everything. Sometimes Mr. Mullins stayed away for days, even weeks at a time, and my father kept things going just as if he owned the factory. He was a wonderful man. He knew everything. He could have managed the village just as well, or the county, or even the State. He used to tell me how they ought to be run, and his ideas were so sensible. Always right!"

"Did he ever hold political office?"

Imogen seemed shocked. "No! No! He would never stoop to that. Politics has such a low type of men, men so filled with hypocrisy, and false statements, and promises they never keep or intend to keep. No. My father never believed in politics."

"Nor did my father," said Peter.

"Then he must have been a wise man, like my father," Imogen averred with a prim little set of her mouth.

Peter was wobbling from one feeling to another. This amusing, ignorant, bombastic, absurd, adorable little girl

was thinking too fast for him. If it were not for that inde-
finable alchemy of her curious personality he would have
no time for her. As it was she was opening new vistas of
thought for him.

However, he did feel indulgent toward her when she
idealized her father. He had always felt that his father was
the greatest man in the world. But he did not want to talk
about him, the eminent Peter Killigrew IV, sound link in
the chain of one of the preeminent American fortunes—
not to this daughter of a village bookkeeper in a tiny bankrupt factory.

Imogen, however, felt she had a sympathetic audience.
She had never before been able to talk about her father very
much, except to Mr. Perkins, and he was skeptical about
Pat Nelson—"envious and jealous of superior ability."

She was voluble, especially after the second pot of coffee,
and the maple syrup on the rice cakes, as they sat back
in lolling chairs, alone on the gundeck, and watched the
morning crowd assembled on the terrace below.

"Did your father care for flowers like my father?" she
asked.

"Yes. Very much." Peter refrained from mentioning the
rack of cups and medals and decorations in the billiard
room on Fifth Avenue taken from horticultural shows by
the Killigrew exhibits.

"Then he must have been a good man. My father said
only good men really cared for flowers. I mean for themselves, not for show. Wicked men, he said, cultivated them
to show off; but good men loved to see them grow and to
bring them up with their own hands.

"I often heard my father say: 'There's old Peter Killigrew

with a regiment of gardeners, and he never knew how to transplant a marshmallow till I showed him.' That was the Mr. Killigrew who died a few years ago."

Peter could have no thought, after this, that Imogen knew his identity. She was not actress enough to look at him blandly as she did when she so casually said that.

"Then your father knew m—" Peter checked himself in time—"knew Mr. Killigrew?" he asked.

"Yes, indeed. He knew everybody, like he knew everything."

Out of the past Peter was recalling what Scroggins had tried to make him hear, the story of the episode of the meeting of the flower hunter on the road near Dobbs's Corners the June afternoon many years before. When Scroggins had told him he had paid little heed, but now there was a sharp click on the plates of his memory.

Peter remembered the old horse-driven brougham, Scroggins driving, young Peter—himself—with his father behind; the old man seen indistinctly across the meadow in some swampy ground; the stopping of the carriage, the calling to the old man; his coming forward, bearing a baby, and a tangled mass of wild flowers; the leaving of the baby while he returned to dig some roots; his—Peter's—climbing down to the grass to play with the baby; he was about eleven then, eight or nine years older than the little girl; the return of the old man with the roots done up in gunny sacking; the offer of payment; its refusal; the return to the brougham; the farewell; the kiss.

It came back to him as if it had happened yesterday. And this was that baby girl—the golden hair red, the soft angelic mouth dropping nonsense and sunbeams.

"What did your father think of Mr. Killigrew?" he asked very gently.

"He felt sorry for him," Imogen replied.

Peter's mouth fell open. "Really!" he stammered. "W-why?"

"Because he had so many gardeners, and knew so little about flowers."

"But—but," Peter expostulated—"it seems to me I remember about reading that Mr. Killigrew often took prizes at flower shows."

"That's nothing!" Imogen airily waved aside the suggestion. "My father said his gardeners took the prizes. Father said lots of people owned flowers and never possessed them. The only way to possess them was to prepare the ground yourself, and plant them yourself, and water and weed them yourself, and pick them yourself. If a gardener brings a flower to you from the garden, or you buy it in a shop it doesn't belong to you. It belongs to the man who grew it. He may sell it, but he never parts with it."

Peter blinked. "But if he takes the money for it," he objected.

"Oh! Money doesn't mean anything!" Imogen airily went on.

"No?" Peter observed, patronizingly.

"No. Father told me that, and I know it's true. Rich people own houses for servants to live in, and they belong to the servants. They own automobiles for chauffeurs to drive, and they have so many, and they can never use more than one at a time, that the others belong to the servants. They own buildings, and the people who live in them and pay rent really have them, while the rich people have nothing but responsibility."

"True!" Peter agreed, sympathetically.

Encouraged, Imogen rattled on: "My father felt sorry for all rich men. I mean men with money; for he was very rich himself, as I told you, in things that don't harm one."

Peter was not quite so sympathetic now, but he managed to ask: "What did he mean by that?"

"He said a rich man never had a friend. Everybody tried to get his money: never could trust a servant; always had to set one to watch another. No relative ever loved him except for what money they hoped to get from him. Never had time for his children, because he had to make more money or keep what he had. Never could be sure of what his own wife thought about him, because he would always have the haunting fear she married him for his money."

A long sigh escaped from Peter. "How did your father know so much about—about rich men?" he asked.

"I told you he knew everybody and everything."

"I see!"

Peter looked out dully over the lake where the hockey players were assembling for the morning practice. He felt the lines deepen in his countenance, and that baffling weariness so much with him began to settle down again, and to rob this rare morning of its buoyancy.

He thought of a line he had often heard, without understanding what it meant, "Out of the mouths of babes."

This girl, prattling of her absurd father, had uttered truths which struck home to him as nothing had ever done before. He had heard things like that said from the pulpit and had read them in newspapers, but they never meant much before, except, perhaps, to describe other *rich* men, never himself.

Now he was hit, hit hard. He felt there might be a little grim satisfaction in rubbing salt in the wound. So he proceeded along a line that was more productive of salt than he had anticipated.

He turned on her rather abruptly, asking: "Have you ever known a rich man?"

"A man with money, you mean."

"Certainly—real riches." He could not let her get away with everything she had said.

"Not very well," she admitted.

"Well, don't you think your father may have been drawing on his imagination, perhaps?"

"Not in the least. I know he wasn't!" she asserted, with a show of spirit.

"Why are you so sure?"

"Because I came in contact with a rich man not long ago. I didn't see him, and he didn't see me; but I overheard him, by accident, and I don't think he has one drop of human feeling in his whole body. He is all eaten up with suspicion; without any real reason for being suspicious, but just on general principles. He doesn't know a thing about life, or human beings, or love, or anything in the world except money—and maybe not that, for he inherited it. If it was not for some kind servants he employs he would be a cruel, detestable little cad!"

Her eyes were snapping, her head in the air.

"A young man, you say?" Peter persisted.

"I suppose so, I didn't see him, I don't ever want to see

him. In fact I know my father was right. I hope I never know a rich man. They must be dreadfully inhuman!"

There was quite a silence after this. Then Imogen became calmer. She turned on Peter impulsively: "Oh. Mr. Jones," she exclaimed, "why did you let me talk like this? I never did before to any one, and I am so happy and have so much to be grateful for I don't want to ever speak ill of any one. And perhaps I was mistaken, too; perhaps I didn't understand the other side of—his side. My father always told me not to make hasty judgments, and that if I waited to understand all I would never condemn anybody."

"But you were right," Peter insisted. "I feel sure you must have been right."

"Well, let's not talk about it any more. Luckily you're just Mr. Jones, and not rich. So we can have a good time, can't we?"

He did not trust himself to speech. He merely nodded his head.

It was mid forenoon by this time. They were made aware of the fact by a precise voice which broke in upon them. It was Miss Petrie. She was much disturbed. Where had Imogen been? Not down to breakfast in the dining room?

Up with Mr. Jones on the gundeck all this time? Why didn't they go out in the snow and have some fun with the others?

To get rid of Miss Petrie they did go out, with their skates, to the hockey rink. They skated until lunch time without a further word about rich men or poor men.

Peter felt well again. This was a splendid vacation. Never had such a good one before. Why had he never thought of

Placid? A bully place, better than anything in Europe; he ought to build a camp up here and come regularly.

Before noon he had made up his mind what to do about Imogen. Of course he would keep out of her way after this little episode. Couldn't afford to see her again, naturally. She called Mrs. Scroggins "Aunt Maria." Ugh! And Scroggins "Uncle Isaiah." That must be his name. His initial was "I."

Nevertheless his personal investigation had satisfied him her case was quite exceptional. He would see to it that she was well provided for. Scroggins would have his orders. There would be no repetition of that curt dismissal of the case as an "appeal to charity." On the contrary, he would take real pleasure in seeing that she had everything money could buy.

In this pleasant frame of mind, whose source, of course, he did not communicate, and quite content with the world, they went to lunch. Peter even permitted Miss Petrie to join them, but he was glad to hear her say she did not like to ski.

So they went skiing after lunch, and upset, as at their first meeting, and recalled that as if it had been ages and ages ago. Were they not old established friends now?

At tea time Peter got a real blow, however. Imogen remarked, casually it seemed, that she was going home that night. He protested that it was utterly impossible. Having seen her letters to Scroggins he felt sure she could stay if she wanted to, but of course he could not reveal his source of information. But he did insist that she stay.

"Miss Petrie has the reservations. Got them yesterday," Imogen explained.

"Have them changed."

"Oh, no! They expect me. I'm going home."

"Who expects you?"

"My aunt and uncle."

"Wire them you are staying on another week."

"No. No. No. I can't. I told them I'm coming to-night. I have to go."

She was adamant. He couldn't understand it. How aggravating! The unreason of women—she wanted to stay; she could stay; and yet she wouldn't stay. And he could never see her again—of course not. For the next time she would surely find out his identity.

The train was to leave at eleven. He proposed they spend the last evening in night tobogganing. She readily agreed.

The slide was illuminated at regular intervals with huge kerosene lamps, and by flambeaux of oil-soaked rags.

It was a popular sport. Nearly every one at the hotel joined in. The scene under the great trees, with the far-set lamps and the intervening deep shadows, was enchanting—romantic!

Peter managed to get the front seat every time, and to put his arms well around her as they started off on the swift glide down the fairway, rendered more mysterious by the darkness.

She snuggled more closely up against his chest. No telling what might be beyond those lights—in the blackness. She felt very safe.

Finally it was almost time for her to go if she did not want to miss her train, and they prepared for the final slide. No embarrassment now about folding his long arms down over her shoulders, and holding her firmly with his huge fur-lined gloves.

This time they had a spill. Every one laughed and climbed uproariously out of a snowbank, and Imogen found herself standing with Peter brushing the flakes from her eyes and hair.

"Thank you!" she said; and the next thing she knew her mouth was closed and arms were all about her, and something was happening that swept her far out of herself—a long, long kiss!

She was not afraid, nor did she resist. She felt again as if the rarefied atmosphere had taken her away—far above the trees, beyond the clouds.

People were all about, too, but neither of them minded. After the kiss she lapsed back to the trail with a little sigh, and started for the hotel, he after her.

She stopped and faced him just before she got to the lights. She put out her hand, and he took it.

"I'm so sorry!" she said.

"Sorry for what?"

"That—that kiss!"

"I'm not!" He drew her close and kissed her again. This time she did not seem to give in so easily. "Why?" he demanded.

"Because—because I shouldn't kiss—people!"

"Oh! People?"

She shook her head violently.

"You are not used to it?" he added, his voice strangely harsh.

She shook her red curls.

"You kiss your aunt and uncle, don't you?" he asked.

"Y-yes."

"Who else?"

"Nobody."

"How about that young man you went up with in the airplane?"

Her eyes flashed as they had on the gundeck when castigating the rich young man. "Oh, him!" she rasped. "I detest him!"

"You never kissed him?"

"Certainly *not!*" He got the glint from her eyes.

His arms were about her; for he had drawn her into the shadows at one side of the hotel. "Tell me," he pleaded, "that you don't feel that way about me."

"You're nice," she admitted. "I know you aren't wrong inside-in your heart!"

For the first time in a long while, a tear came to his eyes.

"Then," he whispered softly, "kiss me once more—just once—good-by!"

She saw the tear. She lifted up her face for the kiss. He felt as he had when the baby tried to pull upon the button of his coat in the car the night before—only with infinitely more poignancy.

After the kiss he said: "Good-by, Imogen, I'm coming—" No. That wouldn't do. "You'll—you'll," he stammered, "you'll hear from me!"

And he rushed off, bewildered.

"Good-by—Peter!" she called, and was gone.

30

TROUBLE

PETER KILLIGREW DID not want to marry Imogen Nelson. None of the Killigrews had ever married beneath them, or outside of their class, except a great uncle, Horace Killigrew, who had become involved with a country school-teacher up in Dutchess County where one of the Killigrew farms was located in the last century.

And Uncle Horace had been a reproach in the family for three generations. He had been obliged to withdraw from all association with the Killigrews, his father—Peter's great grandfather—had cut him off with a meager allowance, and he had lived his life out to a very advanced age, over ninety, up there in Dutchess County.

Strange that Uncle Horace had been contented and had lived so long, but he was looked upon as the black sheep of the family.

Peter expected to marry in due course, but not until he was at least thirty-five, and then a woman of some old family and with established fortune. His father had chosen Ann Hilary and he had been satisfied with Ann; but Ann died, and his father died.

Now he had enough canny Killigrew instinct to believe he should not trust his own judgment until he was quite mature. A wife for the reigning Killigrew, and a mother for the next Killigrew generation must be chosen with a very particular care.

She must be of the most prescribed pattern, hedged in by restrictions of entailed estates as well as of established and unblemished family.

And Peter felt the responsibility of seven generations of Killigrews weighing upon him to make the proper choice in matrimony.

When he got back from Lake Placid—and those kisses under the stars—he felt content for a time, the time during which he considered and reconsidered what he could do for Imogen to establish her so that her future would be secured.

There were a number of things he could do, but, before he decided, and the very first day, he made a short codicil to his will, had it properly witnessed, and placed in the vault. In this codicil, he left a hundred thousand dollars to her in the form of a trust fund, to be administered by his bank.

He told nobody about this. It was only a form of insurance, if anything happened to him. Never before had he thought that he might not live to the customary advanced age of the Killigrews. But you never can tell!

See what happened at Lake Placid! Out of a clear sky!

A bit of stray wild pollen had drifted in an idle wind over the high hedges of the restricted property, and had fallen on the carefully cultivated bloom of the rare, expensive flower in the exclusive estate.

Annoying! Yes. But never mind. The stray wild pollen could be plucked out—as soon as the gardener found the exact spot where it fell.

That was about how Peter felt. He was in love, perhaps, but it would pass, and before he was married, some ten or fifteen years hence, he would have forgotten the adventure. It would have been absorbed in the cycle of romantic experience necessary to all young men, rich or poor.

Meanwhile, he would find the way to take care of Imogen, tactfully, of course, without offense to her; for she must never know that Peter Jones and Peter Killigrew were one and the same.

Probably he would do it through Scroggins. He could trust Scroggins. But he would have to go slow.

It was two weeks before he sent her a letter. It was no use to keep the thing up frantically. He had been indiscreet enough to kiss her. Better let the flame die gracefully.

However, he wrote a number of letters before he sent one. It was no harm to write if you don't send the letters. So he amused himself writing letters and tearing them up and putting them in the waste basket.

Peter faced a good many difficulties when it came to writing a letter. He didn't want any one to know he was writing her, and he didn't want her to connect him with Peter Jones.

He very seldom wrote a letter, his social correspondence being conducted in long hand by Miss Laffan and his business correspondence by typewriter through Mac's or his own dictation. He had never used a typewriter himself.

After two weeks of trying, he evolved a letter which he thought he would be discreet in sending. He need not be harshly judged for thinking of discretion in connection with Imogen. He no longer doubted her innocence or her goodness of heart, but a lifelong training, to say nothing of sad experience, had taught him that no rich man in America in his time could be really safe from the pursuit of the blackmailer and the breach of promise hound. No need to suspect Imogen, either, to recognize these perils. Some one might get the letters from her, or it was not impossible that with the passing of years even she, herself, might change.

The latter was a dreadful thought, to be sure, but it was characteristic of Peter's caution that he did think of it, and, as the lawyers say: "Without prejudice."

So he decided that the letter he should send—for he must send one, as he had promised she would hear from him—would have to be typewritten. To avoid letting any stenographer know what he was doing, he bought a typewriter and had it sent to his house, and set out to learn how to use it.

Slow work, but he accomplished it, with two fingers only, and several wrong keys struck. Finally, he had a single sheet, on which any one might read:

DEAR IMOGEN:

I am well, and hope you are the same. It was a fine vacation, and I am so glad I met you. I hope you will be a good girl, and wish you would write me and tell me all about yourself. With warm regards,

Very truly yours,

PETER JONES.

My address is Post Office Box 211, General Delivery, New York City.

Peter had never been accused of being able to express

himself in writing. The literary was not a Killigrew instinct. None of his ancestors had possessed it.

He went every day to the post office box, privately, of course, as none of his secretaries or clerks knew anything about his having one. To begin with he went twice daily. Then he grew ashamed of himself, and went only once each day.

The answer came a week later. It was:

Dear Peter:

I am glad I met you, too. I don't know how I can be any good-er, but I will try by going back to Dobbs's Corners in the spring. Maybe you can come there some time, and see my garden.

Yours truly,

Imogen Nelson.

This was annoying. It was all right for him to be restrained, but why should she be so? It was hard to get out of the feeling that all others must pursue and play up to a Killigrew.

However, he would prevent that by going to Dobbs's Corners. Plenty of time, though. It was only the end of February.

The day after the letter came, and before he could decide how to answer it, he attended the quarterly meeting of the Charity Amalgamation Board of whose management he was a member. While listening to the reading of a report he looked up and on the wall saw a sepia engraving of the painting: "King Cophetua and the Beggar Maid."

While the cut and dried references to cold statistics were

being glibly restated by the smug secretary he studied the king—the proud arch of his noble head, the kindly glance in his downcast eyes, the youthful happy tilt in his forward reaching hand.

And the beggar maid—her tattered smock, of which she was as oblivious as was the king smiling down upon her under his robe and crown. But that pristine glow of innocence and surging love on her gentle, oval face! "A face beautiful as the day!" That romantic uplift of her beaming eyes as she rose from her lowly station by the side of the road to advance to the beckoning finger of her liege lord, cast before him for sordid trial; then raised beside him as his consort!

Peter was cast into a brown study, which lasted until the meeting was over. He only came out of it as a minister was saying a benediction and then was roused only by the words:

> He hath cast down the mighty from their seats;
> He hath exalted those of low degree!

He went to his office, greatly perplexed. The misery was creeping back on him. It was time for the Tumbleweed to be out of dry dock. He would phone and see about it.

But when he got to the office old Nick Rainey was waiting for him.

"The last cretin's gone—pegged out this morning, Mr. Killigrew," he announced.

"Too bad," said Peter, though now he could take up that recent offer for his grandfather's residence; for the last of

Belle's blood was gone. Old Nick hung by his desk, plainly perplexed, smoothing his hat.

Finally he became bold enough to ask: "What'll become o' me an' the missus, Mr. Killigrew? For I suppose y'll be sellin' th' property one o' these fine days?"

"Don't let that worry you, Nick. I'll look after you and Mrs. Rainey. Stay on there. You'll have plenty of time to turn around, and I'll find you another place."

The old man was vastly relieved. He poured out his thanks volubly. Then, as he was about to go, he turned and exclaimed impulsively:

"Too bad, Mr. Killigrew, there wa'n't new blood in them dawgs three or four generations ago. Because, sir, the property hadn't ought to be sold. Look at how the stuff's goin' up around Fift' Avenue, an' this's just as good. If them dawgs could live on fer five or mebby ten years longer y'd git twict's much's y' will today."

"Possibly, Nick. Well, I haven't sold yet," Peter indulged the old man by remarking.

"It's new blood the old blood needs for mating, Mr. Killigrew," Nick persisted. "It's th' only way t' keep th' line up. I'm tellin' y', sir, an' I know. I've kep' dawgs, man an' boy, all m' life."

And he was off. But it was a long time before Peter could forget that haunting refrain of Nick's: "It's new blood the old blood needs for mating."

The next morning Peter had an appointment with his ship engineer to go to Montauk Point and look at the Tumbleweed; for she was ready to slip from the ways. Instead of going to Montauk, however, he phoned he would not be there that day. Instead he drove to the Towers.

About four months earlier than usual; he had been there only once before in the winter time—at the funeral of his father.

Only half the house was heated. The housekeeper was upset, but dared not express astonishment. She ran the Towers on a small retinue every month in the year except June, and now when the master arrived thus unexpectedly she declared she must have double the help.

Peter compromised with her, and let her get two more maids and a laundress. He said he would be there only a day or two, and would send up his cook from town. Meanwhile, tell Scroggins to see him.

Scroggins tramped in presently from the office, glad to see Master Peter, but not asking any questions. Peter inquired about the dairy, went into details about the Holsteins and their food, examined the charts, wanted to know what was doing on the pine reservation, checked up the new nursery stock, said he wanted to go out and look at the Cochin China boar bought the summer before in Iowa.

Scroggins went over it all methodically, painstakingly, as was his wont, but wondering. This was not what brought up Master Peter.

Finally, making it as casual as possible, Peter asked: "How is the girl, Scroggins?"

The superintendent became immediately troubled. "I'm deeply worried about her, Master Peter," he replied.

"Why—not well?"

"No—she's far from well."

"What's the matter?"

"Nobody knows."

"What does the doctor say?"

"Says it's nothing, or maybe nostalgia, a kind of home-sickness. And I can't believe it. Why, the home she came from, Master Peter, isn't half as comfortable as the stall we made for that Cochin China."

"There must be something more to this," Peter insisted.

"Yes," said Scroggins, "there is. She won't admit it, but I'm afraid it's a man."

"A man!" Peter started. "She's been going out again, then?"

"No!" Scroggins sighed. "Only on a trip we sent her, with a governess, all respectable and guarded, to Lake Placid. I sent Mac the letters she wrote from there. He said you saw them."

"Believe I did, come to think of it. Then you know who this man is?"

"No, we don't. A shady, contemptible devil who made up to her—open and above-board he seemed to be, but a skate underneath, evidently. For while she told him all about herself and who she was and everything, he acted mysterious, gave her no address, nothing, and when he wrote to her did it without even signing his name with a pen, but on a typewriter, and from a post office address. A regular skunk!"

"What was his name?"

"Jones, he told her; but he was probably lying about it."

"Does she think he was lying?"

"No. Not Imogen—she's too innocent. Believes anything. That's the hell of it. Of course, there can't be any doubt he was feeding her hot air—just a lounge lizard-such as they say hang around those fashionable resorts. The trouble is, Imogen took him seriously. I think she's dying of unrequited love—that's all."

"Hum!" said Peter.

"Yes," growled Scroggins. "Wish I could lay my hands on him. I think I'd give him a good charge of buckshot. I've got the thirty-six loaded—both barrels!"

31

THE DENOUEMENT

THEY WERE IN the library at the flat-top desk when Scroggins delivered his threat, and with more heat than his employer had ever seen him display. Peter rose and turned his back, without replying. He walked to the window and looked out. It was still winter, with patches of snow on the lawn, but he seemed to be looking into June.

And this is what Peter Killigrew saw: A boy of eleven and a girl of three playing with a chain of violets and daisies—the white and the yellow. The boy, impatient, tore the stems from the fragile heads. The girl, only a baby, protested, showing him how to unclasp the flowers, one from the other, without injuring them. Then an old man in a carriage near by called to the boy, taking the floral chain gently from his hands and giving it over to the girl, as he said: "My son, you should never crush a flower!"

Peter blinked. June was gone, and mottled March confronted him, bare and bleak. Out of the grave called the voice of his ancestors!

Were the Killigrews degenerate? Were they weaklings? Was their vision as the water that is passed? Were they as half dead dogs, imbecile through sloth and interbreeding?

Could they no longer leap a twelve-foot fence and back again?

The first Killigrew had stalked those fields out there when they were thickets hiding ambushing Indians. The second had risked the fortune won by the first in swamp lands no one else could foresee as the foundation of skyscrapers. The third had flung clipper ships across the face of the world in the teeth of storm and war and alien greed, to treble the gain of the second. The fourth had reached on and up, abreast with the leaders of the nation.

Were these only rich men, sired in fear, bred in caution, entombed as slaves of habit and dull routine? And was the fifth to be one of them, daring to put his hazard to the touch to win or lose all; or was he to be a dullard, inert, passing by the richest gifts of life because he dared not be himself?

Cophetua? Was this king the first or the fifth of his line? Not the last, surely, else why the beggar maid?

Cophetua! Cophetua! The prince of kings! Thrice royal in that he stooped lower and lifted higher than any others of the favored line.

This, with much else, raced across the rapid drift of Peter's brain as he looked out of the window, while Scroggins respectfully waited. It was but a few moments. Scroggins did not believe the moment long; for Peter was disposed to think slowly and to act only after deliberation.

But once his mind was made up he moved swiftly and according to full plan, not to be changed until it was effected.

"Scroggins," he said, "send Carl to the front door with

the Pershing. And on your way out tell the housekeeper to serve luncheon to me here on a tray—immediately."

He picked up a telephone directory, and began phoning. He got a number in White Plains, then two more, then one in Ossining, and finally one in Port Chester before he found what he wanted.

"You'd think the country would be full of them," he complained as his lunch was set before him.

Later he took the Pershing. Carl asked no questions. From Scroggins down no one asked questions.

In Port Chester he found what he was looking for—a used flivver. He bought it, and left the Pershing with the garage man, with the address of the Towers and instructions to hold it for Carl to call for—on the morrow—or himself, later.

Then he jumped into the flivver and started to drive, but it backed and coughed on him, and he could not make it go. Eight-cylinder cars and some sixes he could manage, but not the lowly fliv. He was obliged to employ the garage man to give him a lesson.

This took more time than he had anticipated. It was growing dark as he started on the road up Westchester Avenue toward Purchase. Pretty late for what he had planned, but still he pushed on. He could not bear the thought of another night passing without rectifying the mistake he had made.

Once having resolved to see her, he was now frantic to get there. He began cursing himself for all his foolish dallying. First buying the typewriter, and then renting the post office box, and now rushing 'way off to Port Chester and finding a used flivver so that he could call on her, when she would probably never see it. Traveling around his thumb to find his finger; yet he felt he had to do them all.

Only the motive had changed. At first he had studiously striven to disguise himself through fear he would be injured in worldly esteem or in pocketbook, if he were found out. Now he was consumed with unholy fear lest she find out who he was, and be influenced to overlook his mistreatment because he was Peter Killigrew. He wanted her to forgive his neglect and deception because she loved him. If it were any different than that, all of life hereafter would be stale and unprofitable.

If he could win her as Peter Jones, then he could sing and lift his head and be a man—and a Killigrew again!

Thinking thus, he battered on in the flivver. When he left the cement highway at the end of Lincoln Avenue, and hit the dirt road something went wrong. He tried to speed up before the engine could quit, but stalled, and was obliged to run into the ditch and look for help.

From half a mile away the help came. He was soon on his way again, reflecting on his accustomed advantages with eight cylinders.

It was after five o'clock when he turned in between the granite pillars and came to a tinpanny stop before the Lodge. He, the owner of the estate.

A maid, who had never seen him, having never been in the Towers, came in answer to his ring, took one look at the old Lizzie below and said, "Service entrance to the rear," closing the door in his face.

Dutifully he walked down, cranked up again, and ran the car around to the back. Once there, another maid answered, and he asked if he might see Miss Nelson. The maid seemed suspicious, but he slipped a bill in her hand and said: "Tell her it's Mr. Jones."

"All right. Wait in here," and she shoved him into a small closet off the pantry nearly filled with an icebox. He took off his hat and stood up against the icebox of the kitchen of his superintendent's house while the maid went upstairs.

In a moment the maid returned, with a broad wink, and led him to the servants' "social ball," a dining-living room to the rear of the kitchen. There she told him to wait again, that Miss Nelson was coming right down.

It was the first time he had ever been in this cranny of his domain. He looked around. On one wall was an old lithograph of Washington crossing the Delaware, on the opposite one a print of the Constitution fighting the Guerriere. Oak furniture, plain, serviceable, scrupulously clean.

There Imogen came to him—under a very bright electric light without shades. This cruelly revealed the hollows under her eyes, the pitiful shrinking in her naturally slender form, the wistful pathos in her saucerlike eyes.

The eyes swam as in a fever. She came in, and then leaned back against the jamb of the door for support.

His whole heart went out to her. His fortune seemed like nothing. For the first time in his life he lost consciousness of his millions.

He held out his arms, and she seemed to slip into them. Otherwise she would have fallen to the floor. He kissed her hair on her forehead, and she placed her head in against his heart.

"Oh, my dear!" said he. "My sweetheart!"

She sighed, unable to speak.

Neither knew how long they stood thus, without a word,

when both at once were conscious of a rasping voice calling through the distant rooms, "Imogen! Imogen!"

"It's my aunt!" she whispered. "She thinks I'm in bed—ill!"

"You've been ill. Why didn't you let me know?"

"It's nothing—nothing at all. I'm not ill."

"But you do look so—your face is drawn!"

"Not *now!*"

Confession could have been no sweeter. Her eyes fell before the intensity of his glance, and the blushes mantled over her neck and cheeks. Again he held her.

Again the rasping voice, "Imogen! Where are you?"

She said softly: "I'll have to go. It's dinner time."

"I came to see you—in my flivver," he lied glibly. "It's outside. I want you to come and take a ride with me. I've got to talk to you. I've something to say."

"No! No! I couldn't!" She shrank away.

"But I must see you to-night. I'll come back after dinner."

"How can I see you?" she pleaded. "Aunt Maria thinks—and Uncle Isaiah thinks—" she stopped.

He realized she was too considerate to say what they thought, but he knew—at least what Uncle Isaiah thought.

The voice of Mrs. Scroggins was more insistent and nearer.

"Listen," said he, hastily. "I have a plan. Meet me, right after dinner, in the greenhouse, the last one, up toward the big house."

"They are locked at night. We couldn't get in," she objected.

"Never mind," said he. "I know Verhens. He'll let me in.

You'll find the south door in the middle section open. Be there as soon as you have dinner. I'll be waiting."

She looked bewildered. "But I don't believe Mr. Verhens—"

"Yes, he will. Trust me. Be there."

"Very—very well."

He lifted her for a kiss. She accepted it as a morning glory accepts the first salute of the returning sun—copiously and without shame. Then she ran away, and he slipped out the rear door.

He ran the flivver into some bushes and walked up to the Towers.

An hour later he was waiting in the poinsettia room of the greenhouses, the central section on the south. She came to him alight with mantling dewiness.

"I didn't know Mr. Verhens would do this for any one," she observed, looking at him with awe.

"Oh! Yes. He will for me. Come. These poinsettias are too violent in color." He led her on to the orchid house. In the corner stood a date tree under which Verhens had trained violets to grow. The violets were in full bloom, looking down on the cypropediums with their tawny yellow slippers.

"Do you know what I wanted to tell you?"

She shook her head.

"Can't guess?"

"No." She seemed not to be greatly interested, though she clung closely to him, and let him put his arm about her.

"I wanted to tell you what I've known from the first—but wouldn't let myself believe because it's the first time I ever felt that way, and I wanted to be sure—that I love you."

She nestled close to him. He cupped her chin in his hand and lifted her face to his. Tears were brimming in her eyes.

"And with you—" he asked gently. "Is it that way?"

She nodded slowly.

"And I want you to—to—m-marry me!" he went on.

The tears fell from her eyes, one big drop from each. She looked at him a bit wildly, and then exclaimed with pent-up passion, "No! Not that!"

"But—why—why?" he stammered, nonplused.

"I can't marry you!" she cried, breaking away.

"You must!" He reached out to clasp her in his arms.

She ran from him, out the poinsettia door, leaving him crushingly surrounded by his own orchids.

He was after her quickly, however, and overtook her before she reached the kitchen door of the Lodge. He led her back to the greenhouse silently. Again under the light he searched her face.

"Why can't you marry me?" he demanded.

She just shook her head. It seemed outrageously unreasonable. He had not anticipated this.

"But I can't live without you!" he went on wildly, seemingly as distraught as she was. "It seemed an age while you were at dinner. I have been in a perfect hell ever since I left you at Lake Placid. You are the only girl I ever cared for, or ever can. There is no reason why you shouldn't marry me."

He paused for an answer. None forthcoming, he asked, less confidently, "Is there?"

Now she faced him squarely. She seemed to have conquered her feeling, and became matter-of-fact.

"Yes. A very good reason," she asserted. "I'm only a

pauper living here on the bounty of a dear old man, who is only a servant, and no one could ever really want me!"

He laughed with relief and cried, "Then it's not because my name is Jones?"

She looked at him in amazement. "Oh! I think Jones is the nicest name in the world!" she confessed.

"Darling!" He kissed her.

She added, for further proof of her inviolable contention, "Besides, I will never marry. I am going to die an old maid—and take care of my garden in Dobbs's Corners, and go on dreaming beautiful dreams—like this one!"

She smiled at him, with that roguish little tilt at the corners of her mouth.

"Very well, then," said he. "Then it is settled. We drive to Greenwich to-night in my old flivver out there under the trees, and get married in the old church where my grandfather was married."

"Oh, no!" she pulled away, quite serious again. "I couldn't!"

"Why? Give me another weighty reason like the last one."

"Well," she hesitated, "because Uncle Isaiah would be hurt if I did that—besides, he made me promise I would always live with him."

"I thought you were going to live at Dobbs's Corners?"

"Part of the time."

He felt more assured now—felt his doubts all resolved; and of superior knowledge, the male marauder proud of his skill and craft in providing for his mate.

"All right," Peter agreed. "I'll fix it so that Uncle Isaiah can live with us."

"Why, he has been on this estate all his life. He wouldn't leave here!" she protested.

"Never mind. You saw I fixed it with Verhens. Trust me with Scroggins too. I'll manage him."

"Oh! But Mr. Scroggins is a great man, and very set in his ways."

"The sort I like. Will you trust me to fix it with him?"

She nodded her head.

"Then come!" He started to lead the way.

"But not now—I'm not dressed, and—"

"Never mind—"

He was masterful. Nothing could stop him now. She loved him for himself! And Jones was the greatest name in the whole world!

They rattled into Greenwich in the old Lizzie a little after nine o'clock. The minister he sought was not at home, and he was glad of it when he reflected that with the minister the responses would have been necessary, and his right name would have been revealed. He found a justice of the peace. A little prearrangement with him fixed it so the register was signed by them separately, Imogen first, and the justice never spoke their last name, saying only, "I, Peter, take thee, Imogen, to be my lawful wedded wife," and "I, Imogen, take thee, Peter" and so forth.

So she started back in the flivver thinking she was Mrs. Peter Jones.

At Port Chester he stopped in a garage and exchanged the flivver for a bigger car, a Pershing. She paid little attention. She seemed to be in a dream. Not even when the garage man ran after them shouting, "Hey, mister, what'll I do with the fliv?"

"Keep it!" Peter called back, "for a wedding present!"

Then she took notice. "But, Peter," she objected, "you must not be extravagant. I want to be an economical wife."

Nor did she notice the difference in the riding qualities of the flivver and the Pershing; for she snuggled close to his arm all the way back, not once asking where they were going until they stopped before the door of the Towers. Then she drew back.

"Come," said he, taking out a key and walking up the steps.

She seemed frightened, asking, "What are you doing? Nobody goes in here while Mr. Killigrew is away."

"We're going in," he asserted, "and fix it with Scroggins."

A moment later they were in the library, in a divan on the edge of the Ispahan carpet. When Scroggins came in Peter said, "Well, we're married. I want your blessing!"

"Peter Jones!" Imogen gasped.

The old man began to shout, "You've deceived her, Master Peter. It's an outrage on a young girl to shock her like this. Your father—"

Neither spoke for the next few minutes, for they were both engaged in reviving Imogen, who had fainted.

WHICH IS THE true history of the courtship and the marriage of Mr. and Mrs. Peter Killigrew V.

ABOUT THE AUTHOR

THE AUTHOR OF *Worth Millions*, known as a dramatist, novelist, and war correspondent, has written several serials for *Argosy-Allstory;* in the past year we have published of his "The Big Gun" and "Sea Lure." His "Petroleum Prince," a comedy of New York social life, published first in the *Argosy,* was produced as a play by Marc Klaw, and "Jes' Sal," published first as a serial in the *Argosy-Allstory,* was produced in October, 1925, at the Princess Theater, in New York, as a play under the title of "Barefoot." His story, "The Big Gun," is being filmed by the Universal Moving Picture Corporation as a superfeature.

Mr. Barry lives in Mamaroneck, Westchester County, New York, in the midst of the country he describes in *Worth Millions.* He has made over an old stone earn built for thoroughbred horses into a little theater, christened the Native Theater. There "Barefoot" was first produced in September, 1925. In former years Mr. Barry devoted much research, as well as original observation to preparation for writing "The History of the Four Hundred," which was published serially in *Pearson's Magazine.* Later a series of special articles on "Getting Into Society," published in the *New York Times,* secured from the late Mrs. Stuyvesant Fish, once the chief leader of exclusive society in Manhattan and Westchester, the published remark that "this is the best analysis of polite social conditions ever written." These articles were republished in London and still rank as standard authority on the subject.

www.ingramcontent.com/pod-product-compliance
Lightning Source LLC
Chambersburg PA
CBHW051133030726
47504CB00004B/857